ALSO BY KATHRYN K. MURPHY

The Firemark Series

The Secret About Time
Simply A Matter of Time

The Sisters in Sirens Series

A Touch of Healing
A Touch of Fire
A Touch of Truth

A TOUCH OF TRUTH

A SISTERS IN SIRENS NOVEL

KATHRYN K. MURPHY

Caraway Press

For Kevin

Since the first night when we slept under the stars, I knew this would be a life less ordinary. Your positive outlook and love have enriched my life in countless ways. I've learned so much from you, and I couldn't have written this book without your support and inspiration.

CHAPTER 1

Ted Saunders knew he was dying. The attack had been quick, from behind him right in his own living room. He didn't know who exactly had gotten into his house, but that wasn't important because no matter who it was, he knew who was ultimately behind this.

The injection had been quick like a bee sting right in the side of the neck before they fled, leaving him there to die. The adrenaline rushed through his body, his heart starting to beat faster as he rolled over to crawl toward the office where his files and computer were. They hadn't been taken or touched. Better to make it look like nothing was wrong.

He pushed through the door and struggled to stand, his breath coming in short spurts that were increasingly more difficult. He grabbed his fountain pen, spilling some of the ink, and scrawled out a name on a slip of paper before the weight of his body forced him to sit down in the old wooden desk chair that creaked under his weight. His pounding heart was racing to keep up, but he was getting weaker and weaker.

He picked up the phone and dialed. They wanted it to

look like a suicide by accidental overdose, and he was not about to give them that satisfaction.

"911. What's your emergency?"

"I'm dying. I've been attacked, and I'm dying." His voice was ragged to his own ears.

"Sir, I have your address. I need you to tell me if it's correct." He listened while they rattled off the same street number he had called home for most of his life, and now the end of it.

"Yes." His mouth felt like sand, but he was drooling.

"Okay, we're sending help now. Stay on the phone with me. Is the front door locked?"

It was hard to sit, as his whole body ached to fall to the ground in exhaustion, but he persisted, answering the dispatcher's questions. The pressure on his chest was immeasurable.

The dispatcher's voice kept going, but she sounded faded, as if she was going farther away with every word.

His breathing slowed. His eyes grew heavier, like the lids were magnets begging to be reunited with their other half.

Fighting against the urge, he looked at the photos on his desk. The first was a faded color photo of Jenny smiling up at him, holding a line with a fish she had caught when she was four. Her hair was in pigtails, she was missing a tooth in her bright grin, and she was sitting in what had been her pink, big-girl wheelchair. The next was a smaller black-and-white photograph of Barb, caught midlaugh in her lace wedding dress. He was there too, laughing also as they started to slice the cake together. He had never been a person of deep faith, but he felt tears start to stream down his cheeks at the hope he might see them both again.

Ted collapsed and died on his favorite wool rug while sirens rang in the distance.

CHAPTER 2

Sergeant Ashleigh Myers was in her cruiser when she saw it.

A skinny man in his midtwenties went up to someone, then grabbed some cash in a classic drug deal move before turning on his heel. It wasn't the deal that caught her eye, but the man's patch on his jacket sleeve, which matched the description of a wanted suspect in a series of attacks in a park a few months ago.

"Hey you, stop."

The man glanced back before breaking into a sprint. Ash followed, gaining some ground before he darted across traffic, nearly getting hit by an approaching car. The tires squealed and the horn blared.

Ash saw him duck into an alley when the dispatch went off on her radio.

"Unit 12, this is Dispatch. We have a one eighty-seven in progress. Caller reports a male victim. Over."

Ash swore and waved to the car passing as she watched the skinny dealer run off. "Dispatch, this is Sergeant Ashleigh Myers. I'm en route. Any additional details? Over."

"Sergeant Ashford, victim is identified as John Doe, mid-70s. No further details at this time. Over."

"Copy that, Dispatch. I'm on my way. Notify CSI and request backup. Over."

"10-4, Sergeant. Backup and CSI en route. Approach with caution. Over."

Still pissed she couldn't catch the guy, Ash arrived at a small house situated between the edge of town and the beginning of the woods. She drew her weapon and flipped on her recorder.

"Myers on scene, no sign of forced entry." The door was locked but not dead bolted. There was a floral wreath, faded from the sun and by the looks of it more than one harsh Montana winter.

Johnson and Marshall were right ahead of her, already working on the door, while dispatch answered. "Male called in an attack and is unresponsive on phone."

Once inside, they did a sweep of the rooms and found no one other than the man on the floor. A quick check confirmed he was already dead, but had just passed. They called in the crime sweepers and began to take the notes and photographs before the paramedics would come in to transfer him out to the coroner.

The house was small, warm, and comfortable if not a little cluttered. In the living room, the lamp was still on. Knick-knacks were arranged under a layer of dust on the end table that had a single coffee mug from the University of Montana, a stack of mail, and a basket of various medicines and remotes. The recliner next to it was a well-worn plaid pattern, with a blanket tossed to the side as if someone had just gotten up. There was a matching couch, coordinating rugs, and an abundance of books seemingly everywhere. The bedrooms and kitchen were similar, emphasizing comfort rather than trendy styles.

Neither Johnson or Marshall found anything or anyone on the property. Both began the process of checking for missing or disturbed items. Later they would track down information to notify next of kin.

Ash returned to the man on the floor near his desk in his office, which was off the living room. She leaned down to describe the way his body was positioned in her notes. He had said he had been attacked, but there was no sign of injury. To the naked eye, it looked like a simple heart attack. Quick and painless. He had been in his chair at his desk before he had fallen. The laptop was off and shut. The phone was off the cradle. Nothing appeared to have been stolen, and there was no sign of struggle. Family pictures still were in place, and bank statements with account numbers were untouched. Blue ink from an open fountain pen had dripped onto a pad.

Ash didn't see any paper with blue writing around, but it was unclear how long the pen had been uncapped. Could've happened a while ago. She scanned the room and noted it was mostly neat and organized. Books stood on shelves, ranging from anatomy to genetics. There were some awards and plaques arranged in a somewhat artful manner. There wasn't as much dust here. If there was an ink spill, it wouldn't have been there for long.

Ash went back to her notes.

He was older, but didn't look his age. According to the records, Ted Saunders lived at this house, was a seventy-four-year-old widower who had retired and sometimes acted as an adjunct professor at the University of Montana in Missoula. In front of her now, he lay looking so much different from his smiling ID photo, but it was him. Ted's skin was lined, his hair gray, and lighter at the temples. His glasses had fallen off and were lying on the floor a few inches away from his face. He had on navy pajamas with a white border and bare feet. There was a wedding ring, but no other jewelry.

His left hand was closed. Leaning forward, she saw the paper from the notepad crumpled inside. The man's hand hadn't started to stiffen yet, so she pried open the cool fingers and reached for the paper when Johnson walked in.

"Alright, they're here," said Johnson, coming around the corner to announce the crime sweepers. "Not sure they'll find much. There's no sign of anything being disturbed or banged up."

"Yeah, doesn't look like he has a mark on him," Marshall said when he walked in behind. "If he hadn't said it was an attack, I would've sworn this was a heart attack. Find anything on him?"

Ash stood to face them. "Just this..." her voice trailed off as she looked at what was in her gloved hands.

"Lemme see," Marshall said, coming to look over her shoulder.

All of them stared down at the paper where her own name was written in fresh blue ink.

Johnson read it aloud.

"Ashleigh Myers knows the truth and the lies."

Both men, who she had known for years, turned to look at her. She could feel their gazes on her face, before they exchanged a glance as they silently figured out how to proceed.

"What the fuck does this mean?" Johnson asked.

"I have no idea," she answered. Her mind was racing. Ash ran through her memory to see if she had ever met the victim and came up empty. Clearly he had known her, or at least about her.

"Right," Marshall said. He was always the more level-headed, let's-stop-and-think-this-through kind of person. "Let's finish getting the evidence and then we'll go from there. Ash, try to think if you knew him or any connection you might have. Johnson, find the wallet or any ID."

Ash held the paper in her gloved hands, while Johnson snapped on a pair of his own and gently removed the paper to put into an evidence bag. "You'll need to be interviewed."

"Yeah, of course." Her voice sounded remote and foreign to her own ears. She went on autopilot while her brain struggled to process the implications of what she had just read.

She removed the gloves and shoved her hands into the pockets of her police-issued coat if only to have something to do with them. Given what the paper had just said, she knew better than to continue to mess with the scene or touch anything.

Johnson and Marshall continued to snap pictures and note all of the necessary information, while the crime sweepers did their work. Later, the paramedics came and took the body. When all of the business that came with homicide was done, Ash watched in the freezing November night while Johnson and Marshall locked the door and sealed the house as an official crime scene, wondering who in the hell Ted Saunders was—and how on earth he knew her secret.

CHAPTER 3

Ash didn't know what to think, so like always, she went for a run. Never mind the fact that a snowstorm was on the way. Sometimes you just needed to get outside and clear your head. No music, no podcast, just a human being being alive.

The icy wind pelted her face as she jogged from her Jeep that was parked half a mile away at the local park on the edge of town. From here, trails opened up into the preserves and hundreds of miles of undeveloped land. It was a favorite of backpackers starting out for hikes.

She had come here before for trail running when she was really out of sorts. Running through the dim light over small roots and loose stones kept her attention in the here and now and reminded her of the hills on her family's old farm. Connecting with nature was bred into her and always helped.

Her sneakers hit the ground at an even pace as she hit her stride while jogging. Not too fast, not too slow in her normal running gear. She was a few miles beyond her normal route, but then again, being the person of interest in your own homicide case was a special kind of crazy.

She had already been interviewed, which yielded nothing except more questions and suspicion. At first her coworkers were approaching her just with procedure in mind, but then they started to spin it—asking her as a colleague what she thought the connection would be, which was a classic tactic to get her to confess something.

They didn't have anything, and she didn't know anything. Just a few days ago, she had been processing information on the recent attacks from seemingly normal people in Goldvein, hoping for a break that would lead to a promotion. Now she was quickly being removed from cases.

Ash had never met Ted Saunders. She had looked him up online, found his dissertation, and had fallen asleep several nights in a row trying to read it. Most of it was about the genetic mutation of mushrooms and plants as part of a study to bring about cures for infectious diseases, but the data was a mixed bag and none of it amounted to much.

After getting his PhD, Ted had floated around from different labs and clinics to finally ending up at Rocky Mountain Labs, which was an NIH site that had been in a nearby town for around one hundred years, first as a lab to research and treat Rocky Mountain Spotted Fever. With that work done, it had expanded into the impressive government facility it was today. There Ted continued his mushroom work until he retired with his wife, Barb, who died about two years ago.

They had one daughter who was born and raised here before she died of a heart defect in her early twenties while away at college.

She had looked at all of the possible angles. She hadn't know the daughter, wife, or Ted. She had never been to Rocky Mountain Labs, but knew of it in a neighboring town.

He had no arrest records, and had only ever gotten a speeding ticket once right around the time his daughter died. There was nothing to connect her, and yet, somehow he knew.

Johnson, Marshall, and almost the whole Goldvein Police Department knew about this case, and knew she had been taken into interview as a person of interest, but all of them had the wrong reason why.

They thought she knew about Ted, which was completely false, so it shouldn't matter at all. What scared the shit out of Ash was how did Ted know about her?

No one knew about her, not even her two best friends, Laura and Megan. If she were to tell someone, they would be the main ones, given what Ash suspected. They were like her. They had a special ability beyond what someone should. She wasn't sure on the details, but hey, that was the perk about being able to smell lies. She knew when her friends were hiding the truth, even though they had never talked about it.

Her family didn't know and never would, though her mom would've loved it. Ash had always been so careful to never, ever let anyone at work know. Police didn't use abilities. They used evidence. Good police work was supposed to be facts over feelings. Even when Ash knew someone was lying, she never made a move until she could prove it. Of course, having a handy-dandy ability did give her an invisible edge on where to start.

She headed back toward the parking lot as the sun and temperature dropped. The icy wind was a welcome breeze on her damp forehead. The cold breached her damp clothes, now soaked in sweat from exertion which was a nice change of pace from being soaked from straight anxiety.

Ash was about a hundred yards away from her Jeep when she saw the headlights of an oncoming police cruiser in the distance.

Two officers got out and started milling around, shining a flashlight inside. The skin on the back of her neck prickled up, which was ridiculous. She literally worked with these guys. She was a sergeant. So what, some guy wrote down her name, and now she was afraid? She hadn't even done anything.

She shook her head at the thought, slowed to a walk, and kept moving toward them. They saw her and waved.

"Hey Ash, is that you?"

The scent was faint, but she still caught a hint of it on the icy breeze. It was a pungent, stale taste in her nose and at the back of her throat, growing stronger.

It had always been the same since she was a child. Her power to detect when people were lying had always been her guide, keeping her out of trouble and getting her closer to answers in her police work. She could smell the stench coming off them when there was an untruth or some hidden meaning. Small lies or big ones, it didn't matter. Ash could tell. She didn't know what the truth was, just that this wasn't it.

She breathed in again as the figures approached. In the fading, dim light, Ash studied their body language. It was subtle. A sort of lurch with every step in exaggerated over-confidence in a futile effort to look relaxed and nonthreatening. Johnson put his hands on his belt right near his flashlight and gun. She had seen the walk several times before when they were together at a traffic stop—trying to appear relaxed but on high alert for someone to run. Ash breathed in through her nose again, calling on the depth of her power to know what others didn't. The breeze from the darkening clouds overhead carried the powerful scent of lies, deceit, and danger toward her.

"Come on over. We got a question for you."

It didn't make sense. Why was she afraid? These were the

same people she had shared cake with at their birthday parties in the bullpen. The same people who had her back on calls and in dicey situations. She would have trusted her life to them both, expecting nothing but honesty.

Now though, her ability was giving her some very unwanted news. Marshall was straight up lying to her, and walking right toward her as if she were a suspect.

A voice from somewhere in the woods behind her whispered just loud enough for her to hear.

"It's not safe here anymore. Come with me now."

She froze in place, stuck between two dangers. The voice was low, male, and just more of a breath than a whisper. The man who spoke was hoarse either from the cold or not speaking—she couldn't tell. She didn't move except for the heartbeat in her head, blood thrumming in her ears.

Johnson and Marshall hadn't heard him and were getting closer to the edge of the parking lot, closing the distance between her car and where she was on the edge of the woods. If she turned away now, she would only have a hundred-yard lead. Through the park, then the dark woods beyond. She'd never make it. How would that look? Guilty. All of this for a name on a paper? She was still a damn cop.

"Trust me. We need to get you out of here *now*," the voice behind her said again.

She hadn't heard anyone approach. The parking lot was empty except for her Jeep and the cruiser blocking her in. Who in the hell was it? Maybe she was hearing shit.

Ash took in another breath, searching with her eyes in front of her and through the air around her from behind.

"Ash? Come on. It's going to storm soon. Let's get you home safe."

The stench of the lie was overwhelming her nose. Whatever they wanted, it was not to get her home safe. Every cell in her body screamed at her to run away as fast as possible.

There was no scent of a lie from behind her.

Johnson pulled out his flashlight, and that's when she saw both of them had drawn their guns.

In a split-second decision that would change everything, Ash turned around and sprinted into the woods.

"Stop! You're under arrest for the murder of Ted Saunders!"

Johnson and Marshall each discharged their weapons behind her. The two gunshots rang out in the night, confirming once again that no matter how sad, lies and truth didn't need to make sense.

CHAPTER 4

The movement must have surprised the man in the woods with her, but he reacted quickly. She could feel him more than see him. The heavy footfalls alongside her in the dark were muffled by the frozen pine needles beneath them. He ran at a quick pace, darting among the trees as if it was his nature, quickly taking the lead.

"Follow me and stay behind." His voice was louder now, rough and quick.

Ash fell into step behind him, matching her footfalls with his own.

Behind them, shouts and the beam of the flashlights ricocheted through the woods, casting wide shadows that stretched like claws grasping.

Johnson's and Marshall's voices were chaotic and yelling, but she couldn't make out the words. Their heavy footfalls on gravel echoed through the trees behind them.

The dark figure in front of her kept moving forward, never stopping before turning left and then right, never staying straight, managing to avoid rocks and leaves as they moved away from the path. He brought her down a ravine and through a small creek she hadn't noticed before, pushing through thickets and other pine trees. He splashed through the water. Ash felt the icy water pierce right through her thin running shoes as they followed the water upstream, climbing the nearby mountain, leaving the park territory and the outer rim of Goldvein behind.

It was stupid. What could she say? She had been afraid and ran. Maybe she could say she had her earbuds in and couldn't hear. There had been more than enough pedestrians hit for the same thing in town. She hadn't done anything wrong, though. Why Johnson and Marshall came calling her name with guns drawn freaked her out. Showing up guns blazing made literally no sense. How did they find her anyway?

Shit.

She knew how. Her phone.

The man had started climbing up the rocks now, adjacent to the creek, which was more of a stream, still moving forward at a slower pace, never glancing behind.

Ash powered down her phone before sliding it back into her pocket. Once she figured out who this person was and where she was going, she could turn it back on. For now, she needed to conserve energy, avoid being tracked, and focus on what she was doing. She grabbed the cold, damp rocks and started to scramble up.

The clouds had thickened as the snow began to fall, lightly at first. Her feet were numb with the wet cold, and her thin running jacket was damp with the sweat of running and the fear of pursuit. As they continued the climb upward and into the thicker forest, she became aware that the only sound she had heard for a while was the sound of her ragged breathing as she put one hand in front of another on the freezing slippery rocks.

The man in front of her, who was more of a shadow than

anything else in the dark, could've been mistaken for a bear as he was so agile, climbing with no discernible effort.

The climb turned into a hike where he started to stray more away from the stream, heading again left and then right. Ash focused on his back so as not to get lost, knowing she would never be able to find her way out of here by herself.

It was darker now. Snow fell from the sky, first a few flurries, before coming down faster. She felt it on her face and eyelashes. She reached up and felt her now freezing, wet hair, and tugged up the thin hood on her running jacket.

The man didn't slow down, but her eyes had adjusted just enough to see the snow dust the outline of his shoulders. She couldn't tell much, but from what she could see he was taller than she was, and broader with large shoulders under some sort of coat. She couldn't make out anything in terms of his features, but she got the sense he had long hair.

The walk went on for what felt like hours. Ash slipped and stumbled on a frozen rock, twisting her ankle as she landed on the snowy ground. A thick, meaty hand reached out in front of her to pull her up.

"Are you okay?"

"Yeah, I think I'm fine. My ankle is sore though."

"We won't need to run again for a while. Can you still walk?"

"Yeah. Who are you? Where are we going?"

The bear man paused before turning around. "We're going someplace safe."

"Can you tell me more why it wasn't safe? I didn't do anything wrong."

"Not here." He seemed to look around the dark woods where the snow fell silently around them. "We'll talk later."

He continued forward through his twists and turns, through the woods, through the soft, powdery snow. It was falling faster now, and in the morning, there would be no sign of their tracks, which was apparently a good thing.

The bad part for now was the wind pelting her skin with the icy snow, like little blades of ice scratching at her cheeks. She couldn't feel anything below her knees or her face. She had no other clothes, no underlayer, and only thin leggings and a T-shirt under her jacket. No one but the bear man knew where she was. She had no food, which in grizzly country was a positive, but overall, everything had gone to shit. All she knew was the person in front of her was honest when he said they were going someplace safe.

Ash trudged along behind him, through the deepening snow. If he got tired, he didn't let on.

She went into her focused headspace, putting one foot in front of the other while letting her mind wander. Nothing about any of this made sense. Had she misread the lie? No, there was no way. That pungent stench had haunted her since she was a child, filling her senses anytime someone hid their true nature. There was no mistaking it, and she had never been wrong once, which begged the question, why would they lie about getting her home safe? Why in the hell did they have their guns drawn if they knew it was her Jeep? None of it added up. By now, she was sure that the whole department was looking for her, and she had no idea what they wanted. All she knew was she was somehow safest freezing to death on some crazy hike with a bear man in the woods.

She had lost track of the times they had turned, doubled back, and climbed up more rocks as they weaved in and out of smaller streams. She could've told the bear man they didn't have a canine unit, and the closest one was an hour away, but she let it be. What she thought she knew was all in question after tonight's bizarre turn of events. Despite her freezing toes, she felt safer with every step away from the world behind her.

The pace of the hike slowed to a steady walk as they kept moving until her ankles sunk into the icy snow with every step. She started counting her steps, as the only way to get through, focusing on putting one foot in front of the other and nothing else.

One.

Two.

Three.

Four.

She had done the same thing in the police academy when she had joined. The training kicked in and allowed her to go to a place in her mind where she blocked out all of the pain, and devoted all of her focus to completing the task at hand in a true mind-over-matter exercise.

She was approaching two thousand steps. With little moonlight, she kept following the bear man, more of a shadow than anything until he stopped and stooped into a rock outcropping.

Ash stopped and heaved a sigh of relief, hopeful she might have some blood going back to her feet. Throbbing at this point would be welcome. Her shirt was drenched with sweat and snow that had melted. It was coming down fast now, slowing their progress.

"Are we stopping?" She didn't know the time, but the moon was completely gone along with all of the adrenaline. Surely it must be well past three in the morning.

The bear man didn't answer, but rummaged around farther under the cramped ledge that was more of a hole than a shelter and pulled out a large sack.

"No."

CHAPTER 5

Max couldn't stop now, but he wished for her sake they could, but then again it was because of her that they had to keep going.

He had planted this bag a few months ago, stashing it away in case of a situation like this one tonight. He had been surprised to see her running this late and this close to a snowstorm, then was completely caught off guard when the cops came. He should've stopped her sooner, but had been too far away keeping watch.

This was exactly what he had worked so long to avoid. Leaving her behind would have been simpler, but here he was, reaching into one of the bug out bags to find some outer layers. There was no way she would make it to one of his places with just that thin joke of a jogging outfit.

He thrust the heavy army surplus coat toward her. "Here."

She looked at it and slipped inside. He nodded once when he saw the shoulders relax against the cold and snow. She must be soaked to the bone, but they could get dry later. The more distance they put between themselves and all of Goldvein, the better. Even if they reached his first safe spot, it might not be enough.

He wouldn't put it past them to have surveillance in the woods, but in all of the years he had been around them, he hadn't seen anything yet. Still, he wasn't sure they were safe enough to answer her questions, of which there were probably many and would be more.

"How are your feet?"

The woman stepped from side to side. "Numb. I can't feel anything below my knees."

"Are they throbbing?"

"My right one is starting now that we've stopped."

"Good, that's blood flow; let's keep going."

He hiked the sack on his shoulder.

"Who are you?"

Great, now that he had broken the silence, she was in a talking mood. He had been hopeful they could get along when she was silent for the past three hours.

"No one."

"How do you know I'm not a threat to you?"

Max smiled to himself as he moved forward, hearing the crunch of the snow behind him. Good to know she thought like a survivor once all the excitement died down. That was good. They needed that.

"You're not a threat to me."

"I could be."

Max debated whether or not to answer. Better not. He didn't want to inspire more questions, but the reality was, she should be afraid of him. Very afraid.

"That spirit will help you if needed."

"Why were you watching me?"

"Later."

"Can you tell me anything now?"

Jesus. He was used to silence around him at all times. Had come to peace with it out of necessity.

"No. Just keep walking."

He expected some resistance, but there was nothing but the footfalls behind him, staying in step. He had felt her presence in the woods this entire time. Living alone and off the grid had given him a sense about when others were nearby. Typically he felt overwhelmed, and worked to limit exposure to others.

They walked in silence for several more minutes, Max navigating the way with her behind him, trudging along. He heard the fatigue in her steps, which had gotten heavier. Instead of her fast run, she was pushing herself to lurch forward. Her grit impressed him.

He hadn't expected himself to reach out to her, but he did so on impulse after seeing her jog through the woods. Initially, he had spent the last few hours panicking about the risk a split second had cost him. Five years of lying low, blown to bits for someone who might not be able to keep up. People were a liability.

But she had impressed him, covering over six miles deeper into the mountains. With another two to go, they had made it much farther than he had expected, and he was on his normal pace.

Typically, he would've stopped to rest at the outcropping, but the fact that she hadn't collapsed so far had given him hope to push forward. They would be there in another hour.

"Can I ask you one question?"

Shit. Here we go again.

"You already did."

"You know what I meant."

She paused so long, he thought she might've taken the hint this time.

"Can you tell me if I'll be safe with you?"

Jesus. What kind of question was that? No, of course not. Nothing like putting that kind of pressure on someone, and besides, if she knew who she was with, she'd run screaming all the way back to town.

His silence must have made her worry.

"Do you plan to hurt me?" she asked again.

Max closed his eyes as he moved forward. He never planned to hurt people.

"No."

He expected to hear a follow-up, and was relieved when nothing came. After several minutes ticked by, he turned around to see her, and thought he could make out her nodding as she walked.

He almost asked why she would believe him, but conversation was not their friend. She had a million reasons not to believe him and yet here she was. He hadn't been responsible for anyone else in a long time, and the feeling was a heavy weight he carried with each step.

Her presence was making him even more careful than normal. Best to get as far as they could before rest. Borealis would be looking for her whether or not she knew it.

They had gone another mile when he heard her fall behind him.

He turned to see her lying in the snow, a dark figure spilling out onto the white, being covered with the falling flakes that rained down silently. She didn't move at first.

Max crouched down and turned her over. He cursed the darkness and pulled off his glove to run a hand over her face.

The skin was cold and slick with sweat and snow, but nothing warm, like blood. She was breathing so that was good.

"Sorry. I slipped."

She was exhausted and freezing to death.

"Can you stand?"

She didn't answer, but after a pause started to pull herself upward, failing twice. Max lifted her arm, and she swayed when he took his away, so he steadied her.

"It's less than a mile. After that you can rest."

She didn't answer again but, after a while, took a step forward and then another with him behind her, one arm on her back.

They stayed like that, walking through the snowstorm. They were higher in elevation now, which wasn't helping her, but below the tree line, still obscured in the dense cover. That meant the snow they were trudging through, now up to their ankles, was much deeper farther up, and the icy wind was blocked by some of the trees.

Max had already started to scan for areas where he could make a shelter, but given what was ahead of them and potentially behind, he wanted to keep going. If they could make it to a dry shelter, she would be better off. Staying the night in the storm lessened her already slim options.

Shit. He looked down at her feet, trying to gauge their condition with no luck. It had been hours in cold, wet shoes. She had already fallen once and needed rest.

Questions swirled in his mind about where he could go, how he could get her treated with minimal exposure. He cursed himself again for inviting this upon himself.

The snow fell steadily in front of them and all around. With no light, he couldn't see it, but he could hear the icy crystals bounce off his shoulders and feel them glue to his beard. They kept moving through the unrelenting nature, Max guiding her around various trees on the path he had walked so many times. No one would see it but him. He had been in these woods so long that the original carvings were almost gone in the healed bark, but he didn't need them anymore. This was home.

The woman never stopped again, as he guided her with care around the stones and uneven terrain. When it was time to turn for the last time, he pressed his hand into her back to steer her in the right direction, aware of her presence and closeness.

She didn't say anything or react other than adjusting her pace to match his toward the small building built into the side of the mountain for just this purpose.

CHAPTER 6

Gabriel stood on the edge of the park, knee-deep in the snow that fell silently around the parking lot. He had already talked to the cops who had lost the woman in the woods before the snow had started.

He had returned to the house to verify he had left no trace of his mission. His target had died quickly. Any attempt the old man had in him to fight was a pathetic plea like that of a bug begging not to be squashed like a common pest.

Breaking into the house through the back door had been so simple. The frilly curtains on the door hadn't even moved when he had slipped inside.

The old man was asleep in his chair with the TV on, his feet up in the recliner with the paper folded in his lap. While the commercials rolled, he had stuck the pressure syringe right under the ear against the neck, grabbing him from pulling away with the other hand. That close to the artery was a guaranteed hit. No mess. No evidence.

It was supposed to mimic a heart attack.

Too bad the old man had more fight in him than Gabriel

had expected. He hadn't expected to see the news report on a local homicide.

He could've let it go, knowing he had left no trace and the police would never be able to link him to the crime, but if Saunders had been able to communicate he had been attacked, what else had he said? So Gabriel returned the same way he had slipped in that night. That was when he noticed the pad out of place in the office. A quick shading had revealed one name.

Sergeant Ashleigh Myers.

First female on the force. Admirable. Dedicated. Now a person of interest who was on the run during a snowstorm because she knew something that should've died with Ted Saunders.

As he stood in silence, the only sounds were the wind and the icy crackle of the snow raining down around him. She might have a head start, but he would be there right behind her.

CHAPTER 7

Ash had absolutely no idea where she was and couldn't have cared less. The bear man had been steering her since she fell, which was good because it meant she could close her eyes. Originally she had been just focused with running. Then she had tried to get her bearings in case she needed to escape the bear man or make a quick run if the police had caught up to them. Then it had been counting steps, and finally she was too tired and too cold to care. When she had fallen, she had seriously considered never moving again, and simply falling asleep.

Dying of exposure didn't seem as big of a concern when she was convinced she'd die walking. But of course, she hadn't. Ash had made the last half mile with as little energy as possible, letting the bear man steer her toward whatever secret place he had in mind.

She hadn't opened her eyes until they stopped, where she almost fell face first into a wooden door from the momentum of moving so much.

The bear man dusted off the snow, then shouldered into

what appeared to be a small hut built into the side of a mountain.

Inside, there was a bed, a table and chair, fireplace, and a sink. No bathroom or other room. The plain wooden walls were painted white, but covered in old *Sports Illustrated* swimsuit models from what looked to be the eighties or nineties, with a few cans of food stacked in the corner.

After the night she had just had, it was heaven.

"We'll rest here for a bit then keep moving."

Fine by her. Ash walked in and slumped on the braided oval rug in front of the empty fireplace, curling up on her side with complete exhaustion, already in and out of consciousness. The questions in her mind were many, but floating to and from her consciousness like distant clouds in a blizzard fog. She heard the bear man rummaging, with what sounded like his large pack and some clothes.

Ash tried to open her eyes, but they were glued together, or the energy it took to open her lids was too much for her to expend.

"I'm going to take off your shoes. Your feet need to dry."

Ash mustered up the energy to grunt in what she meant as the affirmative.

She felt the ties of her soaked running shoes which had plastered themselves to her feet.

When he tried to tug them off, her swollen feet clung to the inside of her shoes, and a sharp pang of pain let her know feeling was coming back. She must have whimpered, because she thought he said, "It's okay," but couldn't be sure if she had imagined it.

He peeled off one sock, leaving her bloated, frozen foot exposed to the cold air in the room. God, she wished the fire was warm, but it hadn't been lit.

The bear man read her mind and closed his hands around the icy skin, gently trying to move it a little in a feeble attempt to warm the skin. She could start to feel him as he ran what felt like a thumb up and down the arch of her foot on the tendon connecting to her big toe. The throbbing followed suit quickly.

He cupped her skin, applying a gentle pressure first at her swollen ankle, and then working his way up her calf. His hands cupping her skin felt like a blissful warmth that radiated down to her bone. Each time he shifted his hand away from her skin, she wanted to cry out and beg his touch to come back, but it always did.

His hand grazed a sore spot on the back of her heel, and with a hiss, she yanked away.

There was a grunt and some rummaging in the pack he had carried. Ash could feel his steps through the floor as he came back toward her, popping open a lid.

"I have some cream for that."

She managed a grunt in response, and edged her foot in the direction of his gravelly voice.

He took her foot again, placing it down on the rug then applying the cream on the sore spots so gently Ash wasn't sure he had even touched her. He wrapped the foot in rough fabric, and began to work on the next. He started the same process, gently massaging the life back into her other foot before applying the cream and wrapping it up to match.

"Are you still awake?"

"I don't know how," Ash said, her voice hoarse to her own ears.

"Good. I have water and you, uh, should probably change. Your jacket needs to dry."

Ash could've cried at the idea of sitting upright, but did so, pushing up into his waiting hands.

"I'll give you privacy."

At his words, she opened her eyes to track him. He went to the back corner and turned around, pulling off his own clothes one at a time. She blinked a few times in the dim light, noticing for the first time a small gas lantern on the table, casting a warm glow over the still chilly space. At least they were out of the snow and the wind.

She spotted the breadth of his back covered in an eagle tattoo with its wings outstretched. The shadows from the gas lantern highlighted his muscles as they undulated in the dark while he pulled off his outer layers.

She begrudgingly took her feet out of the wool blanket burrito and got to work undressing, feeling the painful ache in her muscles, screaming for rest. Everything was soaked through.

"I don't have any clothes to change into."

"Check the bed. There's a T-shirt and long johns of mine you can use. They're clean."

Ash laid all of her clothes out and pulled the clean, dry T-shirt over her naked body. It fit more like a gown. The bear man had at least a foot on her height-wise, so it came well down her thighs. The pants bunched around her ankles with the extra length, but she pulled them down to tuck her feet inside in a makeshift footie pajama.

"Can I turn around?"

"Um, yeah. Thanks."

He turned and nodded once, giving her the first full look at his face.

Bear man was accurate. Big-ass Viking would work too. He had long, auburn hair and a large matching beard. He was wearing a matching white shirt and some underlayers that looked like black pants with thick wool socks. Much better prepared than she was. He probably was hitting six feet four, easy two fifty, all muscle, but he was silent as he took a few steps over to the small cabinets that made up the kitchen. He pulled down a canteen and an enamelware cup, pouring out clear water for her.

"Here. Drink. It's not that old."

Throat on fire, she gladly accepted, gulping down the water.

"Do you need some?"

He pulled out another canteen and started to shake his head no. She was already pouring the next cup and drank with greed and relief.

The door rattled with a gust of wind, and a few snowflakes floated in through the crack, which he covered with another blanket.

"We'll rest here tonight until the weather gets better."

"What is this place?"

He shook his head again. "Sleep first. Take the bed. I'll be fine."

She sat on the edge of the bed instead, feeling her lower back decompress.

"Are you sure?"

"Positive."

"I don't—"

"It's fine."

Ash was too tired to argue. She pulled back the wool blanket and thought the sheets looked a little dusty, but there at least weren't any stains. She did one sweep of the arm to clear any spiderwebs off and let herself relax down, tugging the wool blankets up over her.

At first the cotton was cold against her skin, with the heavy weight of the wool warming quickly to her body. The cabin was better than outside, but she could still see her breath on the stale flat pillow.

Fine. She didn't care anymore. Answers were a tomorrow problem; for now what she needed was sleep.

Her feet began to throb, and she was grateful he had taken the time to care for her. Once again, her ability to detect lies had brought her to the right place. He had treated her with such care and kindness. She didn't know why yet, but he was being honest when he said he wouldn't hurt her.

She rolled over just once to see the bear man, lying where she had been on the oval rug with a blanket over him.

"What's your name?"

"Max. Max Grover."

"Thank you, Max. I'm Ash Myers."

"You warm enough?"

Her body was starting to shake, whether from cold, adrenaline, or exhaustion, she couldn't tell.

"I'm fine. Thank you."

With that she closed her eyes and fell asleep, not hearing him get up and put another blanket on her.

CHAPTER 8

Ash's first realization was that her nose was cold. Her face was cold. Her head was cold. Her body was warmer, and everything smelled like the outdoors.

All of it reminded her of when she was younger, staying at her uncle's house. An old hippie, he used a lot of army surplus blankets when he had gone backpacking in his youth. She had stayed over a few times during their visits and always remembered the smell.

Now, though, there was no familiar patchouli or tea or wind chimes.

Someone was here. She heard the rustling of a bag and then a few pieces of plastic tearing open.

The events of the night came back in a full rush. Going for a run to clear her head, Johnson's hand on his gun, the voice behind her...

Ash's eyes opened. It was brighter than last night, but not by much. There was no window. Cracks of dim light came through the door. The only sound was the creaking of the wooden floor around her. She couldn't hear any animals outside, just the muffled stillness of snow.

She sat up to a spinning head and had to retreat to the pillow, closing her eyes against the sensation.

"Here."

A cup was put on the floor next to the low bed.

She glanced down to see a warm brown liquid. Coffee or tea, it didn't matter to her. She propped herself up and cradled the warm mug, glancing with confusion at the still empty fireplace, seeing only a little bit of snow that had made its way down the flue.

"How did you heat the water?"

"MRE."

Meal ready to eat, another military surplus item Uncle Ron had mentioned, but she never saw.

"Thank you."

He glanced up and nodded once before going back to mixing the water into another pouch, which created steam as the food warmed inside the center with the chemical reaction.

"The snow is deeper than expected, of course. More is coming tonight. I don't know how long we'll be able to sit here. You got family looking for you?"

"Not exactly."

His steely blue eyes studied her from under a bushy auburn brow. He looked like a much younger, much sterner Santa Claus.

"Husband? Boyfriend?"

"Neither. I have two friends that will be worried, and I would've said a whole police department who until twelve hours ago, I would've considered brothers. Would've died for them. I have no idea what happened."

She stared into the dented steel mug as the realization hit. She was alone with a stranger, and everything she had known up until now felt different. All she had wanted before was a promotion, to be the first female detective in the department, and to figure out what had been going on in Goldvein. She had worked her ass off, been told no, and then worked even harder. Then last night, she was the target, and all of that work meant nothing.

"You must know something, otherwise they wouldn't be chasing."

"Why were you there?"

"I like to keep an eye on things."

"That's it?"

"Yep. Especially once I saw the police report about Ted being killed."

"Why involve me? It'd be easier to let me get arrested. I'm collateral now."

Max nodded while he ate his meal, sitting at the table. "So what do you know about Ted Saunders?" he asked.

Ash hated to show her hand first, but nothing about him smelled like a lie. She pulled her legs in closer and only then saw the shiny blisters. She glanced up at the table, looking at the tub of Vaseline and seeing her clothes all strung up on the wall, with her poor sneakers turned upside down, and a very small propane heater she hadn't noticed before.

"Ted Saunders was killed in his own home and wrote my name down as he died. It didn't look like the other attacks, but I think it's related."

"The other ones?"

"Yeah, people have been acting crazy. Perfectly normal, and then they'll just fly off the handle and attack someone. The police have been looking for leads for a while now and getting nowhere. One of the victims we put in custody had a blister pack of pills from the lab. Looked like he was in a study of some sort, but when I called to get more information, they cited HIPAA and no one could get through. There wasn't enough for a warrant, and Rocky Mountain Labs has been there forever, so it sort of fizzled."

Max didn't say anything, but kept preparing the food, then stuck a fork in a pouch before bringing it over to where she sat.

"Do all of your guests get breakfast in bed?" she said with a smile.

He grunted in return.

"Ted Saunders was…an acquaintance."

"I'm sorry for your loss."

Max shook his head. "No loss to me. If anything, it helps me. I can't bring them down alone."

"Bring them down?"

He chewed again and looked over at her, sizing her up.

"You're right about the attacks being linked to this, but not in the way you think. The Borealis Project is testing some major shit on humans."

Ash thought of the blister pack she had found earlier on suspects in the random attacks in town. "I take it things aren't going well?"

"That's the scary part. They are going exactly to plan."

A chill went across her skin that had nothing to do with the cold. "They want to make people crazy? To sell the crazy or to sell the antidote?"

"Not sure."

The ramifications and possibilities swirled in her mind. "Are the police involved?"

He didn't answer, but kept chewing and avoided her eyes.

How deep did this go? How many people were impacted?

"Eat up; they'll be looking for you."

"And you."

He shook his head. "I don't think so."

"How come?"

"I've been dead for five years."

CHAPTER 9

Max didn't know if it was because he wasn't used to being around people in such close quarters for so long, but he was more than amused by the look on her face. Ash was only stunned for a moment. Her perfect lips, which were red from being chapped, parted in a quick surprise, but then quickly closed and firmed to a thin line. She must have made a fierce cop in the police department she'd run from.

"So how are you dead but not?"

"There was an explosion when I left. I don't remember much, but I woke up in the woods later. They couldn't find me. I've made sure that continues to be the case."

"I've lived here for a while. I would've heard about an incident like that."

"Yeah, well, it was a happy accident, and I'm sure they kept it hush-hush."

One eyebrow arched with a smirk that made him feel something he hadn't felt in a long time. "Just like Bob Ross."

He almost laughed despite himself, and that had not been the case for a long time. He should be listening for the sound of vehicles or people finding them. He should be shutting off the heater to reduce the chance of any heat signature. He should be readying his pack to keep moving as far from Borealis as possible, but instead, here he was telling stories to the most striking pair of eyes glaring at him from across the room.

They were so blue they almost looked violet. Since she had woken up, he hadn't been able to look away from her whenever she watched him. Her short, dark hair was all tousled in a way that looked so invitingly sexy, he wanted to crawl right into the bed and feel her body all over him.

Seeing her in his bed wearing his T-shirt, wiping the sleep and exhaustion from her eyes, had been enough to undo anyone, but for Max it wasn't just that. She was tough.

Her feet were trashed after yesterday. He had been amazed to see how far she made it with one swollen ankle and the blisters covering the whole right heel and the pad of her foot. He had been glad to take care of her last night, knowing what was coming next.

They couldn't stay here long.

"Ted Saunders was involved?"

"He started it before they forced him out. Had a kid he wanted to save. Born with some defect. I saw a picture of her one time in his office during the intake. They must have killed him to cover their tracks. This isn't what he wanted, and they would want to neutralize anyone that knows too much."

"So how does he know about…me?"

He took a breath and met her eyes. "Ted knew about all of his experiments."

"I'm not an experiment. Never met the man in my life or heard about any of this before."

"That's interesting. What about when you were a child?"

"Doubtful. My family owns a farm—commune thing—in

California. They would be the last ones in line for a program from a government lab."

"Have you ever felt…different?"

Ash's mouth shut.

He nodded. "Did anyone know?"

She shook her head. "No. I've never told anyone."

"And yet…Ted knew."

Ash blew out a breath and stared into the mug in her hands. "He said 'Sergeant Ashleigh Myers knows the truth and the lies.' God, I can't believe I'm even saying this out loud. I've never, *never* told a soul my whole life. I don't even think the other guys knew what it meant, but it bothered me, you know. To see a secret I've guarded forever written plain as day. Not the typical work day."

"Is that why you trusted me?"

"I could tell you were telling the truth from the first whisper."

"And the others?"

"Weren't. Simple. I don't have a lot of information. I just can feel and sort of smell it when someone's lying."

"I bet that comes in handy as a cop."

"Yeah, but you still have to prove it in a court of law. Probable cause and all of that." Ash shook her head again and looked up at him with narrowed eyes, finding her footing again. "How do you know all of this?"

"Like I said, Borealis runs experiments. You're looking at one."

That shocked her. "You were tested on?"

"Yep. I was recommended after an accident. I used to do mountain rescue. Both helicopter and on the ground. Fell off a cliff and broke almost everything. They offered a way to put me back together. To heal faster. Said I was a perfect fit with my background."

"Which is in?"

"Brief stint in the military, then gym stuff, a little fighting, little security, mountain rescue, kind of bounced around."

"Why would that matter?"

"They're interested in people who are naturally gifted in certain talents. When they find them, they run experiments. Some in-house, some outpatient."

"Which were you?"

"Outpatient…at first." He suppressed a shiver against the memories. If Ash noticed, she didn't mention it.

"Do people disappear?"

"Some do, yeah."

"Did you know John Burton?" Ash thought back to Laura's first husband, Holden's father, John. He had worked first in remote tech support as a government contract, but then started leaving for more hours as a big project went underway. According to Laura, he had become more and more erratic and panicked, putting even further strain on the marriage, when one day he didn't come home. Every attempt had been made to find him, but he had simply vanished, until Ash had taken it upon herself to do a little more digging. Lo and behold, he had popped up on a computer search years later. Ash had never believed in coincidences.

Max thought for a moment. "It sounds familiar, but I didn't come in contact with many people."

"Why not?"

"They kept me in isolation, but I would listen to the employees. Pick up what I could."

"Do you remember what happened before the explosion?"

"It's a long story. Not a good one. People got hurt."

"Did you?"

"No. I did the hurting."

He expected her to flinch. Turn away. Something to punish him. But the violet eyes took on a depth as she stared at him with a fierce understanding and nodded.

"The more you tell me, the more questions I have."

"That's how they work."

"Why are you telling me all of this? You didn't know about me. Couldn't I be a plant?"

"Why do you think I led you away from everyone?"

That changed her attitude, but just for a moment. Her nostrils flared as she took a deep, apparently steadying breath. "You said you wouldn't hurt me."

"I said I wasn't planning on hurting you."

"If you meant to hurt me, I doubt you would've given me the shirt off your back, shared what little food you have, information, heat, shelter. You wouldn't have taken care of my feet."

Max pulled a tight smile to himself. "You have no idea how much danger you're in just by being with me."

"I wouldn't have come with you if I didn't trust you more than the people I was running from, which believe me, was a helluva shock to me."

"Now it all makes sense. I was surprised you actually listened."

Her eyes narrowed to slits. "You come out of nowhere from the woods, tell me I'm not safe, and then you're surprised I followed?"

"Most people don't listen to Bigfoot."

Ash broke into a wide grin. "Well, I'm not most people."

"Good company."

They ate together in silence, each mulling over the conversation.

He watched her discreetly, studying her beautiful features. The neck of the shirt was stretched out due to age and wear, which is why it was a backup. For now, it was perfect as it slid over a shoulder, exposing perfect skin, taut over a well-defined collarbone, with visible strength in her shoulder. She was smart, she was fast, and she was fit. But most importantly, she was different. Just like him.

The thought of someone who understood, who knew what it was like, was so tempting to let himself sink into. For the first time in too long, Max felt the glimmer of connection. Sensations of relief, of not being alone to face the world, tempted him to imagine what could be between them. His mind wandered back to the feel of her calves in his hands.

All of it made him feel antsy, unsettled. He needed more action and less thought.

Max stood abruptly, rolled his mess up, and put them in a sealed bag to dispose of later so as not to attract bears. He stood to go out and take a look around before taking a leak, but paused with his hand on the door, unsure of what to do or say.

They exchanged a glance. Why did he feel the need to ask permission? It had been so long since he had been with others, he had forgotten what was expected. Clearly she was looking at him with his hand on the doorknob.

"Uh, I'll be right back."

Ash took another breath, never breaking eye contact, and nodded. "Okay."

Max took this opportunity to check for signs they had been followed this far. He hadn't seen any trackers on her clothes, except for her phone. He would check it was off when he went back inside.

Snowdrifts undulated between trees, nearing three or four feet deep at their highest thanks to the wind. The brief sunshine fought through the dense gray clouds, but he could already feel the icy breeze, which would grow again with the darkening clouds on the horizon. He walked out of the old hunter's cabin, pausing to listen to the silence. He had practiced the art of waiting for a long time. He didn't move, letting his body become still and heartbeat slow, becoming one with the areas around him.

He listened.

There were a few birds off in the distance, hunting by the sounds of it, but nothing else. One abnormally large icicle hung on the south side. He'd need to keep an eye on that so it didn't form a dam and cause roof damage. He finished his business on a nearby tree and was ready to head back inside, when he heard something like an engine off in the distance.

CHAPTER 10

Ash knew what was wrong before Max walked back in. When he did, she knew he had heard the same thing. The steady beat of helicopter blades.

"Is that for us?"

"Not us. You."

He went over and doused the heater, packing stuff in his duffle bag, before opening a floorboard and pulling out an ancient rifle.

"Local woman goes missing, last seen on a late night run." She had heard those words so often, and it was only now that she wondered if the people she had helped find were indeed missing and in need of help, or if help had been the problem.

Ash felt the hair on her neck creep up as the sound continued in the distance. Was it getting closer? She couldn't tell.

"In daylight, they'll be able to track us and spot us against the snow. Our best bet is staying put for now. This hunter's cabin was built into the mountain for more than a few reasons. With the tree cover, we're hidden."

Ash wasn't convinced, and apparently, neither was Max.

Max began loading the bolt-action, with a series of satisfying clicks.

"How old is that?"

"1898. No need to be registered, but it's enough to stop a bear."

"That's our protection?"

"If they find you, nothing will work, but it'll at least buy us some time."

"Why do they want me so much?"

"You're valuable. I wouldn't be surprised if they start trying to get access to your information and computer."

"I've turned my phone off."

Max nodded. "I hope it's enough."

"You said you did search and rescue before. How long until they call it off?"

Max didn't answer, but sat propped up against the door with his eyes closed, holding the gun. If Ash didn't know any better, she'd have thought he had fallen asleep. "The standard answer is three days, but for Borealis I guess it depends."

Ash reached over to feel her clothes. They were still damp to the touch.

Max shook his head. "No need yet."

"You're the one with the gun," she said as she pulled on the clothes. They were cold and tough to get into, but she'd live.

"It's my security blanket."

"Yeah, well, this is mine."

Ash moved to step out of the bed, felt the floor beneath her foot, and winced in pain. She hadn't realized how sore she was. It occurred to her that until now, she'd been lying in bed since he had put her there. She moved to stretch, feeling every muscle ache in protest, some outright screaming. She did a few stretches, and rolled her neck and shoulders in a feeble attempt to warm up her muscles, just in case.

Time crept by in what felt like hours. It was maddening to hear the thrum come a little closer and move away, all the while feeling like prey being toyed with. Sometimes she was straining so hard to hear, she wasn't sure if she was imagining it or not.

"Why aren't they coming closer?"

"Probably think you wouldn't have made it so far. They're working in sections."

"I wouldn't have made it without you. Thank you."

He turned to look at her, and that's when she noticed the striking blue eyes. "You shouldn't be thanking me. I've led you straight into a nightmare."

"It already was a nightmare. I'm just glad I don't have to go through it alone."

His face softened with understanding before he nodded and resumed his post with his eyes closed and ears open.

"We won't be able to stay here forever. I have to get back to tell my friends," Ash said after several more minutes of warming up her stiff body.

"We'll move during the night as soon as you can."

"Where to?"

"I have a few more houses off-grid north and west of here; my main home is farther in the mountains."

"Well, unless you're looking for a new roommate, that isn't going to work."

"What's your angle?"

Ash stretched again and paused.

Before, she had been so set on being the first female detective in the department. Nothing could've stopped her. She dedicated her life to that job.

Now that goal seemed so trivial in comparison to staying alive and figuring out what the fuck was going on with her, her friends, Max, and Borealis back in Goldvein.

"I have no idea."

"When you don't know where you're going, you're not going anywhere."

"Thanks for that. Big help."

Max shrugged. "Just pointing out the obvious. You only have two choices. Run away or go back."

"Running away isn't an option. I still have my friends to look out for."

"That's some fierce friends."

"They're more like sisters. We're a family." More than they knew, since Ash had never told them her suspicions. They had never wanted to talk about it, probably because they had no idea about her ability, but Ash knew they were different just like her.

Whenever Laura had come out of the ambulance with good news, Ash could tell she was lying about the seemingly miraculous turn that had put the patient on the road to recovery. At first she couldn't figure out what was going on, but enough time passed where she could tell Laura was doing something *herself* to heal people. Ash didn't know how, but hey, from where she was sitting, she certainly wasn't in a position to judge.

Megan was similar. She was a paradox. Filled with anxiety, but no fear around fire. Sure, she was a firefighter, but all of them had a healthy respect and fear of fire. Megan didn't. She would march right in, taking too many chances, too many risks, and never had an issue except with smoke inhalation. Megan had also let it slip that as an infant, she had survived a fire that killed her whole family. When she said she didn't know how and it must have been a miracle, Ash could smell the lie. Megan knew exactly how she had survived.

Neither of them knew about her. Detecting lies didn't leave a trace.

Ash peeked through the crack to get a glance at the sky, in

hopes of seeing something, even though seeing something would be very bad. Not being able to see without a window was driving her crazy.

She wished she could turn her phone on to tell them not to worry and not to ask questions, but she didn't risk it. Them playing the role of missing their friend was ideal so if the situation was as bad as Max said, it would be clear they weren't involved. The only way to talk to them would be to go back in person, but now was clearly not the right time. Maybe they could help her get more answers about what in the hell had been going on in Goldvein.

"Will they go looking for you?"

"Yes." And that was part of the problem.

"My friends are relentless. Paramedic and fire. We ran calls together. Started together," she added when Max looked surprised by that answer.

"Sounds like you've been through a lot."

"Yeah."

"So you have your friends, your police department, and Borealis all searching for you."

Hunting her was more like it.

"Why did you bring me along again?"

The helicopter blades grew louder in the distance. Ash stilled her body, barely daring to breathe as the steady beat of the blades grew louder than before. She watched as Max seemed to relax in peaceful repose, his eyes resting, as if he had fallen asleep and become one with the structure around him.

Ash took a page out of his book and closed her eyes, trying to still her breath and her racing heart. She thought back to her memories, to a golden place of peace doused in sunlight. Her parents had lived here a while ago for work, before moving out to California. Ash had come back drawn by the stories they told of their time in the mountains when she was born, and to the only time in her life her family had felt normal.

In her mind, she saw the delicate lace on her bedroom curtains, with the sun streaming through as the fabric swayed in the breeze. It was warm, and she was at her grandmother's house with the smell of coffee and lemon dish soap mixing. The sheets were starched white and clean over a soft bed.

The beat of the blades took a turn and got louder. A rattling teetered on the table behind them. She glanced behind her to see the enamelware cup start to rattle on a plate with the vibration from above.

"Leave it."

Max hadn't moved. Ash stilled, trying to close her eyes to go back to a happy place and finding she couldn't.

CHAPTER 11

Max's hand tightened on the weapon. The gun was old, but it packed a punch. Undetectable and still lethal in the right hands, which he hoped were his. He hadn't done much other than target practice, but the training kicked in when it counted, and his trigger finger was still in the safety position. Thank you very much, Drill Sergeant.

The hairs on the back of his neck all rose. Since living on his own for five years, he had developed a sense of when people approached. He typically noted it and moved on, staying still and silent.

Undetectable and lethal.

But today was different. It wasn't just him.

He broke character again, which really was becoming an unfortunate habit lately, and glanced at his counterpart. He was transfixed. She had her head pointing down, touching the door, with her eyes closed. She almost looked like she was mouthing something while breathing. It couldn't be, but was she praying?

"Hey."

His voice was a whisper and drowned out by all the thundering blades around them.

Ash still heard, but he wasn't sure how, and looked up. "It's gonna be okay."

She gave him a weak smile and nodded before resuming the brace position.

God help him, he didn't like seeing her look like that even though she was the exact reason they were in this predicament.

Max pulled a grim face as he watched her beautiful, elegant form tremble with a steadying breath as she tried to calm herself, despite the deafening noise and the rattling dishes.

Borealis wanted to eliminate her and wouldn't be satisfied until they had proof.

And Max just wasn't going to allow that.

There purposely were no windows, but enough cracks to spy out. He stood and went to the bed, standing on the frame to slide the muzzle through a thin crack in the eaves where he had just enough of a view of anyone who got close to the door.

In glancing outside with what little vantage point he had, he assured himself there was no trace. He had even made sure to step lightly in carefully chosen spots to minimize his footprints when taking his morning stroll.

The helicopter kept coming closer and closer.

Had they found them? It felt like they were right on top of them, but the sound kept moving like a large annoying mosquito, teasing and taunting its prey.

From the sound, it seemed like they were going in a grid pattern. A good sign. As long as they did that they didn't know where they were. With each low swoop, the rattling cup danced around, then stopped before they moved away. Surely they would stop soon with the cover of nightfall.

This cabin wasn't on the map, wasn't visible from the sky, and unless they had good heat-seeking equipment, there was no way they could be discovered. He had avoided a fire, left no trace.

Still the looming helicopter swept back and forth, seeming to go farther away from them up the mountain.

Ash had the same thought and looked over at him with a questioning smile and nod as if to say, "Did you hear that?"

Max nodded, but kept his post as she did hers against the door, until the helicopter was far enough for the cup's liking.

"We can't stay here. We'll need to move tonight."

"I don't want to go farther away."

"You've decided what's next?"

Ash gave him a grim nod, then stood, slowly. He could tell she was still hurting in the way she uncurled her body with a wincing of pain on her beautiful features that vanished as she stood straight and looked at him with complete clarity.

"I'm getting to the bottom of this. It ends now." She smiled enough to reveal a frigging dimple, making her look even more adorable.

"We'll need supplies. I have some at my place, and a small truck. If we can get there, we can suit up and get ready."

Ash nodded. "Perfect. Then we'll head into town and bring Borealis down."

Max stood there, admiring her for everything she was Everything he ever wanted. She was strong, steady, smart and oh so feminine. Everything about her made him want to wage war and go into battle. It was a wonder he trusted himself to be in her company, given what could go wrong, especially considering the effect she was starting to have on him.

Staying calm was best. If he was smart, he would get her supplied and let her go away from him, but the mere thought of it started to blur his vision.

"Max, are you okay?"

She was close now, coming closer, and the clarity of his focus was starting to fade. He tried to hold out a hand and stop her from coming close.

She was reaching out to touch him. God, he wanted her to, but wished she wouldn't. Oh shit—he had two trains of thought. Not good. The sound of his heartbeat picked up and drowned out everything else.

"You're burning up. Are you okay?"

That's when he heard the dogs barking and a man shouting orders in the distance.

CHAPTER 12

Ash had no idea what happened next. All of it happened so fast she wasn't able to process what she was seeing until later.

Max almost turned into a different person. Almost an animal. He was the same man, but was moving too fast, and was too strong. His eyes weren't right, as he looked around and snarled at the cabin around them both.

He snatched the bag and gun, then literally threw her over his shoulder and took off into the fading light.

"MAX! What are you doing? The helicopter!"

He carried her and the gear while running through the snow faster than anyone should or could. Even as Ash bounced on his shoulder with his hand clamped over her legs, he was sprinting through the snow. Had it not been knee-high, he would already have been over the top of the mountain they were climbing. They were under the trees, so she had no idea how far away from the helicopter they were, but she couldn't hear it. She couldn't hear the dogs over Max's labored breathing.

"Max, stop! Put me down!"

He didn't answer, but kept running. Manic and crazed, he kept running forward, carrying her like she was nothing.

She held on to his shirt, and she felt how drenched he was. His body was in complete fight-or-flight mode, and thank God it was the second one. Based on the way he had jerked around the cabin snarling, she felt lucky not to have been attacked.

Just like the men in town.

This is what he had been talking about.

I don't plan on hurting you. The fight left her, and chills ran down her back. Instead of trying to talk or get away, she clung to him and tried to match his energy, keeping her eyes peeled for signs of the dogs. It was dusk, and the clouds were thickening again, thank God. With luck it would snow again and cover their tracks.

Ash held on to his drenched back as he kept going, not stopping for water, rest, or even as the incline and terrain challenged him more.

Her mind was in overdrive thinking back to everything that had happened in Goldvein.

All of the witnesses described being attacked by someone who was unresponsive. Stronger than normal, faster than normal. Almost animal. They were fine one minute and then stark raving mad the next. Ash held on as he bumped and jostled their way through an icy cold stream that didn't seem to affect him at all. The water soaked right through his pants and should've been enough to snap him out of it, but he was transfixed on running to wherever they were going.

Literally, he had just told her they should be safer in the cabin from the helicopter, maybe not dogs, but that didn't matter now. Logic and reason were gone. Hopefully, he knew where he was going in this crazed state. She held on and tried to track where they were coming from, keeping an eye on his footprints, which would certainly lead whoever had the dogs right to them if they found their tracks.

She tried again. "Max, do you know where you're going?"

Just panting was the answer. He adjusted the grip on her legs and kept going once they were on the other side of this mountain, darting from pine tree to pine tree, now on a decline.

By now, Ash had overcome the shock enough to recognize he was not going to drop her. She had been trained on how to get out of this in the police academy, but had been struck by how fast he was moving, and it didn't seem like the better option to get down. He was moving faster than she could, and clearly knew where he was going down the small trail.

Ash felt her teeth gnash together and clip each other, taking care to keep her tongue away from the edge of her mouth in case she bite through when he was hopping and sliding down. She gripped and held on to the drenched fabric, feeling the heat come off his body despite the freezing temps and ice-cold water, never mind the fact he had been running through snow.

He tripped and fell, turning so her face smashed into his side instead of the ground. Ash used the moment to duck away from him before he could grab her again.

"Okay, what the fuck is going on? Where are we going?"

The man who was looking at her sent goose bumps over her body. There was a look in the eyes that was inhuman. She was reminded of seeing *Jaws* for the first time with Megan and Laura. Captain Quint had called them a doll's eyes. She had only seen them a few times before. Both were when she had responded to scenes where people had gone crazy and attacked someone.

Max sniffed and twitched his head as if he was a horse, fighting a bridle, and stalked toward her.

"Max. Max!"

His hands curled like claws and his teeth were bared through ragged breathing. She could see the veins popping out of his neck under hot, slick flesh.

"Max! It's me…Ash."

She stepped back with one foot, bracing herself in case he lunged at her. He had her on height, weight, strength, and unfortunately speed. He still had the rifle in one hand too, not that it was in the position to fire, since he had gripped it by the stock.

"Max! Stop!"

He charged instead.

Ash spun on her heels and ran in the direction they had been going, zigzagging through the trees, panic gripping through her as she sprinted for her life.

The sound of heavy footfalls behind her pumped up her pulse to the max as fear laced through her unlike anything before. She grabbed a tree and swung around, hoping to throw him off. All that weight couldn't stop on a dime. He went skittering down the slope but recovered quick, climbing up with the fastest bear crawl she had ever seen.

Her ankle twinged. It wasn't going to last long. Ash saw a stick and grabbed it as she ran back up the hill, hoping to have something to strike out against him.

He grabbed her arm first, and she could feel the vise grip of his blazing fingers close around her upper arm, dragging her down to the snow.

In a last-ditch effort, she whipped the branch around and smacked him right in the shoulder, hard enough for half of the branch to break away before flying into the woods and sliding down the hill on the snow.

Max didn't even flinch, but he did drop the bag and rifle.

Ash tried to pull away, kick, evade, and twist her way out of it like she had done before, but he was unmoved. When she lunged for his face, he grabbed her other wrist and twisted until she dropped the branch. Only then could she see the blood running down his arm.

Ash had never been more afraid in her life.

"You said you wouldn't hurt me," she said, looking him right in the eyes which were still dead to the world, as his head jerked uncomfortably.

He didn't do anything. For all of that might and power, he stilled, holding her, breathing. Watching.

He was like a snake ready to strike, and she felt the odd sense she was in the position of snake charmer.

"Max. Please. Let me go."

She felt the grip loosen on both arms, but neither hand left completely.

"I need you to tell me what is going on."

He didn't speak, but his breathing settled down.

Ash had no idea how long or far he had run, but she didn't hear dogs anymore. Still wary, she took a step back and then another.

He was watching her, never taking his eyes off her, always twitching like an animal. Everything moved but the eyes. Had he blinked? Max let out what sounded like a strangled cry, less like the snarl that she was used to. He sounded like a dog that was in pain.

"Max." Her voice was gentler now. She was still very much afraid, but less so since he had the chance to break her neck and clearly hadn't.

"Max, talk to me."

He blinked. There was almost a ripple that went through him before he started to howl. It was a low cry as he pulled his arms in front of his face and dropped to his knees before putting his head in the snow.

There was a whimpering, and that's when the shakes started.

"Max!" Ash was already on it, jumping forward to close the distance between them and putting her hand on his back, trying to get him to roll over. God, he was soaked, and his skin, which was so hot before, now was freezing to the touch. His pants were soaked and already freezing.

She didn't know what to do, but she kept rubbing his back and started making a shushing noise.

"It's okay. It's going to be okay."

The funny thing was, Ash had every reason in the world to believe that it was not true, and that was before she heard a growl from somewhere behind her.

If shit hadn't been going well up until now, it was about to get a lot fucking worse. Everything slowed down around her. First, Ash watched as Max crumpled to the snow. All of the frenzy left his body a shell, shaking in the snow.

She looked behind her to face what she was hoping she wouldn't see, only to confirm that yes, there was a grizzly emerging from the trees about a hundred yards down the hill.

The signature hump was covered in loosely packed snow. It was early in the season for a hibernation, and even then grizzlies could wake and rise from their den. It was hard to know if this large one had been woken up, or was just taking shelter from the storm, before two complete idiots made enough noise for everyone to know they were here.

Now would be a great time for the helicopter to scare the bear away.

Now would be a great time for someone on a snowmobile to come in guns blazing.

Now would be a perfect time for Max to fly into a rage.

However, none of those things were happening.

She glanced back at Max, who was shivering with his eyes

closed. The faint tinge of blood seeped into the snow, making it pink around him, highlighting him as the wounded prey for a hungry bear, ready to stock up on calories.

Ash stood her ground between the bear and Max. Her mind raced through the possibilities. Was it play dead or stand your ground? Should she yell or stay quiet?

The grizzly hadn't moved other than swiping at its own nose, as if trying to wake up and see what was going on. The black nose sniffed once, twice, scenting the air for food.

Was it like a shark? Could it smell blood, and would it fly into a feeding frenzy before hibernating? If that happened, there was literally nothing either of them could do without bear spray or—

HOLY SHIT.

While the bear was still taking stock of the situation, Ash whipped around and spotted the bag and the rifle.

She abandoned her position and sprinted for it, hoping the grizzly wouldn't give chase.

Her hands touched the cold, wet steel, and she whipped around with the butt against her shoulder, eyeing the bear.

It hadn't moved since she had run away, but clearly tracked her movements. Now nothing was between the bear and Max.

The bear shook its head, snow falling away from the brown fur as it sniffed again and ambled in Max's direction.

The rifle was bolt-action. Ash pulled the bolt to chamber a round, and clicked it back into place before resuming the sight. She had no idea how much ammo was in the relic, but she wasn't about to waste a shot on a maybe. She also really didn't want to draw any attention to them unless it was absolutely necessary. One shot would hit the bear, but would be a beacon for whoever had the dogs.

"Max," Ash called out. "If you can hear me, I need you to stand up."

He moaned in response, but the bear stopped at the sound of her voice.

"Good, Max, but I need you to give me more. We got company. I need you to sit up."

The rifle was heavy. Ash's heart was pounding in her ears. The wind picked up again, and a shimmer of icy snow covered her face. Ash should've been cold, but the adrenaline meant she felt nothing more than a breeze. It also meant they were upwind, thank God, so maybe the bear couldn't smell them.

It was about fifty yards now. Ash kept the sight trained on the brown coat. It was big, but with this distance and an old, unfamiliar gun, she couldn't take the chance.

"Max, I need you. Please stand up."

Max shifted toward her voice, blinking as if trying to clear his eyes to see her better. She was about twenty feet away from him, and took a step closer.

He groaned again and tried to push himself up, shaking in the process. Whatever the fuck had just happened had left him weak and worthless.

"Just… run…" he said, in a soft, strained voice.

"Fuck… no…" Ash answered, matching his tone.

God, it felt like the minutes ticked by as the bear looked at them both, scenting, swiping, and ambling around. It was in no hurry, and neither was Ash. Max was in no condition to run, so there was no choice but to stand guard.

He was shaking harder now. She tracked Max out of the corner of her eye, never taking hers off the bear for even a second. They were fast runners. If the bear wanted to make a move, Max would be toast if she didn't get a clean shot off. Even if they were bear chow, she couldn't even call an ambulance or get help if he was wounded.

The bear ambled around again, scenting, looking at them, almost more curious than threatened.

Leave. Just leave. Go back to where you came from. We don't want to bother you. Go back to sleep.

It was a beautiful sight if it hadn't been terrifying. Even now, she didn't want to kill this animal. She didn't even want to hurt it unless she had to.

At least the appreciation for animals had stuck. That was probably one of the only things she had left in common with her mom.

Minutes continued to tick by at a snail's pace. The bear stopped again, pawing at its face in an attempt to wake up. It looked tired, which was a godsend. Two weeks earlier, and they would already be toast.

The bear let out a couple of snorts, before checking out some evergreens to sniff around the base of a tree, maybe scenting a small mammal.

Ash risked a glance at Max, who was slumped over again.

"Max, you still with me?"

He didn't respond.

"Max? I need you with me."

A pained groan was her only answer, but at least it was proof of life.

Ash was never one to pray, but she kept willing the bear to leave. Turn around and go far enough for them to move on. She kept the rifle trained in that direction, until by the grace of everything holy, the bear did just that. A few more swipes of the paw and shakes of the coat, before it silently ambled off down the hill the way it had come.

Thank fucking God.

CHAPTER 13

Ash did a quick glance around her to find shelter. She could try to trace their footsteps back, but that would just lead them to the dogs, and heading downhill certainly wasn't an option.

Max was still shaking under her hand that was rubbing his now freezing, drenched back. He was in no condition to run. Whatever had happened was gone and taken all of that energy with it.

She was in charge now.

She did a quick glance around her. They were on the downhill side of a mountain; she didn't know which one. There were still enough pine trees to evade being seen from above. No sounds of helicopter or dogs. It would be completely dark in about an hour. They needed to get to shelter and dry off.

There were two options. Find one or make one. There were enough loose rocks under the snow to suggest crevices and caves. They just needed an outcropping large enough to fit them both and the bag.

"Stay here. I'm going to look for shelter. Do you want a blanket?"

Max shook his head, before grunting, "Head west; I think I remember a few."

"Got it. I won't be gone long."

Ash grabbed a branch off the tree next to her, disgusted at the sticky sap feeling, and plucked a pine needle off, laying it down on the snow as her first breadcrumb back to him. With a quick glance at the sun, she oriented herself and headed west, keeping to the steepest part, in hopes of finding something.

Ash continued, glancing over her shoulder at him. He was huddled down, still trembling, maybe even falling asleep. She pushed forward through the snow, feeling the stinging cold seep right through her running shoes. God, what she would give for a pair of boots.

She continued picking her way through the uneven, snowy terrain, pausing to pick up rocks from her footsteps. She hadn't officially studied geology, but her mom collected so many crystals, Ash could name almost all of them and the healing properties her mom referenced by the time she was five, when the homeschooling officially began. Up until now, she had thought it all a complete waste but had done what she was told to appease her mom.

There were some large stones, mostly argillite. They were getting bigger, which meant she was on the right path. She picked along, starting to spot areas where the rocks had fallen straight down, creating an embankment. The purple stood out against the white snow, sparkling in the brief sun. The next rock embankment was large as well and sparkled with veins of quartz inside. That would be the perfect thing to break it all apart. Ash stopped and made sure she could see a clear trail of pine needles back to where she left Max, before she took a turn around a bend and up a steeper slope. It took some spelunking, but her efforts were rewarded when she found a small cave facing east.

It was dry, dark, and just large enough for two people to lie flat. Hopefully the wind wouldn't whip their way all night. Ash checked for animals and swept out a few abandoned nests before hopping back down and making her way back through the trees.

Her heart skipped a beat when she returned and didn't see him at first, but a few more steps revealed a ghastly sight. He was lying down as if he had collapsed onto his side, looking a lot more corpse-like than she was comfortable with.

"Max? Come on, I found a place where we can get you dry."

His eyes fluttered open but didn't stay that way. A low groan came out of him as she tried to roll him over. She knew he was big, but now with her hands against his chest, she could feel just how muscled he was. As if she needed the proof. He had just sprinted what felt like a marathon uphill carrying her. She knew he was strong, but feeling it was different.

"Come on, I'll help you."

With her body weight as leverage, Ash pulled him up and looped his arm over her shoulders, which was hysterical considering the height he had on her. When it became clear that wouldn't work, she braced his side with her own, propping him up. She slung the bag over her other shoulder for balance and set off, guiding him toward the pine needles as they walked toward the cave.

Ash was sweating by the third needle, which she picked up and scattered as they went. He clearly was tired as his weight bore down on her. Instead of walking, Ash was almost moving him by rocking him back and forth while encouraging him to take steps.

"Come on. It's not much farther."

They continued the pattern and settled into a rhythm. Ash hoped the warmth from her body would transfer to him as they kept it up. It felt good to be able to do something. She could look past her aching feet, freezing toes, and burning calves as she nudged Max toward safety one step at a time.

All the while, she kept thinking and wondering about what was next. He had said he'd been tested on, just like the others. He had clearly been thrown into some sort of rage, also just like the others. He hadn't been hurt, other than the stick she smashed into his arm—which she had completely forgotten about until now. Ash peeked at the arm and winced when she saw all of the crusted blood. Add that to the to-do list when they reached the cave.

She ordered her questions for when he was ready, and kept circling back to one. Why didn't he hurt her? When everyone else that she knew of went into a rage, they attacked, but with Max it was different. Could he control it? Would it happen again? Would he be able to control it again?

She hadn't been able to detect it. She had even asked him if he planned on hurting her. Ash remembered his answer, *I'm not planning on hurting you.* Planning. No control, or if he did, it wasn't much.

Ash shook her head at the loophole. Needed to ask better questions next time.

Could she trust him? He had taken care of her, literally ran her away from danger, and hadn't attacked even though he wanted to.

Something wasn't right, but she didn't have enough information to panic about that yet. Right now, he was in no condition to hurt anything. And the point still remained that whatever Borealis was up to needed to end.

The question was how.

First, she would need to get access, figure out what was happening with the attacks in town, and blow the whole thing wide open to end it all. That might even get answers about John, sure as hell would get her a promotion, and—

Ash glanced up when Max made a grunt with another misstep. His face was dripping with sweat, and deep lines etched in the skin from pain or exhaustion. His face was pale with exertion, trying so hard to move forward with the little steps that had gotten smaller for the last half mile.

Her mouth thinned in grim determination. If what Max was saying was true, all of those people who had been killed or arrested had lost control over their lives. His life had been ruined. Her life and that of her friends were completely different.

It wasn't about getting a promotion anymore. It was about revenge.

Ash shook her head. So much had changed in such a short period of time. She wasn't a vengeful, emotional person. She had prided herself on her level head.

Max was a complete stranger, with this new side that she didn't trust at all. Trauma bonding was not uncommon in the police force. Once people went through challenging times together, they bonded faster than any other relationship. Strangers walked into a foxhole and walked out family. It wasn't a complete shock she had become protective of this person who was now seemingly attached to her hip as she almost carried him to shelter. Nevertheless, it surprised her.

Other than the girls, Ash wasn't one to date or make a lot of friends. Her ability to know the truth often led to sensory overload and a very low tolerance for bullshit.

"You're doing great. We're almost there."

What little strength Max had remaining started to give out before she saw the first tear come sliding down his cheek and vanish into the thick forest of his beard. The sight broke her heart.

Oh yeah, she would end the fuckers that started this. First step was to get Max dry, then she would come up with a plan.

CHAPTER 14

Max came to like always, but this time it was to the sound of the crackling fire. He was a little hazy as he floated back to consciousness and regained control of his aching arms and legs. The pain was like someone had broken all of his bones and overstretched his muscles. He didn't know how much more of this he could take, but he had no choice.

"No fire," he managed to say through the gravel in his throat.

She put something in his hand. It was a small canteen from the bag he must have grabbed. He drank while she spoke.

"I think the benefits outweigh the risks. We're soaked to the bone, and it's snowing again."

He cracked his lids to see Ash putting a few more pine needles on a small fire of mostly sticks and leaves. He hoped to God it was dry, otherwise she would smoke them both while sending a giant signal into the sky of their exact location.

"Besides, if they catch us, you'll just hulk out again, right?"

Max pulled a hand over his eyes. Fuck.

"I don't know."

"I do. I've seen that before with the other attacks in town. It's Borealis's plan, isn't it?"

"Super soldiers with too much adrenaline and testosterone."

"Yeah, it seemed something like that. You're lucky you didn't have a heart attack."

Max blinked and looked at the shadows of the rock dancing with the small fire. "A lot did."

"I'm sorry." The sound of the fire crackled between them. It was dim and low, but warming the rock beneath him. "So can you control it?"

"Not much, but I try."

"You said you hurt people. That's why you've been living alone?"

Max closed his eyes. It was easier to answer that way.

"I don't want to hurt anyone else."

"You said that to me before. Here, take some more water. You probably need that after your, um, episode."

Max took another sip.

"I'm surprised you believed me. It's okay if you don't anymore." It felt like the right thing to say, but he braced for the rejection, then relaxed when it was another question.

"Are you self-aware?" He peeked a glance at her. She wasn't looking at him, just the fire. Rock steady and taking it all in stride.

"No, but I've come to and seen the damage around me I know it isn't pretty. I can take you back into town and then I'll get—"

"No."

Now, she was staring at him. The fire's warm glow cast a gentle light on the harsh, warrior's features. Her eyes and hair looked almost black in the cave, lit only from a black rage within.

"You're not going anywhere. You're going to help me take this down."

"I'm a liability."

Ash turned and gave him a hard look.

"Say you won't hurt me."

"I can't promise that."

"Say it."

He threw his hands up and then wrapped them around his legs, turning away. "Why does it matter? I'm like someone else. Don't you get it? I can't control this. I'm unconscious. It might as well be a seizure. You're asking me to promise something I can't."

"Then why didn't you hurt me?"

"What?" Max turned back to her.

"I cracked a small tree into your shoulder. You didn't even flinch, but you didn't come at me."

He glanced down at his shoulder, admiring the helluva bruise and sticky slash. Now that the awareness was coming back to him, his shoulder hurt like hell.

"Incidentally, that's why I'm boiling water. It wasn't a clean small tree."

"I don't understand. I was told I'd attack any threat."

"Welp, you freaked out—sorry," she said, when he winced. "You, um, changed when you heard the dogs and a man's voice. Snatched me, the bag, and took off. But when I came at you with a tree, you didn't attack me. Chase me, yes, but didn't hurt me."

Max just now realized the rifle and the bag were by him with flakes of snow, melting into droplets. At least he had the decency to think about it. As far as he knew, this was the first time he ran away, other than breaking out from Borealis.

Normally he went for the danger head-on like a shark looking for blood.

"I'm surprised you didn't rip a tree right out of the ground. You sprinted up the mountain, carrying me and all of the crap away from the dogs. Hopefully you know where we are."

Max nodded, while still considering what she just said. "I'll be able to see better in the morning."

"I figured as much. Okay, that looks steady enough to boil water. "

Max watched as she opened the little pot and poured some water inside with a hiss. While that heated, she started opening his first aid kit.

"I'm sorry if I scared you."

"A little. You're a mean-ass motherfucker when you're like that. And I mean that as a compliment," she said with a smile over her shoulder.

"So you're not afraid it'll happen again?"

Ash smiled to herself. "I'm kind of counting on it. Besides, we'll need it to get to the bottom of whatever is going on in that lab."

"For what it's worth, I'm good insurance."

"Exactly."

"But what if I hurt you?"

"You would've ripped me limb from limb if you wanted to and you didn't, so I think Mad Max and I are cool."

Max sat up again and watched as she explained what she was doing as she cleaned and bandaged his arm with careful precision. Her tenderness touched him. It was as if she was speaking to a child as she held the small flashlight up to study what she was doing before wrapping his wound in gauze from the little sterile packet he had carried around for years.

The mix of the fierce warrior's fighting spirit with the

tenderness of a police officer helping a lost child had him confused.

"You should be running for the hills."

"And run right into the people who want to stop me from figuring out what is going on? No way."

"But you saw what I am. You had no idea who you were talking to in the woods. I shouldn't have—"

"Hey." She didn't speak until he looked at her. "It's okay. We're in this together."

Max watched her profile as she looked at the fire. "Do you know…" He didn't know where to go with the question, so he just left it out in the air.

"We're going to get you well and get to wherever your supplies are. After that, I'm calling a few people, and we're going into that lab."

"There's people inside."

"Not for long."

Max shifted toward her, feeling sore and weak. The wind skirted alongside the rock and fluttered the flames, but the fire didn't die out. As he pushed toward her in his damp clothes, the rock felt warm underneath the foil blanket.

"I'll do whatever I can to help. I've been sitting outside those gates waiting for anyone else to make it out alive so I could find someone like me and maybe bring it down together or go somewhere where we can live in peace."

"One step at a time." She looked over at him and smiled. She was beautiful, both in body and spirit. The kind of warmth the sun brings after a blizzard, giving light, life, and hope all in one brilliant sweep. "I have so many questions I want to ask you."

"I don't have a lot of answers."

"That's okay."

Max blinked really fast, feeling the tears threaten to spill again.

"Hey." The tenderness in her voice threatened to undo him. "It's okay. Come here."

Ash slipped her arms around him and held him close as he broke down and sobbed, shaking against her arms.

He had been alone for so long. Afraid of what others might think. He kept watching, always waiting for one of the other guys to break out. Other than a few people he did odd jobs for, he hadn't talked to anyone, but now he had a…friend.

It was overwhelming. Her hair tickled his neck, and her arms applied a gentle pressure as security around them both, while she rubbed his back, and he let everything go.

When he had thoroughly embarrassed himself enough, he leaned back and wiped his fingers down over his eyes, trying to swipe as many tears as he could into his beard so she didn't think him a complete child.

Ash smiled before shivering against another burst of wind. The chill that had seeped in to his bones edged away with the warmth from her body as she slid in behind him and rested against his back. The last thought he had before he fell asleep was that their bodies fit together perfectly.

CHAPTER 15

The next morning Max woke up feeling like he had been hit by a truck. He also couldn't feel his arm, but that was much more pleasant when he realized why. Looking down and seeing Ash's dark hair on his shoulder made him feel warmer than her breath on his chest. She was soft and strong and still curled against him.

While she lay there asleep, he took stock of what he could remember. There was the helicopter, the guy, dogs, and then he freaked out, which is how they got here—no, wait, that was Ash. The rock above him was only a few feet from his nose, so she must have rolled them both in here. He wiggled his fingers and toes, doing a quick check on the damage from the past forty-eight. No broken bones, a few scrapes here and there. He was sore, but in great shape considering what they had been through.

The clothes were pretty trashed, and the food supplies were low. The small fire she had taken a risk with had left a pile of soot, which would be a dead giveaway to the most basic tracker, but that and the foil blanket had kept them from freezing to death on another snowy night.

Right now the sun was trying to break through the thick, gray clouds. Not ideal for marching through where they could easily be spotted from above or behind. They needed to get to a safe spot and regroup. The hunting shack was probably compromised, which was a damn shame because he had loved it. Thankfully, he had three more safe spaces, but there was one main one they would need. If he could leave the other ones secure, that would work for whenever this shitshow ended. Assuming he still was alive and well to see it through.

Ash stirred. She looked up, still sleepy, and then jerked to look at the opening. The fear was evident and very real.

"It's okay, but we should get going."

Ash was already up and pulling on her clothes, leaving his body cold in her wake.

"We need to get supplies and get back into town."

Max was stuffing the foil blanket into the bag again. "I have a house and truck a few miles from here. We should be able to get there before nightfall."

The journey was several hours of wading through knee-deep snow, avoiding deeper drifts, while sweeping the snow behind them to attempt to cover their tracks. It snowed on and off while the wind fought against them. Max's arm had started to burn, while his leg muscles screamed in protest after the episode yesterday. He was sore, stiff, and much slower than he had been. He checked on Ash frequently, who matched his slower pace and was showing signs of limping again, while she marched on with her head down, leaning in to the frozen landscape ahead of them. They took turns carrying the bag and finally made it after the sun had set.

It was a small cabin, but larger than the hunting shack. It sat dark and low, banked into the hill of the mountains, obscured by trees. There was one small, dark window near the green door, which was half-hidden by snow. When Pat had first shown him the place, Max had thought of something between a hobbit's home and a witch in the woods of a fairy tale. He swept away the snow from the keyhole, reached down toward his boot, and unthreaded the key that was there to let them both inside.

Max stomped a few times to get most of the snow off him and on the rug before he walked over to the small kitchen and lit the kerosene lamp on the table, which cast a warm glow over the space.

Ash stepped inside and shut the door. It was the first time he had shared this space with anyone other than Pat who had only come twice. The feeling was odd…and intimate. She was drenched with flakes of snow frozen to her hair. Her face was reddened by the exposure, but her eyes were still clear and alert.

"Nice place you have here. Do you just have these cabins tucked around the mountains?"

"Yes and no. This one is my main one. The others are just shelters for when I'm out. Old hunting cabins and hiking shelters I've taken over as a stopgap. This is where I stay most of the time."

Ash looked around and took the place in. Max's skin felt tight and not just from the pinpricks of blood flow coming back to the numb areas.

"It's nice," she said, and he felt a small relief that it met with her approval. "I like the kitchen. It even has curtains." She walked over to the small kitchen in the living area and looked around before poking her head into the bathroom and bedroom. "How did you manage to get this if you're…?"

"Supposed to be dead?" he offered while kneeling to start the work of building a fire in the wood stove.

"Yeah, exactly."

Max brought the match to the small pile of tinder and watched the flames flicker to life. "I got lucky. When I crawled out of Borealis I ran through the woods mostly, finding the hiking shelters, then the old hunter's cabin, but I was a mess. Paranoid and on the run. I was convinced there was someone behind me for weeks."

"But they never caught you?"

He shook his head while he fed the fire. "No, then I ran into a hunter in the woods. I about bolted, but he must've seen something in me, because Pat waved me down, gave me food, didn't ask questions, and offered money for helping him. His ATV had broken, and he didn't have cell service. I stepped in, and we kept meeting. He gives me odd jobs to make money and lets me use his cabin."

"That is lucky."

"I owe him my life."

"I understand the feeling. So off-grid, right?"

"Yep, so I have most of the basics, and it's all in Pat's name so my name isn't anywhere on it."

Satisfied with the flames, he shut the door to the wood stove and stood. "That should warm us up. We're about three miles off the closest road, so I doubt anyone will see the smoke, and if they do, well, I can explain being here a lot easier than being in the woods with you."

"If that happens, I'll hide behind the curtains," she said with a grin.

"Tomorrow we can go into the closest town and talk to Pat. He has a phone so you can make some calls, and we can pick up supplies."

"Perfect. I need to call my friends as soon as possible. Even though the police have probably gotten to them first. Do you think Borealis has the ability to listen in?"

"I'm not sure, but it's better to be safe than sorry. You can think about what you want to say and do next while we regroup for tomorrow. I have some more clothes you can borrow in here."

He walked into the small bedroom and turned on the LED light.

"I didn't think you'd have electricity when I saw the lantern."

"Yeah, solar, but they're covered with snow now, so I have to use it sparingly. I'll get out some candles in a bit. Here's some old shirts. They're clean and dry, and you can use the bathroom to wash up if you want."

"Oh, I want," Ash said with a smile.

"Okay, I'll heat up some water for us both. I winterized to keep things from completely falling apart when I left, so give me a few and it'll be ready."

"Can I do anything to help?"

"I'll do this if you don't mind cooking."

Ash nodded. "Yeah, of course."

"Pantry's got some cans and whatnot, and the kitchen has everything you should need, but let me know if you need anything. The propane burner is down below, but most of the time I just use the wood stove. Either is fine. Whatever is easiest for you."

"Got it."

Max finished up in the bathroom, then grabbed the bucket to fill the holding tank above the shower since the microscopic hot water heater would take a while. When he walked out, the sight of Ash in the kitchen was so beautiful and foreign he stopped to stare.

She had changed in the bedroom after all and was walking around in his white T-shirt that looked more like a dress, baggy black pants, and dry socks. Her back was to him as she was inspecting another can and opening it up, while a pot heated away on the stove. A tea kettle started to whistle, which made her turn around. When she saw him, her face broke into a smile.

"I found some tea, and figured we'd need water anyway. Want me to get you something before I heat another pot?"

"Ah…sure. Thanks," he said, handing the bucket over to her to fill in exchange for the warm mug. That's when he saw the half-empty bucket of snow by the door.

His brain was still trying to catch up with the idea of her in his space, and here she was taking command. "You got to work quick."

"It's the adrenaline. I'll collapse after eating. By the way, I know we'll need the calories, so I heated up both cans of chili."

Max had been eating the same brand of canned chili for years, and never thought much about it other than as a means to an end, but watching her go over to the pot and stir it, then add a little pepper, he couldn't wait to sit down and eat. "Sounds delicious."

"Do you like spicy stuff because it could really use some hot sauce?"

"Yeah, whatever you think is good."

"Awesome."

He should go change his clothes, which were now damp instead of frozen, but doing so meant he couldn't sit here like a bump on a log and watch her. "Do you like to cook?" he asked, sounding just as lame as he felt.

"Yeah, I guess. My mom taught me all sorts of recipes when I was kid. It's funny, she uses a wood stove too, so this feels like home sweet home to me." She laughed and put the cans in the sink, then sorted through the box of tea to find one she wanted, while Max stood there agape. The woman had just been running for her life after having been almost arrested by her peers, and now she was making tea.

"So do you always whip something up after running for your life?"

Ash laughed. "Not always, but yeah, sometimes."

"I was only joking."

"I guess it's weird, but yeah, after some really tough calls, I think small acts of normalcy bring a lot of peace." Ash shrugged, while her face fell with what looked like some bad memories. Max felt bad he had brought them on.

"Go take a shower. I'll take over and watch everything so we can eat when you're done."

"Okay, yeah. I'll be quick."

Max watched as she turned and walked into the bathroom, shutting the door behind her, and felt himself relax as the small cabin felt like a home for the first time ever.

CHAPTER 16

Ash woke up the next morning and stretched on the couch. Max had wanted to sleep in a separate room, and after…well, seeing him rage like he had, she agreed, but she did draw the line at taking his bed again. After all, he had already let her into his home and given up a bed once.

She heard light snoring from the small bedroom, so she padded around the surprisingly toasty living room and added another log from the stash Max had brought in last night to the dim coals, stoking it a bit to get it going.

She took stock of her body, noting all of the bumps, bruises, and scrapes before working her way through the morning sun salutation. She walked her body through the motions, gently taking time to stretch every area that caught and popped, feeling the blood circulate as she came back online.

The tea, food, and rest had done wonders. She and Max had settled into a comfortable silence, each eating mechanically, fighting off sleep, before he had barricaded the door, showered, and gone to bed. She had fallen asleep under a small mountain of blankets on the couch to the sound of the water and the wood stove.

What she needed now was action. With her exercise done, she checked on the fire and found some instant coffee, which would do. From there she found a box of pancake mix and a little oil and got to work on pancakes in the cast iron pan on the stove. A few minutes later, Max appeared, and the look on his face was priceless.

"Good morning. What's wrong?"

"I just can't get used to seeing someone in here."

Ash froze with the spatula in midair. "Could my being here make you hulk out?"

"No, I like it. I knew it was you. I'm just not used to…"

"A companion?" she finished for him.

"Yeah, Pat's never stayed this long."

She flipped a pancake onto the plate. "Well, hopefully I can get out of your hair soon so you can get back to being Bigfoot."

Max laughed and looked at her with a sparkle in his eye that looked playful and dangerously alluring. Ash shook herself, stepped away, and went back to the task at hand.

"I thought pancakes and coffee would be a good start to the day."

"It's a perfect start to the day," he said, as he poured the coffee into the enamelware mug.

They sat down to eat at the small table, neither saying anything to the other, while Ash considered Max for what felt like the first time.

Initially, she had been so focused on the lesser of the two dangers and deemed him safe. Then he had been unpredictable, violent, then heartbreakingly tender as he had cried into her hair in the cave. Now, though, she considered him in a whole different light.

A flush washed over her skin as she peeked at him in the light of the lamp and the little sunlight coming in through the window. He looked dangerous, like the kind of guy you wouldn't want to meet in an alley unless he was there as your backup. His eyes were blue, quick to crinkle when he smiled at her under his beard and hair. Today, he had tied up his hair in a knot at the back and combed his beard. It came down to his chest, and Ash wondered what he'd look like underneath it all.

When he caught her eye, he smiled again. "What?"

"Just getting a good look at you, Bigfoot."

"I clean up a little better."

"Yeah, I like the beard, though I was kind of hoping for a bow and braid."

"Not gonna happen. I laid out some clothes on the bed for you to wear, at least until we get to Pat's surplus store."

"Won't he be closed because of the weather?"

Max shook his head and finished the coffee. "No, it's in an old mill building next to his house on his family's property. He's always open for the right people."

"How far is this hike?"

Max grinned. "Don't worry. I have an old farm use truck."

"What about the snow or the tracks?"

"I think we'll be okay; there's a road between here and there."

Road was a generous description. When Max first took her to what she had mistaken for an abandoned barn, she wasn't sure the old farm truck would run. It was a light-blue Ford F-150 that needed grease on the doors and had flaking yellowed foam coming through the seats. Max threw the army surplus bag that had the antique rifle in the back and gave the key a turn, pumping the pedal to get it to catch. The engine took some convincing before it came to life with a roar.

"Doesn't this draw attention when you drive around?"

Max popped the parking brake and shifted into gear. "No more than any other old guy in a hunting truck."

"Fair point."

"Would you hop out and shut the barn? I try to keep it dry in there."

With that done, they were off. Ash glanced in the rearview mirror and breathed a sigh of relief as the house and barn melted into the landscape of snow. Even from fifty yards away, you might miss them if you weren't looking for them. Another wave of relief swept through when snow started to come down around them again. Their footprints from last night had been mostly obscured by the wind, but any trace to the house was too much.

They bumped along for what felt like a solid thirty minutes until they reached a larger, more normal road. It still hadn't been cleared, but at least it was level. Ash turned around and again noticed the long driveway vanished almost as soon as they had turned out of it.

It was another thirty minutes to Pat's with the snow. Neither of them talked on the way. This gave Ash time to think. The landscape, when you weren't running for your life, was beautiful. All of it looked like a winter wonderland and reminded her of her childhood home.

Max turned the oversized steering wheel into Pat's driveway, which was another small notch in the forest you could miss if you didn't know what you were looking for. It was several minutes of bouncing and jostling up the steep driveway that had the tires spinning a few times, but the old truck seemed to know its way home and pulled up by an old brown farmhouse next to a large steel building.

A little crusty man, who looked like a mix of ZZ Top and Rasputin, came out carrying a shotgun business end first, before he recognized the truck and waved.

"That's a warm welcome," she said before she opened the door.

"That's Pat."

CHAPTER 17

Gabriel ended the call with the main office on his satellite phone. They were impatient, which made them all rash and worthless. Tracking took time and could not be rushed. Little things would get missed that could derail the mission.

He and the team he had hired had worked with the police initially, offering help as an emergency crew, adept at search and rescue. They had more resources including the helicopter for which the police were grateful. The dogs had not yielded much with the snow, and the helicopter hadn't found anything below the canopy. The police had focused more on calling her family and friends, which yielded nothing but pathetic emotion. They thanked him and his team before calling off the search for one of their own who had gone bad and vanished into the blizzard.

Gabriel smiled to himself. It was easier this way. Checking in with others slowed down the chase, but now he was free to move as fast as he wanted. He slipped the phone back into the pocket of his parka and moved the snowmobile forward. He wasn't worried about the sound of the engine. Let them hear him coming. He enjoyed the chase.

He sent his teams to scout east and west while he headed north, following the river, upward into the hills. It was the most difficult journey, but was what he would've done had he been in her shoes. He smiled to himself as he followed a small path too large to be for deer and was met with fantastic results. It was an old hunting cabin built into the side of the mountain, covered in snow, except for the doorway, which was lower than the banks around.

Gabriel dismounted and pulled out his heat tracker to confirm. His mouth broke into a cold grin again when he saw it was warmer than the surrounding area due to a small heat source in one corner. Otherwise it was empty. He loved being right.

He pushed in the door, and his nostrils flared at the smell of food. She was good. There was no trace of clothing in the one-room shelter. Just a bed with a wool blanket, a braided rug on the ground, and old posters on the wall. There were no remnants of recent fire, which would've been a dead give-away for the chopper. No trash or refuse that might attract animals.

Gabriel went over and felt the heater. Cold, but not frozen. She hadn't been here last night, but he was on the right path.

He pulled out the walkie-talkie from his pocket.

"Both teams report to the north side of the mountain about five hundred yards off the stream. I've got the scent."

CHAPTER 18

The surplus store was filled with olive drab wool blankets, ammo cans, MREs, and all things military. Pat matched the vibe. He had taken off the old army coat and was now seated behind the checkout counter, with the shotgun close by. Ash could clearly see why Max liked him as she listened to their conversation about a job delivering an old chest of aircraft tools from WWII to a client several hours away. It was just business. If Pat was worried that Max drove up after a blizzard with a strange woman, he didn't show it. Instead he sorta shrugged and went back to the matters at hand involving some surplus uniforms for a local play, content to not ask any questions, even when Max explained there would be a delay because of some unfinished business.

Max followed Pat around and started the resupply of winter gear, which included a slightly awkward exchange where Pat sized up Ash with one look before delivering some more suitable clothes from the back. While the pair continued their shopping spree, Ash jumped in to ask if she could use Pat's phone.

"Go ahead; it's behind the counter. Dial *69 before the number. I don't want anyone tracking me."

Ash thanked him and exchanged a glance with Max who was smiling, as if to say, "You see why I like this guy?"

She stepped behind the counter and dialed Laura first, listening to the phone ring while trying to think about what to say. How does one even begin a conversation when they're on the run with no information?

"Hello?"

"Laura? It's Ash."

"OH MY GOD WHERE HAVE YOU BEEN? WE'VE BEEN WORRIED—"

"I know. Listen, I don't have a lot of time. Are you alone? Can you dial in Megan?"

"What? Oh yeah, sure. Hang on. Lemme go to the other room."

Ash smiled as she heard Laura tell Carter to watch Holden, while *Paw Patrol* played in the background.

"Okay, hold on. I'll be back with Megan."

Ash breathed a sigh of relief in the silence while she waited. God, she was so glad to talk to a familiar voice. The line picked up and Megan came on first.

"Oh my God. Ash, what the hell is going on? Everyone at the station has been worried about you!" said Megan.

"Yeah, I know. I'm sorry, but this is the first time I've been able to call."

"What's happening? The police called us both and your mom asking if we've seen you. They've interviewed Carter too."

"They stopped by the ranch, but we didn't know anything."

Ash breathed a sigh of relief that was replaced by panic. They had already contacted her friends, hopefully just because they were connected, but not about anything else.

"Did they ask about me or anything else?"

"Just you," said Laura.

"They think you killed that guy in the house, which is fucking crazy. They're acting like you're an insane rogue cop just like they treated Troy when they thought he attacked that woman in the park."

"After they called off the search, they started saying you were presumed dead," said Laura.

"I can't tell if they're in on it or just know what Borealis is telling them." She kept going when they both tried to cut her off with questions she didn't have time to answer. "I don't know how much time I have, so listen carefully. Ted Saunders wrote my name when he died. He also wrote about how I know about lies."

"Maybe he knew about your history with solving cases," Megan said.

"Have you ever met him?" Laura asked.

"No, but there is no way he knew about me. But he *knew* about me. I can tell when people are lying, always have been able."

"That's *cool*," said Megan.

"How?" asked Laura.

"I can smell it, but listen, I know we never talked about it. Maybe you both have, but I'm different, and I think…I know you are too."

There was silence on the other end of the line. Ash kept going. "Megan, I know there's no way you could survive fires like that. I don't know how you do it, but there must be something special about you. Laura, every time you came out of that ambulance telling me the patient was going to make it, I knew you weren't telling the whole truth. I can tell when you guys are lying, and I knew something was up with both of you." Ash paused and then took a breath as the emotion started to claw at her throat. "I think that's why I've always trusted you both. You're my two best friends, and I'm sorry I couldn't tell you about me until now. I just didn't know how."

Megan spoke first. "God, I'm so glad we can talk about this now. I've had so many questions for so long."

"Oh Ash, I know just how you feel. I should be apologizing to you. I freaked out and tried to leave town when Megan found out back when Carter and I first reunited. I wasn't sure I could trust her, and it took me a lot to even have that conversation. I'm sorry; I should've included you too. I just didn't know how to break the ice. I had a feeling you were like us, but I couldn't tell for sure."

"It's hard when we've all been keeping a secret about ourselves our whole lives. It becomes a habit. I'm glad it's out in the open now."

"It's no wonder we're all such good friends," said Megan. "I've always thought of you both as my sisters, and now we're locked in for sure. It's lucky how we found each other."

"That's why I'm worried now. What if it wasn't luck?"

"What do you mean?" said Laura.

"All three of us are different. We each have something that makes us extremely unique, and we're around the same age in the same town. Ted Saunders knew about me even when I had never told a soul. Borealis knows about me."

"I wonder if they know about us," said Laura.

"But we've been so careful. The only one who knew before Troy was Grandma, and she's gone and would've never told a soul."

"Unless they knew before we did."

"Holy shit," said Laura.

"I wasn't born here though," said Megan. "They couldn't have done anything to me, and I must have had it when I was an infant. Otherwise I would've died in that fire too."

"I don't know how, but I want to find out. I met this guy,

Max. He's different too. Said they experimented on him and others."

"How do you know you can trust him?" Megan asked. "Oh wait, never mind. You can tell, right?"

"Yeah, I can always tell the truth, especially if they're a threat. I just know."

"What else did he say?" asked Laura.

Ash filled them both in on everything.

"That explains all of the random attacks around Gold-vein," Megan said.

"Yeah, I thought it was drugs, but when I went to heal them I couldn't sense anything like that," said Laura. "It makes a lot more sense."

"Right, so Ted Saunders used to work at Rocky Mountain Labs where the Borealis Project is housed. I don't know about him, but he knew about me even though I've never told a soul."

"There must be a record or a connection somewhere," Laura said. "Like an electronic medical record to keep track of everything."

"Max and I are going to track down the other people I had been investigating earlier and try to find out more."

"How can we help?"

"Lie low and see if you can figure out more about how you might be connected."

"Got it. I'll call Mom in a bit and see what I can find out without giving any details," said Laura.

"I can look through the files Grandma kept about the family after the fire. I'm guessing since your number was blocked this isn't your phone. Do you want me to call your mom?"

Ash thought about her mom somewhere making tea or working in the garden. A familiar pang of guilt hit her gut as she realized her first phone call was to her friends. They had never been close, and the distance had grown over time.

"No, I'll call her too. I doubt there's anything, since she's so crunchy, and I won't tell her what's going on. The less she knows the better. It's safer that way."

"What if the police come back?" Laura asked.

"They probably won't if they've called off the search, but there are others involved, so be aware and don't talk to anyone about this."

"Are you sure you'll be okay? Can you trust this guy Max? What if he killed Ted?" Megan asked.

Ash looked up and found Max through the shelves. He was strong enough, even without the rages, and had the training to survive alone in the winters. He had motive for revenge, and the knowledge on how to get the job done. She watched as he nodded to Pat and checked what looked like a first aid kit, before glancing her direction and giving her a questioning thumbs-up which she returned.

He smiled and nodded once before going back to listening to Pat.

"Ash?"

"Yeah, I can trust him. Max is one of us."

CHAPTER 19

Max came back around to the front with everything he thought they would need for whatever happened next. What did you get when you didn't know what you were up against? Damn near everything.

He piled some more winter clothing on the counter, and gave Ash another thumbs-up, but paused when she didn't return it.

"Yeah, Mom, I'm okay." Ash glanced up at him with a weak smile that was not convincing. "I know. It's just a misunderstanding. It'll be sorted out soon. When did they call you?"

A muffled crash came from behind some shelves of clothing where Pat was rummaging around to find his old ammo and black-powder stores.

"Yeah, I don't know when I can come, but I'll try. Listen, this is important, super random I know, but was there ever anything that happened with us and Rocky Mountain Labs back when you were in Goldvein?"

Ash looked up and pressed one hand to her ear to block

out the noise from Pat. "Yeah, okay. Well, let me know if you think of anything."

She paused again and didn't look up. "Okay, thanks. I'll call when I can."

"Well?" Max asked when she ended the call.

"Nothing out of the ordinary. The police called her to see if she had seen me, and she hadn't so that was pretty much the end of it."

"They didn't ask about Ted Saunders?"

"If they did, she didn't let on, and she has never heard of Rocky Mountain Labs, so there's that."

"I'm surprised they didn't say you were connected to a person of interest."

"Yeah, me too, but Mom's pretty new agey, so she and police work never got along."

Max hesitated as he watched her stare at the phone after a brief shrug.

"Was she worried about you?"

Ash smiled. "I'm sure a little, but not nearly as much as my friends were. She and I go pretty long without talking. It works for us."

Max knew she didn't want to talk about it, so he dropped it for now. There wasn't much space for an awkward silence because Pat walked up then with another pile of supplies.

"Good news! I found the ammo. What do you carry?" he asked Ash.

"9mm Glock."

"I got an M1911. That's a .45."

"I'm okay with more of a punch."

"Okey doke." Pat stepped behind the counter and unlocked the glass case. "Be careful with this. This one is documented from WWII, so consider it a loan."

Ash picked it up and tried out the handle in her hand

before sliding it in the old surplus holster. She clipped the belt on and tightened the lower strap around her thigh to anchor it, which made her look dangerous, serious, and sexy as hell.

As if she read his mind, her violet eyes looked up, dark and deadly, and stared right into him. The corner of her mouth tilted up into a smile that made him want to snatch her up and carry her back home. The outfit and the attitude told him she might blow his head off if he tried.

She had changed from the frumpy too-big clothes from him into the sleek, black wool base layers. They hugged every curve of her lean, muscled body. Now with the holster on her hip, she looked like one of the super sexy characters from a video game he played when he was a teen. Didn't matter that he had grown up, served, been tortured in a lab, or lived alone for five years—when he was around her, he felt like a teenager again.

"Feels good, eh?" Pat asked, bringing him back to the present.

"Feels like me again. Thanks, I appreciate it. You ready?" Her violet eyes sliced back over to them with an intensity he hadn't seen yet. Borealis had no idea what was coming their way.

Max popped a few knuckles and nodded before loading the truck. By the time they finished, it was getting dark again and starting to snow.

"Be careful going back down to the cabin, and stop by when you can. I have some fences that need repairs around the mountain, and some rentals in a few weeks. Could use the help."

Max shook the extended hand. "Thanks for the help. I'll be there."

Pat looked from him to Ash and back again. Max wasn't

sure, but he thought he saw the faintest movement under his beard that would've indicated a smile.

"You should bring her around more often. I like her. Not many women who look like that and aren't afraid of a little lead."

"We, erm… Yeah, it's not like that."

Pat didn't seem to listen or care. "She reminds me of someone I knew a long time ago. I think I might give her a call, see how she's doing. Alright, you kids stay safe with whatever you are up to, and try not to work too hard."

"Thanks, will do."

He heard Pat cackling on the way back up to his store.

"I like him," Ash said when he got back in the truck.

"Yeah, he's good people. Doesn't ask a lot of questions."

"That's the best kind."

"Well, speaking of questions, did you figure out where you want to go first?" he asked her while he backed the truck out.

"No, my friends didn't have any leads, and you know how it went with Mom, so the only thing I've got is where I left off."

"Which is?"

"Ted Saunders and the recent attacks in Goldvein. I was working on the investigation when he died and all of this blew apart. All of my research would be locked down, except for my laptop at home."

"I'm sure they're watching that space."

"Right, which rules that out, but there are other people who know stuff." Ash looked over at him and smiled. "I think I need to pick up where I left off and research some of the recent attackers—keep looking for links."

"Sounds like a plan. We can leave tomorrow first thing."

"Good. That will give me a chance to get a list together from what I can remember."

"I'm glad we're working together."

Max watched her face until her gaze flicked over to his. The violet flames in her eyes sent a shiver up his spine, which became stronger when she added a cold grin. "Those fuckers at Borealis won't be."

CHAPTER 20

They got back to the house and unloaded. It was dark, and the snow was falling again, covering what had already been there long enough to form a thin layer of ice on top, making it that much more treacherous.

Max cooked something with chicken that was warm and pretty good considering it was another MRE. Ash sat on the couch feeling toasty. She was wearing her new wool base layers, wrapped in a Pendleton blanket and admiring the flames through the window of the wood stove in front of her.

"Here are the notebooks. Some of the pages are used, but you can flip to the back."

Ash took them and did just that. With the pencil he gave her, she wrote down the names of the attackers she could remember. There was the one that had rushed Megan and Troy when they were on the mountain, the one that attacked Keira in the park, and a few more since then she had been investigating before Ted Saunders had been killed.

She paused and considered if that could've been one as well, but decided against it. It was too calculated. All of the attackers had followed a common theme. None of them had worried about being seen or caught. They all had been perfectly law-abiding until they seemingly snapped and went stark raving mad.

Ash updated her notebook, itching to grab the files she had kept on each one and had spent hours poring over searching for a connection.

Well, that was easy now, wasn't it? In the center of the next page, she wrote Borealis at Rocky Mountain Labs. According to Max, all of them had connections to Borealis. At least one last year had a blister pack of unmarked pills from Borealis. They had given minimal information, hiding behind HIPAA, blanket statements about clinical trials, and their community work running a charity clinic.

Knowing what she knew now, Ash wished she could go back and push harder. She ran out of steam on the information and circled back to questions, listing them out in front of her.

How did Borealis pick their people?

What did they disclose?

Did everyone become violent?

How did the project start?

Where was it heading?

How to stop it?

She sat back and tapped her pencil on the moleskin before it flapped closed.

Max came back in the room with two mugs, steaming with hot chocolate.

Her mouth watered at the rich smell as she accepted the cup. The rich, sweet flavor was perfect and warmed her chest as it traveled south. Ash took another sip and savored the taste, feeling, and company.

It was perfect, really. Sitting here in a small cabin, deep in the woods, with snow falling outside, the fire crackling inside, the blanket, the cocoa, and Max—all perfect.

She sipped again and wondered what her world would've looked like had she not been on the run. Either working late, or being at home alone, doing some yoga, maybe watching TV, but otherwise she had fallen into the sad pattern of work a lot, sleep a little, repeat. Her apartment was more of a crash pad than a home. It was minimal, which she had loved, but it didn't have the same warmth. When she thought of her home, it felt sterile and cold. Even though she was around people, she didn't know anyone else in the complex. Everyone was quiet and kept to themselves. She didn't cook much, and aside from working out, which took place at the gym, she didn't have any hobbies.

Ash used to go out more with Laura and Megan, but since she had moved departments, she wasn't running the same calls as them. When they weren't working or at school, they were spending time with Carter and Troy. Ash couldn't blame them, and was happy for them.

She was fine on her own. She had always preferred her own company to that of others. It gave her a break from always interpreting other people's lies. Sometimes it was information overload, which was why her apartment was quiet, clean, and clutter-free. It was a refuge and a place of rest.

But she had never felt peace like this before. Max, and Pat for that matter, hadn't lied. It had been days since she'd smelled or sensed any untruth. Even though they were on the run and she was so fired and probably would be under arrest for failing to comply, Ash felt peace.

She wasn't looking out the window or trying to lower her shoulders down from her ears. There was no tension or stress. Just cocoa and a fire and Max.

Ash turned to look at him. He sat on the couch, a full

cushion away, wearing a white T-shirt and some loose olive joggers. His legs were crossed at the ankles, as he sipped on his cocoa and stared into the fire.

"How's it going?" he asked, when he realized she was watching him.

"It's good. Is this what you do here every night?"

He shrugged. "I guess. What do you do?"

"Pffft. Work, some more work, maybe yoga or the gym a few times a week, then watch TV or scroll on my phone in the dark."

"I'm sorry I don't have those things. They would have to be in my name, and that's a risk I can't take."

"I know. It's okay. I was just thinking I'm enjoying not having the TV."

"It's peaceful."

"You don't—?" Ash stalled out, trying to figure out how to phrase the question without sounding rude.

"Miss people?"

"Yeah."

"Not really. Sometimes I get lonely, but then I'll go help Pat out in the store, or a few times I'll do some tree work for him with a small crew. One time I even helped wrangle some cattle a few hours from here. Small, odd jobs where no one asks questions as long as the work gets done."

"But what about when you can't get out? How do you pass the time?" Ash asked, shifting to look at him more.

"I'll read. I don't have a lot of options, but sometimes I'll go down to the library and buy a book for fifty cents, a dollar if it's a hardback."

"Would a card be too much exposure?"

"They need a piece of mail. I really want one, but I felt weird impersonating Pat after all he's done for me, so I just make do, and there's a fair amount of options. If I had a card, I could use the computer or check things out, but I might get overwhelmed at that point. I can use the books as long as I'm there, so sometimes I'll go there, read, and put it back on the shelf. It'll take me a few days to finish the book, but it works."

"What do you like to read?"

Max smiled. "Everything, but mainly the mysteries or classics. I've been working my way through the Bible."

Ash raised her eyebrows. "Really? I didn't see that coming."

"Yeah, I figured it was the most read book in the English language, so I figured I'd see what it was all about. I haven't finished it though."

Ash nodded, intrigued. "So you enjoy the time so you can read."

"I guess it's not just that. Sometimes I'll go out and hike around. Just sit with nature and think."

"That's what I do at yoga, but I bet you don't have to pay for the privilege out here."

Max let out a little laugh. "No, so far nature's still free. Sometimes I'll write or draw too."

"Really?" Ash asked, aware her voice had gone from incredulous to awe.

"Yeah, I'll sketch a little here and there. It's not much, but I enjoy it. They're all in there."

Ash looked back at the small notebook in her lap. She opened the flap and gasped at the beauty.

Page after page was filled with beautiful pencil drawings of the room, the sky, Pat, the truck, landscapes of the forest, and then faraway places. She stopped on one of the Taj Mahal.

"I've never been but I saw a book on India, so I kept going back to the library to finish this. I'd like to go there someday."

"I hear it's beautiful. Why India?"

Max gave her a side glance. "Well, you've seen how I am when I…lose control."

"Yeah, that is intense."

"I'm trying to get control of it. Being out here, in the silence, it's easier. I thought that someday I might want to travel to an ashram. Practice meditation, and work on…"

"Peace?"

He glanced up with relief in his features. "Yeah. Peace. I think I'd like that."

"You're never going to believe this, but that's where I want to go too."

"What? No way."

Ash nodded. "Way."

"How come? I mean, not that you can't or wouldn't want that too. I just never expected someone else to like that."

Ash took another sip and nodded. "Yeah, I get it. I guess there are some parts of how I was raised that stuck around. I've always liked yoga. I mean, it was part of my mom's daily life, so even though we have our differences, that's just part of who I am, and I get that from her."

"Makes sense."

"But I can do that anywhere, really, so there's more. I love the healthy eating, since staying fit is part of my job and again how I was raised, but my favorite thing about it is the vow of silence."

"Not a big talker?"

Ash pulled a face. "No, and it's the listening that wears me out." She shifted on the couch to face him. "Remember how you said you're trying to find peace? Well, for me, every day I'm inundated with information. It's overload—completely overwhelming."

"Really?"

"Yeah, so when I walk into the bullpen—that's the main area of the police department— I'm overwhelmed with all of the little lies. I get migraines from it really. It's everything, and every time."

"So every time someone lies, you get hit?"

"Exactly. People asking about the weekend. People saying they're fine when they aren't. People commenting on their haircuts, significant others, what they had for lunch. There are so many lies baked into our society today, and that's just the people I work with. It's the lady at yoga class, it's the kid I've pulled over, and it's my boss."

"Your boss? Shouldn't he be honest?"

"You haven't spent much time in local government, have you?"

Max shook his head.

"His heart's in the right place, but you have to tell things in such a way so as to navigate people. It's the politics of it all that requires little spins about the budget, promotions, or who didn't get the weekend off."

"That is a lot."

Ash let out a sigh and fell back against the cushions. She watched the fire. "I really like the idea of a vow of silence. That sounds peaceful and relaxing."

"I hope I haven't given you a headache," Max said in a voice so quiet, she almost lost his words in the sound of the fire and the wind outside.

She looked over at him. Before she knew what she was doing, she reached out and covered his hands in hers. "No, you haven't."

"Let me know if I do, but you probably know already, I haven't lied to you about anything."

"I know. That's why I'm here with you."

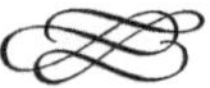

"Are you sure this won't be traceable?" Ash asked as she hopped in the truck.

"It's a risk, but I think it'll be okay. Not a lot of people are out." He pulled the truck out of the driveway, going extra slow on the treacherous ice-covered snow. "Besides, if we go to the one in the next town over where the storm isn't so bad, there will be even less of a chance of someone recognizing us."

"What if they aren't open?"

"Then we head over to Pat's place and at least get a bunch of newspapers."

"This seemed like a much better idea when we were in the kitchen."

Indeed it had been. Over a cozy breakfast and coffee, Ash had gone over all of the questions with Max about Borealis. From there he added some notes to supplement what she knew from her previous investigations. She had tried to come up with a list of names of people that had been recently arrested or detained for attacking, but had come up short. As it was, even if she had a list of names, it wasn't like she could waltz into the bullpen and pull them in to interview.

They had settled on three main questions, all centering around Rocky Mountain Labs—when the Borealis Project started, what it was originally for, and any public information about the project or other people involved.

Ash pulled the drawstrings of her hoodie tight over the beanie. With her hair covered, she could blend in very well, as long as she didn't come in contact with someone she knew directly.

Max edged the truck forward over what felt like hours until they finally reached the main road which had been driven over more than once to create a hard packed snow. He had taken the time to put chains on each tire to help give the old girl some more grip.

They headed out of town and into the next. The roads seemed clearer the farther south they went. Ash's hand closed around the strap to the surplus bag. Inside were supplies for another night out just in case they couldn't make it back to the house. The rifle was underneath the seat, with her M1911.

The hairs on her neck stood as the sight of another truck appeared coming toward them on the two-lane road. Her pulse ticked up and her breathing got shallow, even though the other truck didn't change pace and passed them by with nothing more than a friendly wave from the driver.

"You okay?" Max asked.

"Fine."

"You know, for someone who can smell lies, you can't tell them."

Ash glanced over to see a kind smile before he focused back on the road.

"It's okay to be nervous. I still am. Hell, I wonder if I'll ever not feel hunted again."

"That sounds exhausting."

"It is. And lonely, but then people stress me out. Sometimes I want to live a normal life, at least I think I do, but then after a day in Pat's shop or the library, I'm so worn out from being on high alert all the time."

"What you've been through—I can't imagine doing this for five years."

Max let out a shallow laugh. "Yeah, it's a good thing I'm good on my own."

"What about family? You don't have anyone?"

Max shook his head. "Dad worked in construction when I was a kid. Mom was a stay-at-home mom. It was pretty good until he got hurt on the job. After that he got hooked on pain pills, started selling shit, got mean. He ended up in jail where he OD'd."

"I'm so sorry. That's awful."

"Other kids heard since we lived in a small town and they were pretty rough."

"Kids can be cruel."

"That they can be," he said, nodding slowly. He took a moment, then sighed before continuing. "Yeah so that's that, and then money was tight. Mom got sick and died right after I got out of high school."

"That's terrible."

"It felt like she was hanging on until I got in the marines. She made it to my graduation from boot camp, but after that, she passed."

Ash reached out and covered his hand with hers. "I'm so sorry."

Max shrugged, but turned his hand up and held hers. "Thanks. It was tough, but I got through it."

"You shouldn't have to go through this life alone. Even if it's all you know."

"You do."

"Yeah, but I have friends, used to have colleagues, and even though Mom is…well, Mom, she's still there."

"I have Pat." Max turned to look at her before looking away quickly.

Ash tightened her grip on his hand. "Hey," she said softly, her voice barely above a whisper. She waited until he looked at her. "You have me too, now."

Max smiled under his beard and blinked a few times. They drove the rest of the way hand in hand, breaking apart only when he had to put it in park.

By some miracle, the library was open and empty.

Ash opened the truck door and almost slipped immediately. Max had almost bit it too. They made their way to the glass doors which slid open like arms welcoming them in for a hug. Ash could've wept with relief with being in a semifamiliar space, but kept her head down and hat pulled down tight. A librarian seated behind a desk gave them a smile and polite hello before returning back to their computer.

This one was older and smaller than the one in Goldvein, but had the benefit of grant money and new renovations, creating a mix of towering columns, old stacks, and new technology and furniture. As planned, they stuck together. The police were looking for one person, not two.

Max headed over to the newspaper section, picking up a few of the latest copies to see what had been said about the storm and Ash, if anything. Ash headed for the computer right next to the periodicals.

She glanced over at Max who nodded. It was a risk, and they had gone over the pros and cons at the house, but ultimately decided the information was worth any chance of being discovered. The librarians kept a safeguard over patron information, so the likelihood of someone thinking to pull Ash's computer log-in from the public library during a snowstorm, when she wasn't a regular at coming in, was very low.

Ash typed in the numbers to her library card and the password before the computer came to life, giving her full access to the Internet and research databases. She may not be a regular inside the library, but she was a big fan of the e-books and audiobooks on the app, which was how she had memorized the thirteen digits. Never before did she think that information would be so handy. Max was impressed and gave her a gleeful smile like a kid allowed in a candy shop for the first time in years.

It didn't take long to open up a dozen tabs about Ted Saunders and his work at Borealis and Rocky Mountain Labs. Ash skimmed article after article, including the lab's own history page from their website.

"It says Rocky Mountain Lab has been open over a hundred years. It's in Hamilton now but there have been several different locations," she said when Max took the chair next to her. "They got started to research Rocky Mountain spotted fever, Q fever, and Lyme disease. They even have plague and other diseases there, but there's nothing about Borealis anywhere on the page."

"I bet they don't want to advertise what's really going on."

"There's a library where Ted Saunders's books are, but nothing else here mentions his work."

"Have you searched for any other labs in the area?"

"Yeah, this is the only one that came up. It has to be this one. Does it look familiar from when you were there?"

"I woke up in the woods, but it looks like it's the right size of compound. Is this the place you spoke with on the phone during your investigation?"

"I never went there personally. I was planning on it when everything blew up in my face."

"Can I help you to look for anything?" said a female voice behind them.

Max and Ash jumped apart like two teens caught up to no good.

"I'm sorry, I didn't mean to startle you. We're closing early after all, because the weather took another turn, so you have about thirty more minutes. Is there something I can find for you in the meantime?"

Ash felt Max's gaze shift to her. "Is it possible for you to print this out? We're doing research on Rocky Mountain Labs."

"Of course, I'd be glad to." The librarian pulled up the oversized sleeves of her burgundy sweater and reached over to click a few buttons. "It'll be at the circulation desk. Actually, now that I think about it, if you're interested in the Rocky Mountain Labs, you might be interested in a couple of books in our local history section. I can pull them for you really quick if that would help."

"That'd be perfect. Thanks."

Two hours later, they had finally made it back to the house after what had been a treacherous journey. Ash sat across from the wood stove, wrapped in a wool blanket, reading through the history of Rocky Mountain spotted fever. The icy snow that had fought the old truck tooth and nail pelted on the window like a sore loser. Max passed her another cup of cocoa.

"Any luck?"

"Nothing yet. It's a fascinating story though. Montana had become a state, and because four out of every five afflicted adults were dying from things north of the Sapphire Mountains, the governor got involved. After that, there were several scientists sent who ultimately discovered it was from ticks, and developed remedies to control the spread."

"That's good."

"Apparently the locals didn't think so because they blew up one of the vats that was designed to get the ticks off cattle. The locals distrusted them."

Max joined her on the couch. Ash rested against his arm behind her back, while he read over her shoulder.

"The early labs were primitive, consisting of abandoned homesteads all around the foothills that were vacated after people in the area died of the fever. It looked like black measles."

"That's disgusting."

"Yeah, later, they took over an old schoolhouse lab, and now they have the state-of-the-art facility over in Hamilton."

"Do you see anything about Ted Saunders?"

"Yeah, but a lot of it is stuff we already knew. They talk here about how his work was inspired by his daughter, who had severe cerebral palsy. He retired a few years after she passed."

"I didn't know that part."

"Yeah, it said the move was part of a department-wide restructuring."

"Sounds like he was forced out. When did that happen?"

"Looks like it was about five years ago, which is odd." Ash felt the sinking pit in her stomach while she did the math.

"What happened five years ago?"

Ash turned to look at him, while she redid the numbers in her head again and again.

"My best friend's husband was a computer programmer on a government contract. Five years ago was when he disappeared."

CHAPTER 22

"What do you mean disappeared?" Max asked.

"She and I had just met, and she had been married to this guy named John before he disappeared. It felt like they had gotten married in college because that's what they felt like they should do. John worked in computers as a government contractor. One day he left and never came back. She found out she was pregnant a few weeks later."

"Jesus."

"That's not all. I had been tracking his phone at work."

"I guess there are perks being a cop's friend," he said with a smile.

"Oh yeah. Of course. I figured since it was a missing person's case, it wasn't a complete gross misappropriation of department resources. Anyway, he moved."

"What do you mean?"

Ash shifted on the couch to face him. "When he disappeared, he left for work and nothing was found. Not the car, wallet, keys, or phone, but every once in a while, I'd ping his phone just to see. One day it moved."

"When was that?"

"The first time it moved was August. The second time it came back here was in June. I had just checked after my friend had a house party with her new boyfriend."

"That could be a coincidence, but—"

"But there are too many in a short amount of time."

"Yup. I'll make a note of it."

Max watched her work, poring over her notes to recreate what she remembered, what she found out, and what questions she still had. It was meticulous work. Her handwriting was precise and she carefully printed each letter, drawing lines connecting items, then crossing out others. Her attention to detail never wavered as she filled page after page of his book with her careful notes.

"Do we have anything on him specifically?"

"I've organized them all here for you. This pile is Ted," she said, handing it over.

Ash straightened and rubbed her eyes.

"You're exhausted. You need to stop."

Ash pressed her fingers into the corners of her eyes. "I know, but I just want to get something. I feel like I'm close, but I have nothing to go on. I need to get back to basics. Let me look it over again."

Max put a hand on her shoulder and felt the tension in her back. First she was implicated in a murder by her own department, then she was running for her life through a blizzard with a strange man, and now she was trying to bring down Borealis. It was no wonder she was exhausted.

"It'll be there in a few hours. At least rest. You need it."

She didn't move or shrug him off, which Max took as a good sign. Instead she sat there with her head hanging in her hands. On instinct, Max began to massage the knots in her shoulders. He didn't know what he was doing, but he found a rhythm trying to pull the threads apart with this thumbs, pressing out toward her shoulders.

Ash sighed and began to relax in his hands. Her shoulders dropped and her head tilted back up with her eyes closed, lips parted in bliss.

She was beautiful. The sharp angles of her face were covered in smooth skin, pink from the heat of the fire. Her full, dark lashes fluttered closed over those striking violet eyes. She hadn't worn a stitch of makeup, and used the same basic soap and shampoo he had for himself, but yet she looked like a complete goddess ready for war and love all in one package.

Max kept going, working up the back of her neck for a little, before returning to her shoulders and midback. She sighed again, and he could feel her lean back a little farther into his hands.

Her frame was small. She was short and strong, but now that he could feel her bones, she was incredibly lean, almost delicate. Though he knew she was a fighter, now with him, she seemed so small and almost breakable. Max was tempted to carry her to the bed and lock her in the room where nothing could get to her.

He could see her collarbone from where his large shirt had fallen away down her shoulder. Distractedly, he started retracing their steps since coming on this adventure, adding up what she had eaten and how far they had traveled. Had she been eating enough? Was this typical for her?

Max thought back to the first time he had seen her. It had been dark in the park. He had seen her run at dusk, which caught his attention. With the recent attacks, a woman running alone was an unusual sight. She looked distressed, especially when the cruiser had shown up. From where he had been, he had seen the profile of the guns flash before she could, and in a split second decided to act.

"Ow."

"Oh sorry, I didn't realize I went too deep. I, uh…don't have a lot of practice."

Ash turned back to him. Her violet eyes looked at him, heavy-lidded and dark with relaxation. "That was the best thing that's happened in months."

Max felt his cheeks get hot under his beard for more than a few reasons. There, sitting on his couch, Ash blinked again slowly, barely awake, warm enough to have one shoulder tempting him from where his shirt had conspired against him. He bet it smelled like her, and he knew if he got it back, he would never wear it again. It would stay treasured with his notebook, close to him always.

"Come to bed," he said, his voice lower than expected.

Ash looked at him and nodded before padding over to the room and crawling in between the covers.

"Wait," she said, when he turned off the light.

"What?"

"Lie with me."

Max had a thousand reasons why that was not a good idea, yet his feet had a mind of their own. He lay down in his usual spot, in his usual room, in his usual bed, with a very unusual sensation of the woman of his dreams resting her head in the crook of his shoulder.

For the first time since he had left home, Max felt at peace. He fought sleep as hard as he could, taking care to soak up every sensation and breath of her next to him. The last thing he remembered before sleep won, was that being with Ash made him feel at home.

CHAPTER 23

Gabriel stood looking at the remnants of soot in front of him as his cold smile grew. The black smoke on a rock outcropping had been exactly what he had hoped he would see.

After he had found the hunting cabin built into the mountain, it had taken days to find the trail again. It was clear someone had run, but the snow had obscured much of the trail, and there was no rhyme or reason for the running. Instead of a strategic move he himself would've followed, this part of the tracking had become erratic almost with predictable pattern.

They had run, but it hadn't been planned. It had taken days of searching three hundred feet outward from different points, working in a circle, to find his first tell, but the payoff had been worth it.

A freshly broken branch had been cracked against something hard, splintering and flying away from the direction of the force of the swing. There had been an indentation in the snow, and a dark patch of old blood that still tasted like iron.

The only thing he loved more than the thrill of the hunt was being right about where to go next.

Once he knew the prey was wounded, it was back to easy strategy. The move toward the rock was smart, less likely to attract predators.

Taking shelter to regroup was the logical choice, and it was a pleasant surprise to see that not only was he right, but they had made their first big mistake.

Humans were the only ones who could leave evidence of fires.

He looked up and pulled out his phone, texting coordinates of his newest find to the crew that trailed him. Now that the storm had passed, moving would be easy.

With that done, Gabriel let his eyes track over the landscape, giving time and space to allow the training to work. When it doubt, assess the area as you would use it.

He tracked a natural pattern of where the slope was passable, especially if someone was wounded, and was pleased when it headed back in the direction of roads and rural homes.

Typical. There was only so much time people could survive in the wilderness. It was one of the many things that made them weak and so easy to hunt.

Gabriel followed the path himself, when the phone rang.

"Tell everyone to go house by house within a ten-mile radius. That's where they are."

With the affirmative on the other end, Gabriel boarded back on his snowmobile, a little disappointed the hunt was so predictable. Killing silently while people slept got the job done, but he preferred to do his best work alone and outdoors where he could take his time.

CHAPTER 24

The next morning, Max woke up to the smell of Ash on his pillow. He rolled over and breathed in again, taking an extra-long moment to rest his head on the pillow before the smell of coffee and the sounds of a crackling fire took over his senses. He wasn't used to waking up in a house already warm and ready for the day.

He dressed and came out to find Ash on the floor surrounded by stacks of paper, while writing in his notebook. She looked up and gave him a cheerful smile.

"There you are. I'm glad you got some more sleep. You've made coffee for me, so I wanted to return the favor."

Max poured a cup and sat down. "You're a busy bee."

"Oh yeah, and it paid off. Check out what I've found."

Max listened while Ash pointed to a pile of articles. Each had an interview from Ted Saunders where he spoke about his daughter.

"See here?" Ash pointed where she had starred a passage. "This was years ago, and he's telling this reporter all about his progress with the stem cell research and what potential it could have. He even went into detail about how this could change people who hadn't been impacted by disease."

"He knew what he was doing."

"Yes, exactly. And check out the date. This is thirty years ago. I've had my ability since I was child, so something was up back then. I don't know what yet, but that must be how I got involved."

"Okay, that's one answer."

"Right. It leads to about a hundred more, but at least we have a jumping off point. Now check this out."

Ash riffled through another stack of papers. "Okay, see, this is about twenty years later, or ten years ago. See the difference now?"

She read what she had underlined. "'Jenny started all of this, and whenever I find myself lost, I always go back to the beginning. She is the key to the answers.'"

"So, what? He's not as excited?"

"No, he's not, but he's not divulging what he's up to. Instead he's talking almost in code. On one hand, he's saying it always was about his daughter, so maybe at this point the project started going in a different direction."

"That's five years before the restructuring."

"That's right. He started talking less, because he knew something wasn't the same. It turns out…hang on, that paper is over here." Ash reached over and brought another stack closer. "That's the same time he got promoted."

"Why wouldn't he be happy?"

"Typically, promotion takes people away from the task at hand. He was being shelved, and I think he knew it."

"So why focus on what he's saying?"

"Because he said it a couple of times. Look here, I circled every time he mentioned his daughter. There were two more times in other articles or interviews after that one. In all of them, he said the same thing."

"That's a good script."

Ash looked at him over the papers with a determined gleam in her eye. "Too good. It was intentional. We need to find out more about his daughter."

"How do we do that? The library's closed again for the storm."

Ash looked over at him. "I think we need to look at his house."

"She lived there."

"Yes, and Ted wouldn't have gotten rid of anything. I was in his house before, the night he was killed. He still had her picture on his desk, and I remember the pink wheelchair."

"What else did you see?"

"Not much, other than a cozy home, lived-in, comfortable. He wasn't a mess, but his office was full of books and papers on the shelves. Bedroom was straight out of a Laura Ashley ad from the nineties, so he didn't strike me as one to update anything."

"How would we know what to look for?"

"Ted died in his office. He had been attacked from behind. The coroner was only able to find an injection site behind the ear because he was looking for it. Otherwise it would've been ruled a heart attack. Open and shut case. Because he was able to call 911, and we had the phone record, we had more to go on."

Ash closed her eyes, putting herself in her memory of the night.

"He died in his office. Fell out of his chair, and used a blue pen to write about me."

"Ashleigh Myers knows the truth and the lies… That one, right?"

"Yep, but he was looking at his daughter's picture on his desk when he died. I bet he thought about her too."

"Makes sense."

"Anyone with a loved one has to wonder at the end, but I think this goes beyond love."

She looked up and locked eyes with him. "Do we have her obituary or any information on her?"

Max shook his head. "Not that I've seen."

"We need to start there." Ash began ruffling through papers, sorting and stacking them again, searching for another angle.

"Why do you think Ted wrote down your name?" he asked.

"I have no idea, but probably because he kept tabs on me, somehow knew my secret, and wanted me to make this connection."

Max covered her hand with his own, so she looked up at him. He held her eyes and took the moment for what it was.

"I think Ted wanted you to solve this problem before it gets even worse."

Ash didn't flinch. "How could it get worse? People are being attacked randomly by those who have connections to Borealis, and he's dead."

"I think Borealis hasn't even gotten started yet."

Ash looked at him, and her violet eyes shifted between his own, searching for answers he didn't have, probing what he had said for plausibility.

Max blinked and gripped her hand tighter. "What's the first step?"

"I need to learn more about his daughter. I need to get in his house again."

Max nodded once. "I'll go with you. Make a list of things you need or questions you have."

"Can we get out with the snow?"

"It's not going to be easy to get back to town, but we did it once with the library. It would be good to pick up more supplies. I'll go check the truck."

Ash began her list, while Max suited up and went outside to fire up the engine. More ice had come through last night, and he wanted to get the engine going so it would be warm for Ash and he could get one step closer to getting some damn answers and bringing Borealis down.

Max was halfway to the truck when he stopped.

Something was off.

He strained his ears in the snow. The skin on the back of his neck prickled with five years of good instinct. No one had ever approached this area, or even come close. Even on his worst days, he had never felt this level of anxiety before.

He turned and looked back at the house. It was clear someone was inside. The smoke from the wood stove was clearly rising. It was in Pat's name. No one would've looked for him under it before, but...

Unless they were tracked, there was nothing to implicate this house or location as a place of interest. Could they have followed them through a snowstorm over the mountain?

It was faint, so faint he wasn't sure if he was imagining the sound.

Max held his breath and waited until he heard the distant sound of a snowmobile.

CHAPTER 25

Max had come in from checking the truck white as the snow. He told her about the snowmobile, and how he had never heard one out here before. Both of them had looked at the wood stove and then back at each other before, without a word between them, they sprung into action.

Ash was focused on the research—grabbing printouts, notebooks, and stuffing them in an Army duffle. Max was grabbing supplies, blankets, food, and the old rifle. Ash pulled the grate on the wood stove to cut off the air and doused the flames with some ash, when Max came around and pulled a brick away from the chimney revealing a hidden cubby.

Inside was an ancient Colt .45. He went around the room, moving rugs and pulling up floorboards, and by the end looked like a mountain man in an Old West movie.

Before they ran outside, Ash could hear the whine of the snowmobile herself. Another quick glance between them was the only sign of tension. While Max drove, Ash loaded each gun, then laid them on the floorboards beneath the seat.

Neither one of them seemed to breathe until they turned onto the main road. They didn't speak until hours later, when they were about to turn onto Megan's property. Ash had only used hand signals to direct him.

Both of them were nervous, but they needed someplace to stay that was new and away from the mountain house. They had probably stayed for too long. Now that they were gone, there was nothing there to implicate them. It was just a house registered to Pat. It was best to keep moving.

They also needed something that was closer to town, considering what they were about to do. The library had been enough of a risk, but with her being a person of interest and then a suspect, they didn't need any extra exposure. Plus, the library was closer to the side of town Max could get to, and Ted Saunders's house was on the complete other side, facing the countryside where Megan now lived with Troy.

"You sure no one comes in here?" Max asked her when he cut the engine off. It was the first time he had spoken. Ash hopped down from Max's truck which they had parked in the old shed at Troy and Megan's place. She had been able to call Megan from Pat's store, and the answer had been a quick yes, thank God.

"Yeah, and if they do, they'll see an old truck. It's not like it's my car."

"I know, I'm just asking."

Ash looked up and over at him. He had an army surplus duffle of supplies in his lap, and was fidgeting with the zipper.

"Hey," she said.

Max didn't look up. "What?"

"Look at me."

He fidgeted some more and then glanced up.

She held his gaze for a minute. They had spent a lot of

time together, been through some dicey shit already, and it was about to get a lot fucking worse. She had meant to say something to him, but now, seeing him standing there in the barn with his blue eyes piercing her own, Ash felt herself soften again.

This was the person who had saved her. Who had taken her in at his own personal risk and bandaged her feet, shared his home, and trusted her with his greatest secrets. He had never lied once. She hadn't even smelled the faint tinge of dishonesty. She hadn't realized what a welcome treat that would be until she had spent so much time with just him. It was almost daunting to go talk with others when it had been just the two of them in front of the fire, talking, eating, and resting.

They had spent last night in the same bed, sharing nothing more than space and heat, but the warmth from him had been a comfort more than anything else could've been. At the end of the day, Max was there for her. Throughout everything, he had stood by her, and now was walking into an unfamiliar place, with unfamiliar people for the first time in five years.

"Come here," she said at last.

Max carried the duffle around the bed of the truck and stood before her. He had about six inches, maybe more on her, and a lot more body weight. Ash had never been an affectionate type, usually because people could overwhelm her, but now she stretched out her arms and wrapped them around his neck, pulling him in for a hug.

His breath hitched, maybe in surprise, before he closed his arms around her and held on. He turned his head away at first, and then after a few breaths, turned it in toward her neck. Ash didn't mind. The feel of his quiet strength was a comfort, but it was she who was comforting him.

With Holden, Laura's son, she had learned quickly that you should never end a hug until the kid let go first. That was their cue to you that they had enough of what they needed to regulate their emotions. Ash had always been the last to let go, and now was just the same.

She held Max, just like she had when they had been in the cave together, but this time he didn't cry. He just closed his arms tighter, squeezing their bodies together. Ash knew it was for him, as this must be overwhelming as shit, but she didn't want to let go either.

They fit together. Her head fit perfectly in the crook of his shoulder, as his did with her. They had been inseparable, really, since they came together, and nothing had been hard or awkward after they had gotten to know each other. He was like a big teddy bear of a man who sometimes could go crazy and beat the shit out of someone who wasn't her. He was like *her* big teddy bear.

Ash wanted to kiss him, but just as the thought entered her mind, Max pulled back and sniffed.

"Megan and Troy are good people," she said.

"They won't ask a lot of questions?"

Ash shrugged. "We don't have a lot of answers to give. I think you'll like them. They told us to come to the small new house at the top of the hill. They run a bed and breakfast now, and that's the big one. They live in the little."

Max cleared his throat. "Do you think we'll need to eat breakfast with other people?"

Ash shook her head. "I'll tell them we can stay in the barn or in the truck."

At least that had been her plan until Megan got wind of it.

"Absolutely not," the redhead said, stomping her foot for effect. "You're not staying in the barn. We have other places; don't worry. Very remote."

Ash breathed a sigh of relief. "I didn't want you to have to do any of this. This is already a big risk for you and Troy."

"And we're happy to help in any way. After they tried to frame me, I could tell you something wasn't right," Troy said as he put a plate of spaghetti in front of her at their dining room table.

Ash took another sip of water, so she didn't devour the whole plate in an instant. MREs were great, but spaghetti? And garlic bread? Perfection.

Max sat at her elbow, quietly thanking them when the plate was put in front of him. Megan and Troy had rolled out the welcome mat and included wine, but she and Max had politely declined. They had really gotten the hang of the hosting gig by the looks of it. Neither of them questioned Max. Megan must have filled Troy in from the phone conversation, and while they ate, she could see her friend watching the two of them together.

Boy, what a sight. A cop on the run and a big-ass Viking she found in the mountains.

As it was, Max spoke when spoken to, and answered their questions, asking none of his own. He looked larger at the small dining set than he had in the woods or the cabin, but maybe she just hadn't seen him sit at a table. Ash found she didn't mind at all.

Troy pulled out Megan's chair like a gentleman, taking care to position himself between his girlfriend and Max, which was perfectly understandable.

The evening quickly turned into a round table of party tricks, when after a particularly good cheesecake from Troy, Megan leaned over the table and asked, "So, I haven't seen you since you told me. Can you do it now?"

Ash cracked into a broad smile. "I've always wanted to know how this works. I'll show you mine, if you show me yours."

Megan hopped up and came back with a vanilla scented candle which had been burning near the stove. She put it right on the table, in the center, and with a giggle stuck her finger right on the flame. Not near, not above, right on it, so the flame had to curl around her skin to find the highest point of air.

She waited and waited, while Ash, Max, and even Troy leaned in closer to inspect with childlike smiles of amazement on their faces.

Troy took her hand when she pulled it out of the flame, and personally inspected to find no burn. He looked up and still touched the abused fingertip to his lips anyway, before holding her hand on the table, as if he still wasn't quite sure it was safe and was worried she would try it again.

"Well, how about you? Your turn."

"Mine's not as fancy, but yeah, let's do it."

"Okay, so this is tough because you know almost everything about me, so let's go around the table."

"And do what?" Max asked.

"Play two truths and a lie, of course! Okay, I'll go first. Hmmm, I love painting the rooms upstairs, I aced my last test on small mammal anesthesia and surgery, and this necklace is real gold."

Ash didn't even need to try. The scent from Megan's little lie was like a pungent old friend she hadn't smelled in a while. "You can't have failed, did you?"

"Wow. That's good, and no, I didn't fail, I just got a B."

Troy turned to Megan, "So you really do like painting? You're not just saying that to be nice?"

"I *told* you I love it. It's so satisfying."

"Your necklace is beautiful, by the way," Ash said, nodding to the piece. It was irregular, like a small teardrop hanging from a gold chain that was just about to fall.

"Thanks, it's like the nugget Troy and I found after the

party that night. We've found a few more in the river. Okay, Troy, your turn." Megan flung her red hair over her shoulder. "This will be a real test since you don't know him as well."

"Alright, let's see." Troy thought for a moment and threw a smile Megan's way before facing Ash. He arranged his features in a flat, nondescript sort of way, hiding all emotion as he spoke. "I made a banana bread last week, Dad took Levi to poker tonight, and the farrier is coming tomorrow to put new shoes on Braxton since he misbehaved the last time."

Megan flicked a nervous glance over to Ash, who was already shaking her head.

"You're not playing fair. All three were lies. The first and third were little lies, so maybe one word off. The second is way off."

Megan's mouth fell open a little before she broke into a grin. "That's incredible. It was pumpkin bread, the farrier can't come for another week, and we've been begging Troy's dad to join his poker buddies and go out every once in a while."

Troy leaned back, with a bemused smile on his face. "Yeah, he says he's too busy. That really is incredible. You can pinpoint by strength too?"

Ash nodded and turned to Max. "Do you want to play?"

Max gave a quick glance around the room and took a breath, while sitting up a little straighter in the chair. "It's up to you. I don't have to if you don't want, because they won't know for sure."

"I will," Ash said with a smile.

Megan and Troy nodded, convinced.

He looked back at Ash, who nodded. "Go ahead, try and stump me, so nothing I already know."

"I'm not that fancy, so let me think of something." He paused for a moment and looked down, reaching way back into the memory. "Okay, my nickname in the marines was

Smokey the Bear, my favorite food is chili, and I used to wear a St. Michael medal from my mom every day."

Megan and Troy turned to Ash, who let a smile spread across her face at Max.

"You forgot to include the lie."

After the dinner, Max offered to help Troy with the dishes, while Ash sat across from Megan.

"You're going to bring them down, and Troy and I want to help. Laura and Carter too. You just say the word and we're in."

Ash shook her head and took another sip of coffee. "Being here is more than enough. I don't want to risk anyone more than we already have."

"The house is toward the edge of the ranch, away from everything. It's older, but it's furnished. There's no heat though, just a fireplace."

Ash laughed again. "Believe me, after what I've been through, a roof over my head with a fireplace will feel like home. Thank you."

"You know, you could stay here with us if you want. I'd have to ask Troy about Max, since we don't know him like we do you, but if you want to stay with us tonight, you're welcome to. I know you've been with him for days because you had to, but if you needed some space or just wanted to be alone…" Megan's voice trailed off, with the unasked question hanging in the air between them.

Ash looked over toward the door to the kitchen where she could hear the deep murmur between Max and Troy with the soft clinking of dishes in the water.

"Thank you. I appreciate that, but I'm going to stay with him."

Megan didn't look convinced. "Are you sure?"

Ash thought about Max and all he had done for her, how it had been with the two of them lying together, with her head resting on his shoulder as they pored over papers looking for answers together.

"Yeah, I'm sure."

"Ash," Megan started, looking more uncomfortable by the second. "It's just you've been through a lot, and Max is wonderful, and I know you said he's one of us, but I just want to make sure this is what you really want, and not some trauma bonding shit."

Ash reached across the table and took her friend's hand in her own. "And that's what I freaking love about you. I'd expect nothing less, but really, I'm good."

"For real? I've never seen you take to someone like this before."

"You're right." It was then, at the small dining room table, with the candle still burning next to them, Ash said what she hadn't even realized herself. "I've never felt this comfortable with anyone else other than you and Laura. It just is."

Megan's face broke into a wide grin. "I knew it, and I can't wait to tell Laura. She's going to be begging for the deets."

With that settled, Megan was quick to arrange for Troy to deliver them to the old cabin by the creek that they sometimes opened to tourists and local field trips to let them pan for gold. They stopped off and grabbed the supplies—and

Max's small armory—from the truck before all traveling together, since they agreed to leave the truck in the shed in case it would be seen.

Megan and Troy went in ahead and lit the candles and started the fire before saying goodnight. Megan made sure to give Ash two big thumbs-up when they drove away, leaving her and Max in the small, rustic one-room cabin.

It was furnished in a matching style; the bed, nightstand, and two chairs all were wooden with exposed bark as an artistic feature. The linens and cushions on each were a Pendleton wool, in light blues and whites. The candles from the lanterns flickered on either side of the bed, while the crackle from the fire Max was tending gave off most of the light and the heat for the room.

"This is the nicest cabin I've ever stayed in," Max said, still poking at the fire.

"Megan said it's popular for people who are looking for a more authentic experience, and they have it booked fairly often, though not usually in the winter."

Max didn't say anything. Ash looked around and slid the primitive lock in place in the wooden door behind her, then drew the handmade woolen curtain closed, not that she would be able to see any light outside. They were at least a mile from anyone else, but still the idea of who might be looking in lurked at her.

With a shiver, Ash closed them all and stepped closer to the bed. The warmth from the fire heated the space, but as she pulled off her shirt, the cool air bit at her skin. She stripped from her pants and slid into the cold linens.

"You didn't have to stay with me," Max said, facing the fire still.

"Did you hear Megan offer?"

"No, but I figured she would. I know how close you are."

Ash looked at the back of him, silhouetted against the fire. "I wanted to stay with you."

He didn't say anything to that.

"Were you hoping you'd be alone?" she asked, holding her breath.

Max didn't answer, but stood and turned to look at her.

The light from the fire flickered over his beard, picking up the strands of gold and hints of red. His eyes looked dark and focused. The effect of him should've scared her, but Ash loved the sight of him like that. He was sheer power and peace all in one.

Max stepped forward and sat on the edge of the bed, so her body naturally rolled toward him.

"I like being with you."

"I like being with you too."

They both looked at each other in the silence, neither one looking away, neither one uncomfortable with the quiet. Both acknowledged the unspoken exchange that was happening. Ash naturally sniffed the air and detected no lie again.

Ash sat up to face him, holding the covers to her chest and feeling the cold air on her shoulders.

Max moved first, slowly reaching one hand toward her face. She didn't pull back, letting him go at his pace. When his finger touched her jaw, it was so light, she shivered with the anticipation.

"You're cold."

He stood and looked around for another blanket, finding one in the closet before bringing it to wrap around her.

"Are you always going to be bundling me up?" she asked with a coy smile.

Max stopped and looked at her like a deer in headlights.

Ash slid her hand over and pulled back the covers on the other side of the bed. "Come here."

Max did as he was told, pulling off his outer layer, so he was just in a T-shirt and shorts. He lay down, and the weight pulled her closer to him where Ash curled right up against him.

He was warm and solid. The feeling was addictive after having been in the cold bed alone. Ash nestled her head in the crook of his shoulder. His arm swept around her and cradled her as she lay on her side right against him.

"I'm glad you're with me," he said, his hand slowly stroking her back. "I don't think I could've slept if I didn't know where you were."

"Really?" Ash said, propping herself up to look at him.

Once again, there was no lie detected. That was when she noticed the loaded gun on the nightstand next to them. It was a sobering reminder of everything they had been through, what they were about to go through, and just how much they had to lose.

"I was in and out when you were gone looking for the cave, and I was scared out of my mind. I haven't been able to sleep without being near you since."

Ash smiled. "No one has ever said that to me before. I'm usually the one that can take care of myself."

"Well, it's the truth."

"I know," she said with a smile, and she leaned down and kissed him.

CHAPTER 27

Max was warm and smelled lightly of the smoke from the fire. The hair from his beard tickled her face as she held the kiss, letting her tongue and her hands explore.

He was strong, and not just gym strong. These were the kind of muscles that were lean and hardened with survival. She greedily traced all of his chest with her hands, desperate for more.

Seeing Megan and Troy had been so surreal, talking about their powers so openly and watching them as a couple over a meal at a table.

It was then that Ash had realized just how much of a couple she and Max had become. They had been too busy running for their lives and looking for answers to acknowledge just how much had grown between them.

But now, this was a taste of what life would be like when all of this was over. She and Max having dinner, chatting with friends, and coming back to a bed together. They just were.

God, Ash had never thought it was possible. People usually overwhelmed her senses.

But not Max. He was everything she needed.

She pulled back from the kiss and searched his eyes. This was a lot for him too.

"Are you okay?" Ash asked.

His blue eyes were dark, the pupils wide and searching her own face, before he reached up and touched her cheek.

Ash let her head fall into his hand, knowing full well he could support her weight. There, in the cradle of his hand, she rested her eyes and cheek against his rough warmth. Leaving her head there, she opened her eyes and saw him smile under his beard. He blinked a few times and pulled her face toward him, to rest his lips on her forehead.

"You have no idea how much I've wanted someone just like you. And now that you're here..." Max let out a half laugh on a breath and shook his head, as the emotion thickened his voice.

Ash found his free hand and gave it a squeeze.

"I've just been so alone. I never thought I'd be able to be close with anyone. I've always worried about their reaction or if I lost control and hurt someone... I don't think I could live with myself if I hurt someone I cared about." He looked toward the fire and took a breath to steady himself. "I just never thought...I'd see what I did tonight, with you and Megan showing each other how you—we—are."

Ash smiled. "Me neither. It's so much nicer than being alone."

"Yeah, I figured I would be like that forever—that it would be better that way. And now, I can't imagine sleeping somewhere without you nearby."

Ash gave his hand a squeeze and pulled him closer, so they were both nose to nose on the pillow.

"I used to sit alone and imagine what it would be like to be out and feel normal again. I haven't felt that since I left Borealis. Then you came."

"Well, you're the one who found me."

Max smiled and looked at her with a sense of awe like a kid on Christmas. "You know, the weirdest thing was I never would've gone into town to try and find out more information about Ted like that if something hadn't been telling me to go. I just had a nagging presence telling me to get down there."

"It's almost like fate," Ash said with a smile.

Max stilled and got serious. "Do you believe in that sort of thing?"

Ash thought and looked up past his shoulder at the darkness. "My mom did. My brother does, I think. I stopped as I got older, but I think part of me wants to believe. I mean, hell, there must be something out there, considering we're different. If I can't even explain myself, there's got to be something bigger, right?"

Max nodded, his eyes wide. "It's just that…you're so beautiful, and so strong, and you're like me."

"Well, I don't think I'm strong enough to take a small tree to the arm and keep going," she said with a wry grin, running her hands over the nasty scab and scrape that had healed over since his episode on the mountain.

Max didn't laugh. He looked at her with a serious reverence. "You are everything I've dreamed of for five years. I would've never called out to you in the woods, but you look like…well, let me just show you."

Max got out of bed, the floorboards creaking under his feet, and rummaged in one of the bags, where he pulled out an old sketchbook she hadn't seen before. It was an olive color, probably from the surplus store, and worn at the corners. Max opened it and let the pages flutter before he passed it over.

"What is this?" Ash asked, before the breath left her lungs when she saw the inside.

As before, his drawings were so realistic, but it wasn't the style or detail that caught her eye. The first page was a drawing of a woman from behind, looking out the window. The hair was a little longer than Ash's, but not by much. The next was a woman, curled up with a mug, reading a book in front of a fire. The profile was much like her own, blowing over the steam. The one after that was Max standing behind her smiling, with his arms wrapped around her shoulders. There were dozens of them, more than he could've done in the time they'd been together.

There were two figures resting on the couch, watching the fire, with her head resting on his shoulder just like they had been. One of the woman at the counter at what looked like Pat's store. A snow scene, a forest scene, in hiking clothes, underneath the starry sky—they went on and on, and all of them had the same woman in the center in more and more detail with every passing page. There was a dinner scene, with two other people in the distance, so their features weren't as clear, but the woman was on full display, laughing in the freest kind of way.

Ash's breath left her body as she turned to the last one. It was beautiful. A clear shot of the face, and the resemblance was uncanny. There was no doubt, it looked just like her. She was tangled in bed, with the sheets draped over one of her shoulders, sliding off the other. The eyes were wide and set over an inviting smile, while the bangs fell in front of her face.

"Max, I—" Ash stalled out, without words to describe what she was looking at. "These are beautiful."

"I've worked on them since I met Pat and got settled. I never expected you, this, any of it…" He shook his head, and cleared his throat again. "So I would sit and make up the world I wanted. I never expected you to come to life."

Ash blinked and felt the tears fall down her cheeks at his pure honesty. "So when you saw me in the park?"

"I just had to do whatever it took to get to you and keep you safe. You're all I've been dreaming of."

Ash couldn't speak, so she reached for him instead.

Max took her and held on tight, pressing her into him and wrapping his arms around her like she was life itself.

"Why didn't you show me this before?" she asked with her face pressed into his shoulder.

Max pulled back and wiped his eyes, before raising his arms and letting them fall. The slap of his hand against his thigh sounded like acceptance and resignation all in one sound. Restless, he rolled out of bed and stood.

"I wasn't sure until we were all sitting around tonight. I figured if I could get you safe, and help bring down Borealis together, that might be enough, but after the past few days, and then sitting together tonight, it just all felt..." his words trailed off as he looked at the floor.

"Impossible?"

He nodded. "I imagined what my life after would look like, but I guess I had given up hope it would ever happen without even realizing it."

Ash got up and came forward. Her body, small and soft compared to his, pressed into him to fit perfectly. "When I go home, I want you there with me."

Max searched her eyes and smiled, while a little laugh escaped him. He picked her up and spun around while she wrapped herself around him and pressed her face into his neck.

He stopped and put her down, before Ash pushed herself onto her tiptoes to kiss him, greedily. Their mouths inter-twined, hungry to claim each other.

Ash pushed him on the bed, before straddling and looking down at him.

"Come here," he said, and flipped her so he was on top to pick up where she left off.

Ash loved the feel of him around her and arched up to meet him. He returned the favor.

Hands pressed and pulled, desperate for connection, like two lost souls who finally found one another.

Everything about him felt right. They fit together perfectly. He was pure, honest, strong, and gentle all in one quiet package.

Ash wanted more. She pulled his hand up toward her breast, until he found the skin that was desperate for his attention.

Max's breath caught. The rough skin of his callused hand sent a shiver of anticipation through her body.

"You're cold. I'll cover you more," he said, his voice low and rough.

Ash reached out to stop him from sitting up. The light from the fire sent a cascading array of colors over his face, making the gold in his beard and hair shine.

"No. I want to see you. All of you."

His eyes were dark with desire. "You're so precious to me. I can't see anything else."

It was in that moment, she knew she had never felt this way about anyone else.

CHAPTER 28

Max was awestruck.

With the waning light from the fire washing over her bare shoulder, Ash was quite simply the most beautiful person he had ever seen in his life.

He took one hand and slowly traced the delicate line of her jaw, bringing his fingertip down to the point of her chin, letting it rest there.

Ash slowly closed her eyes and leaned into his hand. When his hand stopped, her violet eyes, almost black in the dark, fluttered open as her lips parted, inviting him in for more, which Max gladly accepted.

She was so perfect.

Max let himself get swallowed in the sensation of her closeness, of her hands on him, and his on hers. The feeling sent shock waves up his arms and down the base of his spine.

Never in his wildest dreams did he think for a moment he'd ever have this. He had never known someone so much like him.

Ash pulled him closer, and he gladly followed her as she

fell back into the pillows with him on top of her, scooping his arms deep in the covers to envelop her like the precious treasure she was.

Her breath filled his ears. The feel of her smooth skin against his own, the light of the fire on her skin, all of it was so much. He began to feel a familiar ringing in his ears, which stopped him.

"Max? What's wrong?" Ash sat up, her lips swollen from their kiss and her face full of concern. God, he hated that she ever needed to look that way.

"I just…feel so much. I don't want to lose control."

Ash's lips formed a small O, followed by a gentle, siren smile as she crept closer.

"You didn't hurt me last time, remember? I'm safe with you." Ash slowly sat up and let the sheet fall away so he could see her breasts, taut stomach, and smooth skin. The sight nearly undid him.

"I want to believe that," he managed to say through gritted teeth.

"I know I am. If anything comes through that door tonight—"

"I'll rip them to shreds," he said, in a much lower tone than normal. He had never heard himself when he lost control, and had the strange sensation he was somewhere in between now.

"Exactly, but I'm safe and so are you."

"Right. We're safe." He would make sure of it.

"And I want to kiss you," she said, bringing herself over him and looking down at his eyes.

Max closed his eyes, as her hand traced the line of his jaw just as he had done for her.

"Do you want that?" she asked, her voice barely above a whisper.

"Yes."

Ash closed the gap, bringing the warmth back to him.

Their tongues explored each other, as she raked her nails over his chest and arms, tracing the outlines of muscles.

Likewise, he ran his hands over the arch of her exposed back, warming the cool skin and feeling the shiver run through her body as he did.

The heat between them built until Max couldn't think of anything else but wanting her and having her.

As the fire died down until all that remained were red hot coals and an occasional pop, the pair took turns touching and entwining their arms around each other.

Max could've stayed there forever. With Ash in his arms, their mouths together, and skin pressed against one another, he felt complete. Time stood still as they explored each other's bodies. Ash felt every scar from his surgeries, tracing them with the tips of her fingers and massaging the tattered skin with the heel of her hand.

"I want to see you," she said. Max pressed a kiss to her temple and nodded.

She peeled back the sheet and in the dying firelight took in the mess that was his body.

"They did their best," he said, when she didn't say anything.

"Who?"

"All the king's horses and all the king's men."

"You are nothing like Humpty-Dumpty," she said with a wry smile, touching a very excited part that made him strain backward with the sensation.

"Depends on the day."

Ash didn't answer, and closed the gap to kiss him again, lightly, before she turned her attention to his shoulder. She pressed her lips with the lightest touch to every jagged map line and knotted tissue, where the skin had knit itself back together. It was agony of the greatest pleasure.

He knew them all, but avoided looking at himself in the mirror. Feeling her lips on each one reminded him how much he had been through even before Borealis. His stomach was mostly okay, so Ash moved on to his right side and sent a shiver up his spine when she reached the part by his ribs and hip. He rubbed his hand on her back again as she moved down his right leg that had taken a particularly bad hit in that fateful jump.

"Does it hurt?" she asked when he shifted.

"Not anymore."

"Good, I'm glad."

She moved all the way down to his foot, which had mostly been saved by the boot. In the dim light, her profile was exquisite as she sat up and looked at him, silhouetted in the dark.

"Lie down," he said when he saw a puff of her breath.

It was warm between them, but they had cooled, and he couldn't stand the idea of her being cold any more than she had been. Max stood and put a log on the fire, stoking a few times, sending sparks flying upward before he turned around and saw her lying there naked in the bed, looking up at him with dark eyes.

She was the most perfect thing he had ever seen.

"Come here," she said, pulling him on top of her.

Like before, they fit together perfectly. Max braced himself so that his weight wouldn't crush her.

"I need you now," she said simply.

Max cradled her head in his hands and kissed her deeply, trying with every cell in him to communicate how much of a treasure she was to him. He shifted so he was between her legs and with a thrust of his hips brought them together with a satisfying shiver from both of them, as two became one.

CHAPTER 29

Ash lay in the crook of Max's shoulder after what felt like the best night of her life. He had fulfilled her every desire and more. They had taken it slow, gentle, and been met with one release after another.

Max had been so strong and powerful over her, before she had flipped him and taken control, riding him until they had both found a release together. For minutes after, he had lain there watching her catch her breath as he ran his hand and lips over her back, sending shivers over her flushed skin, until she could stand the waiting no more and rolled over to meet him again.

There was no need to rush or explain. No mission, no impressing, no shame. There was just the two of them finally together. Two people who had been loners with secrets, now together with a partner who understood intimately. Someone who offered protection and admiration.

Ash felt Max breathe heavy and slow, content to rest after what must have been hours of connection. Even in sleep, his hand was pressed against the small of her back. If she rocked away even the slightest bit, he pressed her back into him, the message clear.

Stay.

She didn't even want to think of the times with other guys in her bed, but they were completely unmatched by what she had with Max. Everything about this had felt different. It was as if someone truly saw her for the first time and offered nothing but complete acceptance.

Ash felt the sting before the tear slid down her cheek and ran onto Max's skin. She swallowed the others back, hoping he wouldn't wake or notice. She *never* cried. But how could she explain what it had felt like? She never once felt like she could truly relax around anyone, and now she was...

The big hand swept around to her shoulder and then her cheek.

Busted.

He slid his arm out and turned to look at her.

"Oh no. Did I hurt you?"

The horror in his voice melted her heart.

"No, no, it's nothing like that."

"Then why are you crying?"

"I guess I'm just happy."

Max didn't answer, just kept combing his fingers through the side of her hair, tucking it behind her ear.

"Is that unusual?"

Ash thought about that for a moment. "I didn't think so before. Maybe I just had gotten used to how I felt all of the time and considered it good enough."

"You deserve to be happy and relaxed."

"I'm a cop."

"I understand, but that's not all of who you are."

Ash opened her mouth to speak, but closed it. She wanted to disagree, but the fire in her belly was dimmer.

"I've gotten so used to that being my whole personality." Even now, she winced at the thought of her usual routine. Work, work out, home, yoga, shower, dinner, prep green juice for tomorrow, paperwork, sleep. Maybe meet up with the girls once a week or month, but otherwise it was rinse and repeat. Her apartment was sparse, utilitarian, and had felt like a refuge from all of the overstimulation and lies that bombarded her every day. Now the memory felt empty and sad.

Max ran his thumb along her chin. "You're so much more."

Before she could open her mouth to protest, he closed the gap with yet another heart-stoppingly tender kiss, which turned into more passion that she met gladly.

He rolled her onto her back and covered her, until she looked up at him, raked her nails over his chest, and found what she was looking for again below the sheet. Once again, he was hard and ready. The sight of him was almost as impressive as what it had felt like. Ash gave him a sly smile and bent down, taking care to pleasure him, while getting her own from every gasp and breath he took. His hand tensed off and on as it ran down her side, reaching for her hip, until he gripped her so hard and didn't let go. Only then did she stop and sit up.

The dark blue eyes were intent with a desperate need, and she felt more powerful than ever before.

"My turn," he said, flipping her again and pushing her legs wide before he returned the favor with spectacular results. The sight of his broad shoulders beneath her hips was enough to make her feel like a complete goddess. What he was doing there put her over the edge and sent her quivering to another plane.

After she was spent, Max sat up, completely striking with his strength and size, and thrust home, sending them both over the edge into oblivion.

Sometime later, they came back to earth in each other's arms, their breath heavy and thick. Max still had his arms around her, when he pushed back and kissed her.

Ash was the one who spoke first, her voice more breath than sound. "I've never felt like this before."

"I'm scared to call it what it is, because I don't want it to go away."

Ash smiled. "Then we won't say anything."

Max hadn't stopped petting her until now, and cradled her cheek before pulling her in for another kiss.

He was warm and so tender, so afraid of hurting her, which was so far from the reality. If she hadn't seen him in his episode in the woods, she didn't think she'd believe he could hurt anything.

Now, however, he gently turned her away from him and brought her up against him, bracing her and supporting her from behind. His arm swept around the front like a loose blanket of its own. The warmth of his breath was on the back of her neck and ear, making her shiver.

They lay like that, resting together, finally at peace while the night was still and quiet. The log he had added to the fire had burned away, leaving the red coals, and a small residual flame flickered, resilient in the night.

It was funny in a way. They had been together for days, but now lying here after everything they had done, Ash expected it to feel different somehow. The feel of Max's beard on her shoulder tickled, but the sensation wasn't overwhelming. She didn't need to squirm away, or find space for herself to think or process all of the emotion and contact. He was there, and it was perfect.

CHAPTER 30

The next morning, Ash woke up to Max brewing coffee over a small fire. He poured her a cup and sat on the edge of the bed. It was early. The sun was nothing more than a hint on the frozen horizon through the glass windows that gave everything a bluish glow.

After a chaste kiss that lingered with the memory of last night, Max passed her a cup.

The mood turned more serious. They sipped their coffee in silence and suited up for the day. Max packed everything up. They didn't know if they'd be coming back or not, so it was better to keep everything with them. Ash fixed the bed and pulled on her own base layer, followed by some jeans and a sweater Megan had given her.

She sat on the braided rug, pulled on her boots, and checked her gun before tucking it into the ankle holster.

Max came back in and extended a hand. Ash took it, and he pulled her up into his warm embrace.

He smelled the same. Smoky warm strength with a hint of the pines outside. Ash drew in a long breath and let herself relax in his arms before looking up and kissing him.

"Let's go get your answers."

They set off in the truck for town, now much closer than before. It felt odd riding the familiar streets in the early morning light. She felt too exposed. It was too bright, too open. She wondered how Max was feeling, having been in hiding for years. Max reached over and held her hand, giving it a squeeze.

Ash returned the favor and pointed him toward Ted Saunders's house. She hadn't been back since the night of the attack, the one that changed everything.

The neighborhood looked more pleasant than it had on her first visit, but usually murder had a tendency to stain even the nicest of settings.

There were fenced-in yards that looked neat even with the snow. Some houses sported snowmen or evidence of snow angels in the front yards. It looked charming and like a nice, quiet area to raise a family.

The side roads were still covered and icy, so it was quiet. No one was leaving for work or school. Only a few cars had even been dug out.

Max navigated the old truck through the area, slowly, toward the older homes on the edge of the neighborhood.

Ted's house was at the end. Max drove by as they had discussed to park in the alley behind. As they passed, Ash noticed the wreath that had hung was gone. There was no car in the parking space, probably removed by the distant family—a niece somewhere in another state if she remembered from the obituaries. The house wouldn't be listed soon, but once the investigation was completed, it was almost sure the family would sell it sight unseen to a company that bought houses in these tragic conditions. Once that happened, Ted's whole life would be thrown in the dumpster. Kitchen counters where the family had cooked holiday dinners would be ripped out for new ones, probably white, and with new floors and a fresh coat of paint, the home would be stripped of all memories, then sold as a clean slate to begin anew.

Would the family that moved in ever know what had happened here? Probably not, unless they pressed the realtor or the neighborhood gossip let it slip at the Fourth of July picnic.

It wasn't unrealistic to think she and Max might be the last ones to go into Ted's house as he had known it, for the sole purpose of getting to know him, his daughter, and trying to make meaning out of his life's work.

It was a tall order. One that Ash loved. This was the work she had always wanted to do. This was why she had become a cop.

"You ready?" Max asked, looking over at her.

He was handsome in his sweater. It was a navy V-neck, rolled at the collar and untucked over dark jeans that Troy had stored away. Thankfully they were long, since Max was taller than Troy by a few inches. Neither of them looked tactical, which was the point.

"Just a nice couple, checking out a house that was soon to be on the market. An investment property? Maybe a starter home? Maybe someone from the family coming to assess the estate and begin the liquidation process," he said, trying to either calm her or himself down.

It worked. "Alright, I like that. Let's go," said Ash.

Max was out first and came around to her door, opening it up with a smile that looked and felt genuine. Ash slipped her hand in his and let him lead her toward the back door. They were crunching on the ice-packed snow leading up to the small, covered back entrance. There were no other footprints. Icicles hung from the edge of the roof, glistening in the sun, one in the light dripping one slow drop at a time.

It was quiet, just the sound of icy wind and heaters

desperate to keep up echoing from around the other side. Even if it was empty, it would have to be kept at sixty degrees to winterize and make sure nothing would burst and wreck the crime scene.

Ash pulled her hat down to cover her hair and pulled up the hood of the winter coat Megan had lent her and let her eyes start tracking over the scene. The front door hadn't been disturbed, but the lock on the back had been thrown the night of the attack, so whoever had killed Ted came through just like they were.

There were two windows on the back of the house. One was high and probably over the kitchen sink looking out. Another was farther down and obscured by curtains, most likely a bedroom. The attacker could've seen where the light was, and noted if Ted was in the living area or farther back.

Lucky for her, Max had learned a few things on the run. He bent down and, with a few clicks, opened the deadbolt then the door, checking inside first before waving her in. There was no reason to suspect anyone would be inside in this weather, but still it hadn't been all that long since the attack.

Ash stepped over the threshold, taking care to step into the shoe covers they had brought. Max walked off to check every room and verify they were alone and to check for any security measures, just like they had planned. Ash took in the space around her and put herself in the space of the attacker.

Not much had changed. The recliner was facing away from the back door toward the TV. Someone could easily walk in, peer through the glass to see an older man watching TV a little too loud before swiping a credit card to gain entry. Same thing in the office, with the chair facing away from the door. Boom, injected and left for dead. Slip out before anything else happens or anyone comes.

However, Ted didn't go quietly into that good night. Ash switched now to Ted's perspective.

He knew, she thought. Ted knew what had happened and he knew exactly why.

"What did you do, Ted? Did you fall out of the chair? Turn to look at someone and see the person who killed you?"

He made it to the office, off the living space through a door, and sat at his desk. Ash followed the imagined scene and stepped on the greenish carpet in the paneled room filled with bookcases.

"We're good. I'm going to sweep the bedrooms," Max said when he poked his head in the doorway.

"Got it, thanks," she called back, letting her eyes follow what Ted had done. He had made it to the desk. The pad and the blue pen were gone. Ash gave herself a shake and got back to focusing on what was left behind.

No computer, of course. Pictures of his daughter and his wife. Pens, notepads, a few bills showing typical expenses for an older man living alone and well below his means.

She slipped on her gloves and opened the drawers of the executive desk, revealing typical files. Mortgage, electric, old taxes showing a decent check from Rocky Mountain Labs.

Medical files from his wife, and then daughter. Ash pulled out the daughter's and riffled through. Typical stuff from the pediatrician, physical therapy, and other specialists. There was a lot, but nothing out of the ordinary for her condition. Certainly nothing about experimental treatments. His wife's signature was on several of the copies requested by the school. Not Ted's. These were her records of her daughter. Did she know what Ted was doing? There was no indication of anything but an involved parent keeping good records.

Ash slipped it back into place and went through a few more, revealing nothing more than a shocking collection of paper clips. Now, the bookshelves.

Apparently, Ted was a fan of thrillers. John Grisham, James Patterson, and Dan Brown's hardbacks all lined the shelves. What would Ted think about how he died? Would he have gotten a kick out of this? Maybe so.

There were some medical journals, a few astronomy books, books on woodworking, masonry, and some historical biographies, mainly Galileo.

Ash stepped back, doing a final sweep of the home office.

Home office. This was where Ted's household and personal life was, not his work. That was clear. Ash spun on her heel and made a pass through the kitchen, dining room, laundry area, and poked her head in a few closets before going upstairs to find Max.

She found him checking the master bedroom.

"Nothing in the guest or the master bathroom. So far, nothing in here other than clothes and pictures."

It was a small bedroom by modern standards, but the house was older and felt warm. The dressers were lined with pictures from family vacations, parents, grandparents, a wedding portrait, baby pictures, and a simple prayer card on what must have been his wife's side. There were still clothes in the drawers, but it looked light as if someone had picked through most of it and left only what had special meaning.

Ted's stuff was much more lived in. Nothing was out of the ordinary though. There was the passport in the underwear drawer with a few hundred dollars' worth of twenties in an old bank envelope. T-shirts, slacks, and a vast array of holiday ties.

She and Max exchanged a glance, and even Max cracked the ghost of a curious smile. He had no reason to like Ted, considering what he had told her in the woods, but if Ash was reading him right, seeing the humanity he had left behind peeled back the layers on Ted Saunders for Max.

Ash kept going, looking through suit jackets in the closet

and the standard variety of shoes, when her hand hit something cold, hard, and metal on the top shelf of the closet.

"Here we go," she said, bringing down a nine millimeter in her gloved hand.

"Not the biggest piece, but a standard size. Is it loaded?"

Ash nodded. "It's chambered."

"Sounds like Ted was expecting company."

"That's not that out of the ordinary. It's high up, out of reach."

Max looked at her and pointed to the bedside table. "That's the second one in this room."

Ash put it back where she had found it in the dark closet and followed Max over to where he opened the drawer in the bedside table, revealing a smaller piece.

"It was lying that way when I found it, handle toward the bed."

"Easy to grab," Ash said more to herself than anything. There wasn't anything else of note in the drawer. Some nasal strips, heartburn medication, and a few phone chargers. "Why would he have these here but not arm the door? Not even better security?"

"Typically people secure first, and then defend."

"Right, but Ted's ready for a fight with the door open. It's like he was waiting for them?"

"But it wasn't by his recliner."

Ash went back to the drawer and checked the boxes of medicine. "This heartburn medication is expired."

"Not unusual, right?"

"By about five years."

"Okay, so he's not going in here that much anymore."

Ash looked at Max. "What if he worried more about it when his daughter and wife were alive?"

"Now that they're gone, he's less likely to carry. Makes sense."

"Let's check the last bedroom."

Max and Ash walked across the hall to the daughter's room, opening the door with a creak.

The walls were a pale pink with a full-size bed in the center of the room and a simple white headboard. The bed was made, but everything had a layer of dust on it, suggesting it had been closed off for some time. A few pictures of different sunflowers were on the walls. There were some old trophies and medals, some for Special Olympics basketball. Hanging nearby was a framed photograph of a much younger Ted with dark hair, pushing a smiling girl in a pink wheelchair across a finish line, both of them wearing racing bibs.

The closet mostly had boxes of clothes, again a few sentimental pieces, like a handmade sweater with a bear on it, a couple of blankets, and a stuffed dragon with a torn wing that had been reattached.

"She looks like she had a wonderful life with a loving family," Max said, running his gloved finger over the mended wing.

"I don't get it. I thought something would be here. What am I not getting?" Ash said, spinning around.

"We should go," Max said from behind her. "A car circled the block."

"Yeah, okay. Let me just make one more sweep."

Max opened his mouth to protest before he thought better of it, nodded, and walked silently out of the room.

Ash checked for any journals, diaries, or notes she might have kept and came up empty.

"Come on, Ted. Where would you hide something you wanted me to find?" Something must be hidden for her. Something wasn't what it seemed. If only she could talk to someone, then she could smell the lie.

Ash closed her eyes and breathed in deep, trying to sense

what wasn't right, what was different, what was hidden. There was something. Almost like a perfume after someone had left the room. She was in the right place. Something hidden was here.

It was odd to use it after so long without, but the feeling came like muscle memory. She cleared her mind like so many times before, and focused on the sense within her searching, feeling, sensing.

There.

Ash opened her eyes and looked at the framed picture. She stepped forward and noted how thick it was, more of a shadow box than a frame.

With her gloved hands, she pulled it off the wall, but it wouldn't come easily; instead the front part came away. Ash went to catch it thinking it had broken, when the front frame swung open on a hinge.

Ash pulled out a small notebook and flipped through, seeing Ted's scrawling notes in blue ink. Before she shut the frame, she took one final glance at the picture. On the back in blue ink, Ted had written, "Jenny and Daddy's big race."

Max walked in, the smile gone from his face. "We have company. Time to go."

CHAPTER 31

Ash followed Max down the stairs and out the back door. Over the thrum of her heart beating in her chest, she heard Max shut the door behind them.

Both pulled off their shoe covers and gloves before walking the short distance to the truck. It took everything not to make a run for it, not knowing who or what had stopped in front.

As if he could read her mind, Max reached over and grabbed her hand, walking with her to the car, side by side. Just two people, a nice couple, looking at a house.

Given the situation, Ash tried to shake him off when she reached the door, but Max stayed by her side and opened it for her.

Ash went to reach for the bag under the seat to hand him a gun, when Max held up his hand and shook his head. He gave her a kiss on the cheek and shut the door before slowly walking to the other side.

That's when a bald man came around the corner, getting one shot off before Max could finish a sentence. "Hey, what are you—"

Ash ducked down to grab her own gun.

Max ripped the door open, jumped in, and slammed it shut. The man ran toward them, and Max cranked the Ford, which came to life with a roar and lurched backward into the alley.

Shots were fired from behind them and pinged the side of the truck, hitting the tailgate, but they didn't slow down.

"Bad luck or monitored?" Ash asked.

"I think monitored or he was waiting for us."

"Shit," she said, looking in the side mirror. "Hardly anyone's on the road, so they'll spot us no matter where we go."

"Let's not panic yet," Max said, making one turn after another onto the main road. Thankfully, there wasn't a cut through from the alley to the main road.

A black car peeled around the corner in front of them, driving toward them head on.

"Okay, ready to panic?"

Max floored the engine and took off with a black cloud of exhaust, blowing past them when he hopped the curb.

Ash clipped her seatbelt and held on to the chicken handle, as he veered onto the main roads.

"Isn't this truck recognizable?"

Max squealed through another turn, shifting into second gear like a pro. "I'll figure that out; you read what's in the book."

"Got it."

Ash flipped it open and tried to calm herself down enough to focus on what she was seeing. At first, there was a short inscription followed by a series of medical entries.

FIRST DOSE ADMINISTERED *on second birthday. Three rounds of treatment for six weeks each. Dose was given orally in the form of a liquid vitamin. Patient preferred cherry-flavored drink. Muscle strength remained unchanged. Balance improved. Cognitive function remains normal for that of a typical two-year-old. Gross and fine motor skills are delayed.*

PAGES AND PAGES of blue ink filled the little notebook, its pages frayed from use. Max jerked the truck around and shifted into another gear before hitting the gas pedal enough to throw her back.

"See anything helpful?"

"It's a lot of medical stuff. Dosage information. He was trying to save her, just like we thought. It's all here."

A different black car peeled out from another crossroad, trying to cut them off.

"Keep looking so we know where to go next."

"How about we deal with one crisis at a time," Ash said, pulling out the antique rifle and pulling the bolt to chamber the bullet, before cranking down the window and taking aim at one of the cars.

She squeezed the trigger right as it pulled alongside her. The recoil threw her back into the seat, while the window of the other car shattered.

"One down. Where's the other?"

"Behind us," Max said, taking another steep turn, heading for the highway.

"Can you outrun them?"

Max chanced a glance in her direction with a you-got-to-be-kidding-me face.

Ash pulled the bolt again and slid open the glass window in between their seats.

"Say when," Max said.

Ash tugged on her seatbelt to make sure she was locked in.

"Now."

Ash fired, right as Max slammed on the brakes. This time the windshield had a clean bullet hole. She didn't miss her chance. Pulling the bolt and snapping it back each time she fired to load again.

Max shifted again and throttled the truck away in a triumphant roar.

"Good eye."

"Not too shabby considering it's not my first choice."

"But it's good, right?" Max shot her a grin, with a bit of sparkle in his blue eyes like a kid proud to show off a bike. "That's why I picked it when I had to choose one. I figure old enough to not be registered, somewhat fast, and does some damage."

"I like how much thought you put into this."

"Well, you know, safety first."

"Damn straight. We're going to have to lose the truck, right? I'm sure the cops will be on this."

Max shrugged. "Not necessarily if Borealis doesn't want them involved, but yeah, better safe than sorry. Where to now?"

Ash thought for a moment. She didn't want to go back to Megan's and involve them. If the truck was found on their property that would be bad news, and Troy had already been involved too much for his liking. Max's house was out.

"Any chance you have more safe spots?"

"Any chance you have more friends?"

"Yeah, actually, but I really don't want to have to involve them."

"We're kind of running out of options if you want to stay in this area."

Ash waited a beat. "Head uptown. I'll show you where."

Once Max was underway, now driving the speed limit, like they hadn't just totally been in a car chase, Ash slid the rifle back under the seat and turned her attention back to the little book.

Ash flipped it over to read the last entry.

Daddy loves you more than anything. I'm sorry I wasn't enough to save you.

"God…" Max said, puffing out his cheeks with a long breath. "I can't imagine."

"You seem less angry," Ash said, looking over at him.

"I just… I don't know anymore. I thought my life was over, and now you and your friends, and all of this." Max shook his head and glanced over at her. "It's hard to be mad at a guy who was trying to save his kid, you know?"

"Yeah, I know." Ash flipped through the detailed notes again, watching the blue ink flutter by in the pages, when she noticed the back cover had started to peel away at the corner. Now that she noticed it, the whole back cover almost looked like it had gotten wet, but none of the pages inside were damaged. She ran her fingernail over the peeling corner, and it came away, revealing some more blue ink.

"Hold up, there's more inside the cover."

"We were due for a break, to be honest," Max said, still checking the rearview mirror every few seconds.

Ash took a breath and then read it aloud.

If anyone else finds this book, it explains everything. All I wanted to do was save my daughter. I'm sorry for everything that happened after. I didn't mean to do any harm. Before I knew what was happening it was too late. Borealis had become weaponized. I never meant for that to happen. I know they'll come for me. They pushed me out when I didn't want to go with their plans. I wanted to heal. They wanted to create Violence.

When I was young, I was Reckless and misused clinical trials. I didn't disclose everything and I regret it all. Those patients didn't know what they were putting into their bodies or their children. Now, I'm older. I lost my daughter. I realize what I was Gambling with. I was so focused on the idea of saving her, I didn't take into account the lasting effects on other people's lives.

I kept records on all test subjects Elsewhere. I'm sorry for my Actions. I'll be gone because as long as I'm here I'm a liability. But you all won't be. I hope you can find it in your heart to forgive me, though I understand if you can't. I'm truly sorry for what I've put you through. I've studied you from afar, and you're doing amazing things to help others. I know you didn't have the choice to become what you are, but you chose to be brave. Never forget that.

"OH MY GOD," Max said, pulling a hand over his face. "This is everything. Just like we thought." He let out a rueful laugh. "I can't believe it."

"He knew they were coming for him. He was waiting." Ash read it again, and then once more. "He wrote down my name, and now this."

"He was hoping you'd find it."

"Then there must be more to it."

"Like a secret code?"

"Bingo. It's the capital letters. Some are wrong."

"I was never any good at word puzzles, but let's hear them."

"V, R, G, E, A."

"Well, it's not her name, and it's not yours."

Ash shook her head. "It's grave. Where's that file? We need to figure out where Jenny's grave is."

"Check the green duffle behind the seat. All of your notes are there."

Ash rummaged around, leafing through pages of research.

"Got it. Turn around. It's at St. Mary's-Turner Cemetery."

CHAPTER 32

The entrance to the cemetery was clean, neat, and somber. Gray bricks and slightly purple stones from the local quarry stacked at the entrance to the now open gate were an imposing welcome. There was snow on the ground, but it had been cleared from the main driveway through which they entered.

The drive was on the north side of Goldvein, far enough they didn't see much traffic or any more suspicious cars, but close enough Ted could've visited frequently.

As cemeteries went, it was a nice one. Not only was the road cleared, but the headstones were in neat rows, and the flowers families left were fresh, not faded. The trees and hedges were neatly trimmed, and the headstones were clean.

"Any idea where to start?" Max asked, when he stopped the truck.

"Someone must be here, if they opened the gate."

"Unless the caretaker just drove by and then left."

"Maybe so." Ash looked out the window at the ones around her. Some were old, dating from the late 1800s through World War I and a couple of World War II. "I think we're in the old section. Let's keep going until we see some newer dates."

The truck crept along, each spying what they could see through the window from the warmth of the cab. The icy wind still swept across the open landscape, scattering the snow in a magical swirl much like a ghost.

Ash couldn't help but wonder where Ted would have been buried, which made her wonder where would she go? Would anyone remember her? Did anyone remember these people? Was Ted the last one who remembered Jennifer?

"There's a new one, back there," Max said before pulling the truck closer and hopping out of the cab.

They split up, each walking the long row looking for Jennifer Saunders, who had died ten years ago at the age of twenty.

That's why she was here in the first place, because they were the same age, Ash thought. She was the same age as his daughter. Laura was three years older, and Megan was four years younger. Wasn't that called standard deviation or some shit? He was taking a sample size. How had he done it? Laura wasn't from here originally. Megan's grandma had moved her after the rest of her family had perished in that house fire. Ash's mom would've looked askance at anything with a needle from a doctor. Ash had been missing several vaccinations as she had painfully learned when she entered the police academy. Where was the link to them?

"Over here!"

Ash ran over to meet Max in front of a fairly traditional grave marker in size and shape. There was a simple cross carved along with her name, dates, and a few bronze stars.

"Jenny Saunders. Beloved daughter, now with the stars forever."

"The dates match what you read in the car."

"Yeah, so that doesn't really help us," Ash said, circling the space, looking for what, she didn't know.

"Had anyone else been here recently?"

"No, there weren't any tracks in the snow," Max said, matching her energy, looking at every letter.

"Thank God." Ash reached her fingertips out toward the cold granite, feeling for any breaks that might lead to more. It was solid and smooth polished stone on the front with carved letters. The edge was rough in a stylistic choice.

Ash took a step back and looked around her, hoping for something to point her in the right direction.

It was a pretty location, even in the winter covered with snow. There was a small grove of cherry trees next to them that would most likely flower and bear fruit. The stone faced east with a clear view of the sunrise.

Ash looked back down at the headstone in front her. "Jenny Saunders. Now with the stars forever."

She reached out and touched the bronze stars in the pattern of a horseshoe. They were linked with a series of small etched lines, mimicking a constellation she didn't know the name of.

Ash followed the pattern with her fingertips, stopping at each star until she reached the last one.

It moved.

"Max."

She could feel the warm breath on her shoulder as he crept right behind her.

Ash grasped it with the tips of her nails, then spun it while pulling to reveal a small bronze cylinder.

"Holy shit."

CHAPTER 33

Max watched Ash slide out the bronze cylinder from the granite headstone. At first glance it looked to be sealed, until Ash twisted the star at the edge and a slip of paper came out.

"It's an address."

"That's a lot of effort to hide an address."

"Yeah, it doesn't make sense," Ash said, checking the cylinder for anything else. After she made sure it was empty, she put it back into position and walked with him to the truck.

He opened the door for Ash, who blushed at the gesture and climbed in, before he went around, got in his side, and cranked the engine.

"What do you want to do?"

"I'd like to keep going. I won't be able to sleep, and the truck will be harder to spot at night."

"Let's do it. Where to?"

Ash squinted. "This would be so much easier with a smart phone."

"I'll go slow since it'll get slick. I need gas anyway, so we can ask at the station."

They drove in silence to the nearest service station. Ash was deep in thought. He glanced over in her direction several times, noting her furrowed brow, clearly thinking everything over.

He didn't want to distract her, so he said nothing until they pulled into the gas station.

"Want anything to eat?" he asked her.

"Oh yeah, I guess we haven't eaten since the morning."

"Here." Max peeled off some bills and gave them to her. "Tell the guy to put forty on pump three, and grab me whatever is warm-ish."

Ash took the bills and looked like she felt weird about it. "I'll make sure to pay you back for everything. Pat too. You know, once I get home."

Max smiled and shrugged. "We've only had MREs and chili. The gas station hot dog can be on me."

Ash didn't look convinced. "What do you want to drink?"

"It's been awhile since I've had a soda."

"Do you have a preference?"

Max shook his head. "Surprise me."

Ash walked in with her hat pulled low and her hood pulled up and came out a few minutes later with a bag, while he was pumping the gas that had switched on while she was inside.

"I can finish filling up if you want to walk inside for a minute, go to the bathroom and all that."

"Sure," Max said.

He tried to ignore the feeling of familiar anxiety tugging at him as he headed toward the bright interior of the store. Even just being under the bright lights of the gas station cover were unsettling, but going inside always raised the hair on the back of his neck. Since he had to pay in cash, he had to do it this way all of the time, but that didn't mean he liked it or was used to it.

He gave a brief nod to the woman behind the counter, who was helping a lady pick out lottery tickets. Neither looked up at him.

Max finished his business in the surprisingly clean men's room, and instead of rushing out like always, this time he studied himself in the mirror while he washed his hands.

Jesus. That was the first word that came to mind. No wonder Ash had called him a big-ass Viking. He certainly looked like one. None of the cabins had mirrors, so he only caught passing glances of himself in truck stops and service stations. The bathroom at Pat's store had one, but it was small, scratched, and the lighting wasn't great. His beard had been big since he had been on the run, but this was out of hand.

Max wet his fingertips and tried to run them through his beard and then on his hair in an attempt to smooth it all down. He had taken to tying it back before, and it seemed like he might need to get back to it or get a full haircut considering he had a beautiful woman waiting in his truck now.

God, he looked like a homeless person. No wonder she wanted to pay him back for the gas station hot dog or whatever it was that she bought him.

He picked up some money from under the table from Pat, but not much. He didn't have an official ID anymore or social security card. He remembered his numbers, but all of the official paperwork had been taken from him during the intake at the lab. He had never sought to retrieve it during the explosion. Since then he'd been so set on finding others and getting revenge, he never even dared to dream or imagine what a life would look like after this.

Ash had mentioned home, and her mom. She had an apartment, a job, a car in her own name, and family waiting for her.

After all this was over, what could Max even offer her? He didn't even exist, let alone have a bank account. Would he even be able to open one or get his ID back?

Shit.

With that sobering thought, he walked back out to the truck to find her sitting inside.

"What did you get?"

"A hot dog and a Cherry Coke."

"Oh, that's my favorite one."

"No shit," she said, looking over at him with a smile. "Me too."

"I knew you had excellent taste," he said with a smile that made him feel sad on the inside.

"I also asked the lady in there about the address and got some directions. Told her my phone was dead."

"Did she believe you?"

"Oh yeah," Ash said in between bites of hot dog. "In fact, she used that to go on a rant about how much technology is setting humans back. We can't remember what we used to and kids these days are lost without them."

"That's a little rude."

"Yeah, but she wrote down where to go right here."

"Excellent," Max said, finishing his own hot dog and washing it down with the rest of the soda, which really did hit the spot.

He cranked the engine, which roared to life so well, the old engine laughing in the face of the cold air. Even with a shot tailgate, the old truck seemed to be somehow getting better.

They headed out into the dark night. The gentle flurries

came down and danced on the wind over the glistening ice and sparkling snow.

Neither one of them saw the police cruiser pull into the gas station or the two officers who got out to go talk to the woman behind the counter who had just gotten off the phone with them, reporting exactly where the wanted woman was heading next.

The woman's directions from the station had been perfect, including her country markers which denoted at which farm to turn. First it was the highway, then it was a small byway that took them by a large lake uphill into the mountains. Gradually as they drove, they moved away from the mostly cleared valley into the dark woods, where the road conditions deteriorated quickly, and visibility into the trees on either side made Ash instinctively watch for deer and other animals.

"Any idea what we're going to find at this address?" Max asked.

"Nope, so we better go in packing."

"I never leave home without it."

"Yeah, but considering your ability, you may not even need it."

Max flinched a little bit. Ash saw him in the dark and put her hand out. "Sorry, I keep forgetting you're in a weird place with it."

"It's okay. I'm still getting used to the idea that it's here to stay and I don't have to be angry about that."

"I guess it's different for me, since it's always on. It's been a really nice break being with you. I feel like I can finally relax and get some peace."

Ash let her head fall back. "Sometimes it's exhausting. It's just overstimulating getting all of that information at once. Even if I don't need to unpack every little lie, I still wonder."

"How do you deal with that?"

Ash let herself look out the window. "A lot of time alone. I'll go to yoga, work out, listen to music, and just go run. My friends used to make fun of all of my green juice and soothing teas, but I can't control what's around me, so I try to over control what I can."

"Does it work?"

"Sometimes. It's like I have to decompress all of the time. You must stay pretty relaxed too."

"I have to, so I don't let it out."

"Yin and yang. You need to prevent yours and I need to recover from mine."

"I guess so," he said, glancing over at her.

"We're getting close now," she said, giving his hand a squeeze. "Then maybe we can go to yoga together."

"I don't even know what Pat would say." Ash could hear the smile in Max's voice.

"He can come too, you know."

Max let out a laugh. "Yeah, that'll be a no. Maybe I'll suggest it just to see what he'd say."

"We'll pick up some green juice for him afterward."

They tossed a few more highly unrealistic scenarios back and forth, until Ash pointed out where to turn.

It was a snow-covered road in the middle of a densely wooded area. They hadn't seen another car since they had left the gas station, almost an hour ago. The only way they knew it was gravel was from the crunch of the tires through the untainted snow.

Ash leaned forward, as did Max. Both of them palmed guns. Ash slid the rifle out and locked the doors. They leaned forward as the old blue truck edged forward deeper into the forest.

"I should've backed in," Max said, implying what neither of them wanted to say out loud. One way in, one way out. Easy to trap.

After what felt like an age, they came on a small clearing of a simple concrete building with a single flood light on the outside. At first glance, it looked like the kind of building one would find on a highway weigh station. Simple, stout, without any markings on the metal door.

Max looked at her and with a quick nod, backed in, facing toward the exit, then killed the engine, plunging them into silence.

"Doors unlocked, but let's take the key so no one can move it."

Max handed it to her.

Ash looked at it and then him.

"If it goes down, and I freak out, just get the fuck out of here."

Ash opened her mouth, but he shook his head. "I can't guarantee I won't hurt you if we find what I think we might."

"Do you think this is where you were?"

"All I know was when I was a subject, I was in the woods when I came to, and a doctor led us here."

Ash took in a breath and let it out slowly. "Okay, but if that happens, I'm coming back for you, guns blazing."

Max didn't answer, just closed the key in her hand, and pulled her in for a quick kiss.

Ash took her gun, and Max took his.

"On three."

Both swung open their doors at the same time and

crouched down outside before walking over toward the pool of friendly yellow light on the untouched snow.

"At least we know no one's been here," Max whispered.

Ash swept around the corner and checked the meter for the little shack. "It has electricity, and I'm sure this is more kilowatts than that light needs."

"Alright, here goes nothing." Max shot the door handle clean off in one go.

The ping of the metal echoed through the dark, empty woods. Ash braced for an alarm, and when none came, they kicked in the door.

Ash when low, Max went high.

He had never been a cop, but was the best partner she'd ever had. They cleared the small room that held a few bags of ice melt and a couple of snow shovels. Max nodded to her, and Ash did the same, both standing and looking at the door in the back. It had a small glass window through which they could see a lit concrete staircase descending below them.

"Ready?" Max asked.

"No, but Ted wanted us here, so here we are."

They swung open the door and descended, Max first, Ash covering from behind. All that was around them was silence, except for the buzz of the fluorescent lights above them.

The stairs were painted as was the metal handrail that wrapped around the wall as the staircase doubled back on itself. If she didn't know better, she would think she was in a hotel heading to the gym.

They kept going until they reached a small landing at the bottom with another unmarked door. Ash and Max exchanged a quick glance. With guns drawn, Ash nodded, and Max pushed the handle to swing it outward.

They were standing in a hallway. Well lit, with painted concrete below them. It felt like a warehouse. The door behind them closed, with a sign reading "Emergency Exit."

Nice to know OSHA was on the job here. Ash wondered if they had set off a silent alarm, somewhere else, but it was too late to worry about that now. At the end of the hallway, there were a series of doors with windows.

The first few looked like standard office rooms with conference tables and decent chairs. The end of the hallway split in a T.

Max went left, Ash went right, checking in all of the rooms as they went. Some looked like meeting rooms that hadn't held anyone in years. Others looked like hotel rooms with a single bed, a bedside table, lamp, and a small desk.

Ash glanced back over her shoulder to see Max checking rooms. She scanned the ceiling looking for cameras and found none that she could see.

Where the hell was she? Was this is a back door to the lab built into the mountain or something separate entirely?

She reached the end and was at a corner where it continued on deeper into this odd labyrinth. There was nothing wrong with what she had seen so far, but the entire atmosphere was unsettling and creeping her out. She turned around again to look for Max and saw him moving in her direction. For as big as he was, he moved silently like a ghost. His voice was barely above a breath when he spoke.

"There was another corner at my end too, but I don't want to split up if this is what I think it is."

"You know?"

"Containment facility or intake."

A tingle of icy cold dread slid down her spine.

"How many staff stay?"

"Depends who they have in here. When I was in, well…it was a lot."

They crept around the corner, her low, him high. The windows got smaller, but the rooms were larger and more medical like. Several were outfitted like hospital rooms, with beds, ports, and IV poles. Everything was off and stored away, with the wires wrapped neatly and put on the countertops next to the sinks. Everything else on the countertops was standard, each room holding wipes, cotton, paper towels, soap, and a small sink. Sharps containers were mounted on the walls over trash cans.

They kept moving down the long hallway that ended in another corner, suggesting a square layout, until the space in the middle opened up into what would be the nurses' station.

Max and Ash didn't even speak, but went to the computers, files, and drawers.

Everything was off, clean, and neat. It was as if it had been an office closed for the holiday. There were still pens in the cup, but no personal items. No Post-Its with stats, pictures of kids, or even coffee cups in the trash cans.

"Have you ever seen anything like this?" Ash asked, picking up a wipes container. It wasn't brand-new, but wasn't expired either.

"No. There were always staff around. Maybe they moved since Ted was involved."

Ash looked up behind her and saw the clock was correct. She opened the wipes to find them still damp.

"If they moved out, it was recent."

"Let's clear the rest and see if there's anything here at all."

They had just set off again, moving faster and more confident they wouldn't find anyone, when Ash heard it.

She stopped and so did Max. They froze in place, straining to hear anything in the silence of the space around them.

Beep.

It wasn't the kind of beep from an alarm or security system, but the small, high-pitched beep from medical equipment. Ash went to drop low, but Max stepped in front her, with half of his body blocking her view of the rest of the hallway.

They stepped forward, each with their gun drawn in the direction of the sound, which was consistent, but slow. There was one more room on the hall. It was lit like all the others, and appeared no different. There was a hallway to the left just past the door. Max stepped a few paces ahead of her and looked around the corner. Ash covered him. Both saw it was empty and completed the square floorplan they had predicted.

Ash rested her shoulder on one side of the door to the room, while Max did the same on the other side.

She took a steadying breath like Max did, before peeking up through the glass with the gun.

What she saw made everything in her body want to race forward.

Max caught her hand as she was reaching for the door-knob to burst through the door.

Ash shook him off, until he turned her to face him.

"It's John."

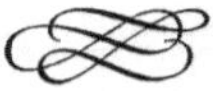

Ash pushed into the room where her best friend's missing ex was unconscious.

This room was different from the others, only because all of the machines were on and working.

Ash didn't know shit about anything medical, but she could tell his heart rate was steady but low. He was breathing with oxygen support, but not intubated. There did appear to be a feeding tube and catheter, in addition to the IV bag which was empty.

How often were they checking on him? How long had he been here? She remembered seeing his phone move when she would ping him back in the department. Back then it had been so simple. Her best friend's husband had vanished, leaving a pregnant wife with nothing but unanswered questions. She had taken on the role of protective best friend, treating Holden like any overprotective auntie would.

He looked so much like Holden, Laura's son, but then he was his biological father who went missing five years ago.

"He might not be the person your friend married."

Good reminder, but Ash hoped with everything that

wasn't the case for Laura's sake, for Holden's sake, and fuck, for John's sake. How the fuck was he involved?

"Check for his stuff?" Ash was so focused on the man in front of her she didn't hear the sound of the door behind her.

A cold voice answered instead.

"That won't be necessary."

Ash went to swing around with the gun, until she felt the cold barrel at her back of her neck.

"No, no. You stay right there."

The voice was male, but high-pitched and breathy like someone who had just run up the mountain or was getting a hell of a kick from this power move. Ash figured it was the latter.

"I've spent a lot of time trying to chase you down. It would've been easier if you had just gone with your coworkers when they tried to arrest you, but then"— the man's voice lowered to a whisper as he got closer to her ear so she could feel his breath—"it wouldn't have been as much fun."

"Why are you chasing me?"

"Easy target. You were a prize. I didn't expect you to find my trap so quickly, but here you are. Smart cookie."

Ash could've thrown her head back to take him out, but she couldn't see or hear Max. Was he still in the room? Had they gotten to him first? She needed more information about John. If she died right here, they'd rot together and no one would know.

"They'll look for me, you know."

"They're idiots. Just like Ted didn't deserve all this anymore. He couldn't appreciate it." He was breathing hard now. "Those weaklings gave up after a few days in a snowstorm. I haven't had a hunt like that in years." He sounded wistful.

"You were behind me in the snow?" Ash almost let *us* slip, but couldn't be sure he knew there were two. He had to. There was no way he hadn't seen Max. Where was he? She tried to angle her head to see him from behind, but couldn't.

"Every step of the way, sweetheart." There was an accent there, very slight from South America. "This is even better than I imagined, though—that you're here." He leaned in and took a deep breath, smelling her hair.

"It's like the fun is over now, huh?" He wouldn't shoot her. He wanted to enjoy this. Torture or rape, either way he was jacked on the power.

"Oh, it's just starting for me. I should just put a bullet in your brain stem, but that's not how I roll."

"You injected Ted."

The man made a spitting sound in disgust. "Didn't even put up a fight. No use of my skills." Sadly, there was no lie detected.

"And what are those?"

"You'll see." The thick fingers clasped around her arm and pulled her back to him, so she had to strain with the gun barrel at her neck.

That was when she saw Max sprawled out on the ground, unconscious with a syringe in his neck.

She took a breath to scream, but caught herself when he jerked her back again.

"Move, bitch."

Ash made her move and threw her body back against him, crushing his hand to the door frame.

It wasn't enough for him to drop his gun, but his grip loosened enough for her to drop and stomp on his inner arch.

That was when she got her first good look at her attacker. The man was bald with bloodshot eyes, with irises so dark they looked black. He was dressed in lightweight tactical gear, and lunged for her quickly.

Ash fired her gun. The bullet skimmed his shoulder, just as he threw his whole body at her. Ash tried to move out of the way, but he caught just enough of her to take her down. The gun skittered across the concrete floor down the empty hall. He landed partially on top of her, with one knee planted and a boot on her face. Ash screamed as she fought back, clawing for anything while he pressed the side of her face harder and harder into the concrete with his boot trying to break her jaw.

She swung her leg up to kick him in the back as she screamed, clawing for anything to fight back with. She would not die now. Her vision swam with the pressure and the pain.

Ash kept kicking and flailing, weakening until the man drew out a knife and ran it down her cheek, drawing blood on the way to her eye.

The scream that came out of her could've woken the dead, but didn't stop the man from bending down to lick the trail of blood off of her cheek as he pressed the knife in farther until he suddenly jerked up and away.

Ash didn't waste time to wonder but scrambled across the floor to the gun. She swung around and aimed while still scooting back to see Max pinning the man against the wall by the neck.

The man's feet were kicking to find the floor but were about six inches too high. Max was lifting him like he weighed nothing, with his veins popping from his arms as he breathed in that odd animal way he had when they were in the woods.

The bald man was struggling to breathe, but still grinning in a way that made Ash's blood run cold. She grabbed the man's gun that had fallen to the floor and aimed with both in his direction.

Max leaned in and sniffed, his eyes dilated like a wild beast contemplating whether or not to eat his prey whole. The man tried to kick and jerk free. Max took him away and slammed him into the wall so the back of his head bounced off the wall like it was nothing.

"Max, stop! We need him to confess. He killed Ted."

Max's head swiveled over to her, and his face twisted into the most terrifying snarl she had ever seen before he let out a most unholy roar and tossed the bald man like a doll on the floor before dropping on top of him. Max moved faster than anything Ash had seen. He flipped the man over and pulled both his arms back to the point of almost dislocating them, then wrenched his head up and to the side.

"Max, no! Stop! Stop!"

Now, he wasn't even looking at her, ready to break his neck. Ash reached into her pocket and pulled out the phone she had been keeping off since this whole thing started and dialed. It took forever to load. Ash prayed there was service, while she ran to the nurses' station looking for anything like duct tape or cuffs.

She came up empty, but at least the phone came on. It buzzed, alerting her to low battery.

"No shit," she said, hitting the first number she could find. "Come on, come on, come on, pick up, pick up, pick up."

Another roar and a scream echoed down the hall.

"Max! Hang on!"

"Hello, this is 911. What's your emergency?"

"This is Sergeant Ashleigh Myers from the Goldvein Police Department. We have an unconscious hostage and a murder suspect in our custody."

She rattled off the address, then turned around to find Max standing right behind her.

She screamed and dropped the phone which shattered and went dark.

He wasn't right; his eyes were dilated still and his face was twisted in the angry snarl, making him look unlike anything she had ever seen before. Ash moved backward and started to run, but not fast enough before he caught her arm and spun her around, clasping her head between both hands like a vise grip.

"Max, it's me, Ash. Don't you recognize me? You didn't hurt me in the forest. It's Ash. I love you. Please. Please," she begged on a choked sob.

That's when she felt the rough thumb trace the line of the cut from her jaw to her ear. He jerked her face forward and grunted at her until she opened her eyes.

He still wasn't right, but he was looking at her so intently as if he recognized her, not from what happened today or even yesterday, but from that time in the forest. It was like he was a different person.

"Hi," Ash said, trying to think of what to say and control her breathing at the same time. "Where's the man?"

He dropped her face and pulled her arm in the direction of another room where the bald man was tied down with makeshift rope made out of sheets, lying face first, trying to fight against the restraints.

"You fucking bitch! You and your goddamn freak are what's wrong with this whole fucking world!"

Max let out a fucking huge roar and lunged at him, picking him up by the ties and dropping him back down.

"Don't hurt him; we need him conscious when the police come."

Ash went next door to find John still unconscious with all machines in place, beeping along in the silence like nothing had happened. She slumped against the doorframe to catch her breath and then noticed that her face was still bleeding, when she felt breath behind her again and jumped.

"Oh my God, how do you keep doing that?"

Max pushed past her without even acknowledging she had spoken and looked at the sink like he had never seen one before, decided against whatever had been in his head, and grabbed a fistful of cotton balls and brought it to her in a tight, angry fist.

Ash looked up at him to see him breathing in that odd, hungry way, staring intently at her like she was some prey.

"Thank you," she said, reaching out to take them, but he avoided her hand and pressed the cotton directly to her face.

It was rough, and hurt a lot more than a little bit, but Ash smiled and let out a laugh before she relaxed her head into his hand.

"You know, I like you. I always have."

He grunted and, apparently satisfied, let go of the cotton and stalked off back to where the bald man had started blaring obscenities again.

With as much running as she had done lately, Ash would've never believed she could be so grateful to hear sirens off in the distance and a metal door open far away.

Ash sat wrapped in a foil blanket with Laura in the back of the remaining ambulance. They were finally alone, but Laura closed the door anyway to give them some privacy.

"I've been waiting to see this firsthand, you know," Ash said, trying to break the tension.

"Well, ever since it didn't work on Holden, I haven't relied on it as much, but here we go. I can't promise it will work or it won't scar." With a snap, she pulled the gloves off.

Ash watched as Laura closed her brown eyes and took a steadying breath before putting her hands on Ash's face. Her touch was gentle, and so soft Ash didn't know if she was even touching her or if she was imagining it. At first it just looked like Laura was meditating, but Ash felt a warm tingle start on her cheek and saw a glow from somewhere to the left of her face. While the glow grew, she felt a rush of blood to the area, and the pain dimmed as if someone had just given her one hell of a nerve blocker.

Laura inhaled a strong breath and opened her eyes, taking a step back.

"Holy shit, that's awesome."

Laura let out a laugh and looked Ash's face over. "Thanks. It's handy for sure. Now that it's settled, come here." Ash let Laura press her into a warm, tight hug, the kind that only best friends who hadn't seen each other in too long could give.

"God, I missed you. Holden's going to freak out when he finally sees you. He's been missing you like hell."

"I missed you too. I'm sorry if this screws everything up for you."

Laura pulled back and dragged her hand over her face before putting up her hair. "Well, we don't have enough information yet. John's in a medically induced coma. They will know more when he gets to the hospital. I mean, legally we're divorced and I'm married to Carter, so that doesn't change anything in my world, but…"

"Holden."

"Yeah, I'm John's only next of kin, so I'll make sure every-thing is done right and follow up, but I'm not bringing Holden into the mix until I know more. He's never met John, and now we know that's not John's fault… No lie, that's going to take some getting used to. I was angry for a long time."

"Yeah, that's not a today problem. I'm just sorry, you know. I thought answers would help, but now it's a mess."

"Don't apologize. You didn't do anything wrong. In fact, you saved his fucking life. God, it's just a lot to take in right now." Laura puffed out a breath. "My therapist is going to love this, you know."

"I'm going to need one after all of this."

"Yeah, I'll give you her number if you want. She's good."

"Thanks, I'll get there. I don't even know what to do right now. I've got to get my car, get to my apartment. Shit, I guess my stuff is still there. I've lost track of the days. I don't even know where to begin to pick up the pieces."

"And you have Max with you."

Now it was Ash's turn to puff out her breath. "Yeah, that's going to be tough," she said as they walked out of the ambulance together to find him lying on a stretcher being treated by Jordan while the other cops had the bald man, known apparently as Gabriel Silva, in the back of the cruiser.

Max had run out of steam and collapsed when the police had arrived at the bottom of the stairs to take in the situation. First they had taken Silva, who was screaming how they finally caught him but couldn't pin it on him, laughing in their face with the lack of evidence. It took three cops to get him up the stairs.

A whole team of paramedics followed and took John up on a backboard to be driven straight to the hospital for treatment. Ash watched as Laura took part in it since it was all hands on deck. Her face had been a little pale, but she was nothing if not professional and revealed none of her feelings. She had stopped running calls that often, but must have come straight from home for this since she was still wearing her jeans.

"He will need to go in just to get checked out," Laura said behind Ash.

"Yeah, I'm going with him. He doesn't have paperwork or anything."

"I can have Carter make some calls to find out where to start with all that."

Ash turned and smiled. "Thank you. This will be a whole new world for him after five years."

"He looks like he's in rough shape. Do you want me to try and heal him?"

"I think he'll be okay. He's like us, but his has a recovery."

Laura's mouth formed an O as she understood what Ash meant.

A truck pulled into the clearing where they all were standing, screeching to a stop by the blue truck. Megan and Troy hopped out.

"I came as soon as we could get away," Megan said, running to give Ash a hug and almost knocking her over.

Troy jogged up, close behind. "What can we do to help? Where's Max?"

"He's waiting over there by the wall with an EMT. They're probably going to take him soon."

"Okay, I'll check on him and bring his truck to the hospital so he has it when he's ready."

"Thanks, babe," Megan said, wrapping him in a hug and planting a kiss on his cheek. "I'll follow you there when we're done."

Troy gave the three of them a nod before he left them to it.

Johnson and Marshall, the two cops that had tracked Ash down before, came forward, backlit from the glow of the floodlight. "Myers, we owe you an apology."

"I know," she said, her voice flat, revealing nothing. She still had run from the cops, and all three of them knew it.

They popped their hands on their hips, not their belts this time. "We were wrong. All charges will be dropped in the morning. You know how it is."

Ash nodded. "Yeah, I do. Does the chief know?"

"Yeah, and he said he wants to talk to you as soon as possible. Sounds like you're finally going to make detective."

Ash smiled and let out a laugh. "I smell paperwork."

The cops laughed. "Yep, a whole bunch."

The older one clapped her on the shoulder through the blanket. "We're glad you're back. You deserve the shit out of this."

"Thanks," she said and watched the two of them walk off to where Silva was yelling about someone's mother in the back of the car.

"Congratulations!" said Megan. "It's about time they saw how great you are."

"That's literally the least they can do," said Laura. "You should get the friggin' building named after you."

A groan came from where Jordan had Max sitting upright. He was holding his eyes, while Jordan had a light in his hand.

"Careful with his eyes," Ash said, losing the blanket to run over. "They're really sensitive to the light."

"Let's get him in," Laura said, hopping up to bring down the stretcher. Megan and Jordan helped lift Max who was covering his eyes and rolling on his side looking like he might vomit. Ash hopped in, while Megan got out and ran to get the truck to follow behind.

Laura and Jordan went into business mode, talking about stats and numbers that faded into the background, while Ash took Max's hands in her own and leaned in to whisper.

"It's going to be okay. We're going home now."

CHAPTER 37

Max hated hospitals. The nurses in and out. The doctors asking questions then disappearing for hours with no explanation. Everything was overwhelming, overstimulating, and freaking out wasn't going to make anything better, because the second his vision started to blur again, the monitors he had been hooked up to starting showing signs of high blood pressure which meant he got poked and prodded even more.

Not that those memories weren't triggering at all.

The sooner he got released and could head back to the cabin the better.

"Hey you," Ash said, poking her head in the door.

Max tried to smile and ignore the tension thrumming through his whole body.

"Waiting to get out of here."

"Yeah, that's probably most people. I talked to the nurses and they're just monitoring you for blood pressure."

"Can I just leave? I don't need that."

"Yeah, technically, but it's better if you don't. They get

nervous if you walk out before your discharge. Worried you'll try to come back and blame everything on them."

"Yeah, the registration lady wasn't too thrilled I didn't have insurance, credit cards, or my ID. She seemed suspicious when I gave my address."

"Which one did you give her?"

"Pat's store. It's the only one with a real registered address."

"I have a feeling he doesn't like that."

Max let out a wry smile. "No, he doesn't, but he tolerates it to run a business."

"The hospital has programs in place for people in your situation. I don't think they'll bill you."

"I have the money for what they did to clean out my shoulder from that branch, but it's just cash."

"Did the registration lady say something about that?"

"Not too much. Went on about the billing department and how to get in contact. I'll sort it out eventually. What did they say about your face?"

Ash ran a hand down the now pink line edged into her perfect skin. It looked great, like it had healed up quickly.

"It's on its way to getting better. Might scar, but too soon to tell."

"I'm sorry," Max said. He couldn't look away from it.

"You have nothing to apologize for. You saved my life and John's life and you know it."

"How's he doing?"

Ash let out a sigh and sat in the visitor's chair. "He's been in a coma for a long time. They're slowly assessing him and will try to bring him out of it. Brain scans are normal. They're unsure what he will remember and what he won't. He has a long road ahead of him."

"He may not be the same or even safe to be around."

"I know; I told Laura that. She's being very cautious.

Honestly, she's handling the whole thing well. She's his next of kin, has his child, and even though she's moved on, she's doing right by him."

"That's good," Max said, resting his head back on the pillow to look up at the ceiling. "I didn't do anything but lose control."

"Well, *he* saved my life then. It's amazing you came back from whatever he injected you with."

"I heard you scream and that's the last thing I remember. It scared the shit out of me. Still does."

"I know, but you were in control. You may not realize it, but you stopped yourself from splitting Gabriel Silva in half, which by the way…he's confessed everything."

Max looked up again to meet her violet eyes. They were creased at the edges with a smile. "I'm free and clear and heading for detective after the press conference at the end of this week."

"Congratulations."

"It's over, Max. We can go home now."

Max should've felt relieved or happy, but he didn't.

"Pat'll be glad to see me."

Ash reached out and grabbed his hand on the bed.

"I'll be glad to see you too. Do you want to come home with me? At least for a couple of days? I've gotten to see your place. I'd like for you to see mine. Come to the conference and the ceremony with me."

Max smiled. "I like being with you."

"We can even get more than a gas station hot dog to eat too," Ash said with a laugh.

Max was released later that afternoon, which he highly suspected had something to do with Ash talking to the charge nurse.

He walked out into the well-lit lobby where people milled

about looking at magazines or their phones, then through the sliding glass doors into the parking lot.

It felt odd. Exposed. Uncomfortable. Vulnerable.

"Here's your truck. Troy parked it for you last night after everything went down." Ash passed him the key and stood facing him with a smile.

His vision blurred again at the sight of the thin pink line on her face. A hazy memory of that asshole's boot on her face floated from the depths of his screwed-up brain when he noticed the bruising on her cheek. It was yellow, which was odd because it hadn't even been twenty-four hours yet.

"My Jeep is over there. You can follow me to my place."

Max did just that, and even though everything was fine, he kept checking the rearview mirrors and tugging at the back of his neck, trying to get the nagging sensation to go away.

They pulled into what looked like a newer apartment complex. Ash pulled into a slot with some numbers on it, and Max took the visitor's spot.

"I haven't been home since, well, you know, so don't expect much."

They walked up to the second floor where Ash let them both in.

"Well, make yourself at home. It's not very big, but it works for me."

The apartment made the cabin look like an abandoned shack, which Max realized for the first time in a long time, it pretty much had been.

The foyer opened into a neatly decorated walkway with a table that had a sleek glass lamp and white shade, with a dish where Ash tossed her keys. There was a stack of mail, probably picked up by someone who stopped by while she was gone.

The whole place was white and gray, with a few tropical

plants. The larger living space had a kitchen with a small table and chairs, a couch, and a TV on a very modern, geometric set of shelves.

"It's really nice in here."

"Thanks. I tried to make it my sanctuary where I can come home and decompress from work. The bathroom and bedroom are back here."

Max followed her past baskets with neatly rolled mats, blankets, and blocks, probably for yoga. Even those all matched in color. They rounded the corner past the floor-to-ceiling windows out to the balcony to find a bedroom and bathroom in the same style. Everything was crisp, clean, and in soft whites and gray. The whole place smelled and felt clean, not like the woodsmoke and pine he was used to. Everything here smelled like lemon.

Ash switched on the lamps by the bed. Both of them were sleek glass with perfect white shades, like two drums that emitted a soft light.

Also on her bedside table was a small plant and an unlit candle. She put her cracked phone on a small black pad, and the shattered screen lit up.

"Thank God. I was hoping it had just died and wasn't completely broken. It's been through a lot. I guess we all have."

Max stood there, feeling too large for the small white space, not knowing where to sit or what to do.

"Do you want to get your things out of the truck?" Ash asked, stepping toward him. "I know this has been a lot for you."

Max nodded. "Yeah, I'll be right back."

"Do you want me to order in some food?"

"Sure, that sounds good."

"Any favorites?" Ash asked, hesitant and looking at him with anticipation.

Max racked his brain to come up with what he liked back when he had choices.

"Here," she said, moving out into the kitchen. "I have some menus in a drawer."

The kitchen was neat too. The cabinets were a clean white, with black stone counters that had little sparkles in them. That was the closest thing in here to the night sky he had become accustomed to.

"Chinese sounds good."

"Cool, anything in particular?"

Max shook his head. "I want to try what you love."

Ash grinned. "Well then, you're in for a treat. Let me grab my phone. Go get your stuff and we can shower and change out of all of this."

Max watched her walk back over the gray carpet in her sweater that was stained with blood down one shoulder. She didn't match this environment, but she would. He hoped he could too.

Max stepped outside into the freezing air and felt like he could breathe again for the first time since the hospital. He walked over to the truck and got his bag out without any issue. There wasn't any snow beneath his feet, but there were some crunches from the rock salt reminiscent of the texture of the actual earth.

Max came back in, and Ash met him at the door, taking his bag to the laundry area, which turned out to be a small room with a utility sink.

"I'm just about to wash these to save what I can since they're not mine. Do you want to throw yours in too?" Ash asked while hitting a remote that brought down a soft gray shade over the windows.

"Sure," Max said, stripping down and tossing the blood-stained clothes into the washing machine. She had a point. It wasn't his clothes, and he appreciated the hell out of Troy, so he'd like to get them back or replace what he couldn't clean and fix.

He wasn't a complete barbarian. He went to the laundromat twice a month, and had been a fully functioning adult before.

He just hadn't realized how different his normal was from others until now.

Ash stood naked in front of him in the light. She stepped closer and stretched up to give him a kiss, wrapping her arms around him and holding him close. Max did the same.

Everything about her was wonderful as always. He just wasn't sure he was enough.

CHAPTER 38

The next few days were a blur of catching up and getting settled. Max checked in with Pat and started the paperwork process to begin to get his identity back. It would be a long road that was made shorter thanks to Carter putting in a few phone calls with his legal team.

Max and Ash put in some time together, running errands and exploring her world as a couple. After he got some new clothes and a haircut and beard trim, they went to the coffee shop, went out to Joe's Diner, and once he had his first piece of mail, walked into the library to get his own card.

Ash headed back to work to a surprise cake welcoming her back, and was able to finish the enormous amount of paperwork all before her ceremony that Saturday.

Everyone turned out for the event. Laura, Carter, and Holden sat in the front row next to Megan and Troy, who kept Max and Pat company on the edge of the row. The guys from station three all took the second row to see her moment.

Max was first, receiving an award for outstanding service to the community. He looked handsome as hell in his dark blue suit, with his tawny hair trimmed and styled. The beard was still there but close cut, giving him less of a big-ass Viking vibe and more of a GQ look. He nodded, smiled for the camera, and accepted the award with complete grace. Most people never would've known he had been so nervous in the days leading up to it. He was still getting used to the idea he didn't have to hide anymore. Getting him to tell people his real name had been a shift, but he was warming up to the idea. Five years in hiding and on the run would stay with him.

Ash wasn't positive, but she thought she had heard Troy talk to him a few times. They seemed to be bonding over the military and working on the ranch, since Max had offered to help out Troy and his dad on a few occasions. Megan had told her that Troy was comfortable with therapy. Ash made a mental note to ask for the name and recommendation. Max might need support readjusting to everything after all he had been through. Even as the idea crossed her mind, she knew it might not go far because of Max's unique situation. He was still working on telling the librarian his name when he had a hold to pick up. Telling a therapist about his uncontrollable rages when he shifted into someone else completely might be something to work toward in the future.

A huge round of applause and cheers pulled Ash from her thoughts, as she heard the chief say her name. She walked up in her dress uniform to accept the promotion to detective and the medal for outstanding service to the department.

After the big show was over, Laura stepped out with Holden to find cookies and lemonade somewhere since he was getting antsy.

"Wish I could go with you, buddy," Ash thought as the program entered the adults talking part.

A good thirty minutes went by because all of the brass wanted their time to shine. Finally, Ash was able to be released to the small reception room where they found Laura and Holden waiting.

Holden's nice clean dress shirt now had strong evidence of cookies all down the front. He ran up and gave her a powerful hug tackle combination.

"Congratulations, Ash." He looked up and placed a chocolate kiss on her cheek. "Do you want a cookie? My mom says if you have one, I can have more too."

Ash raised an eyebrow, smelling the obvious lie. "I don't think she said that, and if I tell her you're lying, you won't get any more."

"You *always* can tell," he groaned. It was true. They had been playing the lying game since he was three, and he hadn't won yet.

"And you always try to trick me."

"Ugh! Fine."

"If you're sweet, she'll say yes and you know it."

"He he he," he said, making a little devious face and rubbing his hands together with the idea of a plan, heading straight for Laura. She saw him coming and raised one eyebrow, ready for whatever he was getting ready to try and pull.

With her simple black dress, Laura looked great. She had an easy grace that she always pulled off. Even when she looked a mess and was under a great deal of stress, she looked elegant and at ease. But today, Ash could see the shadows under her eyes.

John had been having some ups and downs and hadn't regained consciousness yet. Laura had been checking in daily, in addition to setting up paperwork for when he came back and found his life completely different than he had remembered it.

That it was taking a toll wasn't a surprise.

Megan and Troy walked in, her red curls escaping from a

clip that was trying its best to contain all of that energy. She wore a flowy green dress that made her look like an earth goddess. Being with Troy was good for her. She was more confident and doubted herself less every day. Troy gave her the support she needed and the space to grow. It was a joy watching her bloom.

Ash turned to find Max in the crowd and frowned when she didn't immediately find him. She started to search him out when a tall, blonde woman in a sleek, black jacket cut in.

"Excuse me, Detective Myers?"

"Hello."

"My name is Dr. Rose Mallory, and I have been interested in your work on the Borealis case."

"Thank you, Doctor. Did you follow it closely?"

The blonde woman's features deepened with sadness. "Yes, a great deal. I'm from Rocky Mountain Labs."

Ash couldn't help herself. "Did you work closely with Ted Saunders when he was there?"

"Yes, I worked with Ted Saunders as an intern and followed his work closely thereafter. He was a brilliant man until his work consumed him."

"I'm sorry for your loss."

"Thank you. We hadn't spoken in years, actually, but he was such a formative part of my career and will always hold a special place in my heart. I've tried looking for information about the service arrangements. I'd like to go unless it's private to the family. "

"I don't believe his next of kin is local, but I'll make sure you are kept informed."

"Thank you. I'd appreciate that, Detective."

Maybe it was that she heard her new title and liked it or that she was the closest thing Ash could get to Ted, but she was spurred on to ask more questions.

"Of course. Actually, I had trouble following some of his

work when I was researching the case. I reached out to the lab at the time but wasn't able to get anyone to contact me with any details. I was hoping to have someone walk me through what it was I was reading."

Dr. Mallory nodded. "It's unfortunate that our public liaison recently accepted a position elsewhere, so I'm afraid you caught us in between staff. I'd be happy to talk with you more if it would be helpful to your investigation."

"I'd appreciate that. I've read so much about the place; it would be nice to see the inside."

"Of course. We'd be delighted to have you as a guest. I'll arrange it with security this week. You're welcome to bring Max as well if he would like since he was a part of the investigation."

"Thank you. I'll ask him and let you know."

"I'm still amazed you both were able to survive in the woods."

"Thank you. Most of the credit goes to him."

"I'm sure you both made a great team," said Dr. Mallory with a smile, "but you're not giving yourself enough credit."

Ash found Max toward the edge of the wall by the door, but couldn't make it over to see him until the very end of the reception.

"Congratulations," he said, pulling her in for a kiss. "You did great."

"Thanks, I forgot how much all of this is. Are you ready to go home?" Carter had offered to take everyone out afterward, but Ash thanked him and suggested another time since she had been so worn out. As it was, Holden was probably heading home in a post sugar-high coma.

Max smirked. "Yeah, let's go."

He held her hand, but didn't talk much on the way home, and for that Ash was grateful. It let her have time and space to churn over the events of the evening in her mind—everything the other cops had said, the chief, the mayor, Dr. Mallory.

Out of everyone in that room, Dr. Mallory interested her the most. The woman looked to be in her fifties and had worn simple but elegant clothes. The black dress was fitted and accented with a gold belt that looked designer, matched the handbag, and made the woman striking. She had worn minimal makeup other than a little lipstick, and had a single strand of pearls and clear-rimmed glasses. She was everything you would picture about a sophisticated virologist at the peak of her career.

As they had chatted, she had expressed interest in the run through the forest as she admitted to always wanting to try through hiking on various trails around the country. Ash had liked talking with her and hadn't detected one lie, which gave her a sense of comfort.

Max pulled her Jeep into the parking space, and they walked into the apartment together.

It was good to be home.

The scent of pine and woodsmoke from her new candle welcomed her back into her space with a warm embrace. Ash took her uniform off and started hanging it up in the back of the closet to rest until the next special occasion.

Max stripped out of his own tie. "Can I bring you anything?" he asked.

Ash let out a laugh. "It's my place; I should be offering you something."

Max stepped behind her and ran his hands up her arms. "I like caring for you."

"Really?"

He planted a gentle kiss on the back of her neck. "Really."

"I'm so tired, I don't even know what to ask for."

"I'll take care of that too."

"Ooh. I like that. You can make the decisions from here on out."

"Done."

Ash heard him tinkering around in the kitchen while she slipped into her white waffle robe and came out to find the most handsome man she had ever seen carrying two mugs of lavender and chamomile tea. They sat on the couch together, and Ash let her hand fall on his shoulder.

Ash grabbed the remote to the TV and found a video of a fireplace crackling and let it roll before she dimmed the lights.

"Now it feels like home," she said with a smile, sipping her tea.

"I can make us an MRE for breakfast tomorrow."

"Sounds delish. It's funny you mention that because one woman was really interested in that part of the story."

"Oh, was it that blonde woman with the glasses? I saw you talking to her."

Ash filled him in on everything she had said.

"What do you think? Was she telling the truth?"

"Yeah, I couldn't smell one lie. Not even a little fib."

"Okay, well, it'd certainly be interesting to have her take a look at the book."

Ash sat up and looked at him. "So you don't think it's crazy? I mean, Silva's confessed. We found John and the place they kept people. It's all over, but I just feel like it'd be good to talk to her."

"Maybe she can tell us how you're connected."

"And what happened to you," Ash said.

"I'd love to know what happened and what they put in me."

"Same," Ash said. "I really think since we can't ask Ted, she would be the closest one."

"Silva didn't break in interview?" Max asked.

Ash shook her head and sipped her tea. "He laughed in our faces. Said he enjoyed the hunt. Apparently, he had been hired as security for the Borealis Project to bring down people who had been compromised by the project. When he realized the power behind it, he wanted it for himself."

"It's good he didn't get it."

"Not for long at least," Ash said. "So you're coming with?"

"I think so." Max sipped his own tea and stared at the artificial fire.

Ash reached out and took his hand. "I know how much this must be for you."

"I guess I'll just need to get used to it all again."

"You're doing great."

"It's nice to have my driver's license back, but I still tense up every time I drive around."

"It'll take time. You know we have some staff in the department you could talk to if you wanted to."

Max sipped his tea. "Troy mentioned that already."

"He's a good guy, but it's understandable if you're not ready."

"Maybe I will be soon. I'll keep it in mind."

They were silent until the tea was cool and the mugs were almost empty. Ash spoke first.

"You don't have to come if it doesn't feel right. I don't want to pressure you."

Max swallowed. "I was determined to find answers for so long, so I'm going."

Ash sensed a "but" was coming.

"Do you think they'll have them?"

"I hope so."

Ash looked up at him and saw how tired he looked. She took the mug from him and set it next to hers right by his library book and sketchbook.

She straddled him on the couch and framed his face in her hands. In the dim light of the living room, she was reminded of those nights they had spent in the cabin. Max put his hands on her hips right as she kissed him, taking care to start slow, building fire and passion as she went.

It was gentle and perfect. Their tongues each reached out

to taste the other, and their hands pulled the other one closer.

Max parted her robe, revealing her heated skin to the cool air of the room. A chill of goose bumps spread across her, that was replaced by a shiver as his hand caressed over her skin, sending a thrill through her body.

Ash arched her back, wanting more, as he ran his thumbs over her breasts. She could feel he was ready for her beneath him, so she slid down the couch to pleasure him in the way she knew would release all of the tension from the day and more.

Max groaned and strained backward, arching with pleasure before he stopped her and peeled off his own clothes and met her on the floor, laying her flat on her abandoned robe. Max started at her mouth with kisses before moving toward her ear, neck, and down to her collar bone.

He took his time planting the kisses on her chilled skin, sending shivers of anticipation down her spine when he reached her hips, legs, and down to her feet. He took the time to press his thumbs into her arches, running them up the length of her foot in a way that was relaxing and sensual at the same time.

"Max," Ash pleaded.

He settled between her thighs to return the favor of pleasure, until her hands fisted in his long hair and dragged him to cover her.

With his thrust, Ash cried out in pleasure. They found their rhythm as they clung to each other, and the powerful release sent them over the edge together.

They lay like that in each other's arms on the floor of the apartment, their breathing matched, until Max propped himself up on his elbows. He framed her face with his hands and whispered. "I was afraid to say it before, but I want you to know I love you. And that's the truth."

Ash reached up and cradled his face with her hand, when he came down to give her a tender kiss. "I know it is, and I love you too."

They retired to the bedroom and fell asleep in each other's arms.

CHAPTER 40

Many miles away, someone threw a file with Gabriel Silva's name in the fire without even a casual glance. One of the greatest of assets was just another disappointment. Just like Ted.

It wasn't a shock. Silva had been a means to an end. Borealis needed cleaning up to reach its real potential. The solution had been to hire someone with experience in this line of work to eliminate mistakes Borealis had made. At least he had reached some of his targets before getting caught at the end.

Unfortunately, that yielded another loophole. John Burton was in the hospital trying to be revived. With any luck he would have no working memory of what he had witnessed when he had been working IT and dug a little too deep into the records for his own good.

John was an excellent asset to the program, which was why such expense had been made to keep him alive for future use as a sort of insurance policy. If the project went down, or operations slowed, John could be called upon to do the work under immense pressure. Ted and Gabriel had become too hard to control once they had nothing to lose. But John…well, threatening to kill his wife and child was a powerful motivator.

John hadn't been drugged in the beginning, but as time had gone on, the agitation had arisen to where there was little choice. Alas, another mistake in the long line of errors made in the history of the project. Now he was out with the public and the police. He would need to be dealt with eventually. To do so now would be the wrong time, unless it was done with perfection. A quick plunge of a syringe would lead to multiple organ failures. He had been in a coma for so long, it would hardly come as a surprise. Then again, any suspicion would be too much. As it was, getting into the intensive care unit where he was would require access and questions from the guard stationed outside the door.

Such actions might not even be necessary. As it stood right now, everyone thought the whole project ended with Ted Saunders, Gabriel Silva, and John Burton's recovery.

They had no idea how wrong they were, and that was perfect.

Detective Ashleigh Myers was on TV now on a late-night rerun of the evening news. She stood in her shiny uniform, accepting awards and applause from nonsensical people who clapped every time someone paused to take a breath. People were stupid. They weren't paying attention to the meaning of the words or seeing the evidence themselves. All they wanted was someone telling them they were safe and everything was going to be okay, so they could go back to their simple lives living in pleasant, comfortable ignorance. None of them knew how much others did to protect or organize their lives. They expected lights to come on with a flick of a switch without any thought to the people working to make it happen or the engineering bringing the grid. All they wanted was to charge their phones so they could play their trivial games or watch their shows. They didn't want to live life for themselves. They wanted to watch someone else live life from the safety of their climate-controlled homes.

They lived in luxury, designed to keep them pleasant, quiet, and occupied. Designed to tell them what to wear, what to eat, what to buy, and what to think.

The news went back to the clip of Max Grover receiving a made-up award. Appreciation meant nothing. People clapped again without realizing who or what they were clapping for.

Ashleigh Myers was a given. Max Grover was a bonus. He had evaded capture for too long, but now he was back in public, thinking it was okay to come out.

The new director of Borealis smiled in the dark, opened a spreadsheet of all of the known test subjects. They scrolled past Ashleigh Myers, Laura Burton, and Megan White, and clicked to turn Max Grover's cell from red to green.

"Gotcha."

CHAPTER 41

Max drove them to Rocky Mountain Labs and stopped at the gate outside. The black fence around the National Institute of Health campus looked out of place in the residential area. Unlike the side roads behind them, the entrance and parking lot had been cleared of any snow. The guard did an ID check on both of them.

Max passed his new driver's license over and gave Ash a small smile. She rubbed his arm, proud of him for another small victory.

"Alright, you're cleared for entry. Visitor parking is over there, and I'll call reception and let them know you're here for your appointment. They'll take you to Dr. Mallory."

They thanked the guard and did as they were told.

The campus was beautiful as all new government buildings were. It was nestled in the side of a quiet neighborhood of older houses with mature trees not unlike Ted's. It looked like the kind of place kids would ride on bikes and go trick-or-treating around Halloween, but there were plenty of no trespassing and no stopping signs around with two gates, reminiscent of a military base. The Sapphire Mountains were directly behind the buildings, framing them like the background in a painting with no other buildings for miles. Ash wondered how much land the lab owned.

"What exactly do you think they have in here?" Max asked.

"They must have something, that's for sure."

They walked across the empty visitor lot and stepped inside a glass reception area that smelled like new paint.

A young woman with a tight brown bun and a round face stood to greet them. She was wearing a dress with a jacket in brown and tan hues.

"Good morning, my name is Sarah. Here are your visitor badges. Would you like something to drink or to use the restroom before we go back to meet Dr. Mallory?"

Ash and Max both declined, before she directed them to a small waiting room that was well appointed like a new doctor's office.

"You will need to watch this safety training video before we go any further. Please let me know if you have any questions. I'll be back to check on you at the conclusion of the video."

Sarah hit play and stepped out, her small heels clipping across the floor back to her desk.

The video welcomed them to Rocky Mountain Labs and gave a brief version of the history that Max and Ash had researched on their own at the library before beginning a training video on how to enter a biosafety level four lab. The model in the video demonstrated the proper way to wash hands, apply personal protective gear, including gloves, shoe covers, hair covers, and a fully sealed suit.

Max and Ash exchanged a glance before the video moved on to talk about blood-borne pathogens and the necessary showers when leaving the containment facility.

"I feel like I'm watching a video on a plane," Max said, leaning over as they watched a person model the correct way to remove gloves.

When the video was complete, Sarah appeared in the doorway. "Alright, please follow me."

They followed her down an empty hallway toward a set of locked double doors. With a wave of her card, the light turned green, and Sarah stood back to let them go first.

To their left was an open door to a room filled with stacks. The sign said library, which caught Max's attention too. To the right there were a series of doors to what appeared to be offices. Down the hall stood another set of double doors with a keypad, into the more secure areas.

"Here you are. Dr. Mallory will be with you momentarily," she said, directing them to the last office. Inside, everything was impeccable.

There was a large L-shaped desk in the middle, flanked by windows. The desk had next to nothing on it and felt sterile compared to the police department. There was a slick thin computer, keyboard, mouse, and phone all in white, blending in with the furniture. To one side, there was a mini-bar elegantly lit with dark cabinets and glossy white stone countertops and a shiny coffee machine as the crown jewel. Through the glass of the fridge, expensive waters stood like soldiers in a perfect line. Facing this stood a line of floor-to-ceiling bookcases, artfully arranged.

Most of the pieces were curated but not personal. Random bits of sculpture punctuated the volumes of journals, stacked on alternating shelves so as to be pleasing to the eye. Had it not been for a few service plaques and one framed certificate from the local theatre thanking Dr. Rose Mallory for her support, it would feel as though this office was vacant.

Sarah followed them inside, offered them another drink,

which again neither accepted. She grabbed a yellow legal pad and had just sat down with a pen when the door swung open.

Sarah stood so fast, she almost knocked the chair over. Max and Ash exchanged another glance and stood as well.

Dr. Rose Mallory stepped in and smiled at them both, before reaching over to shake their hands and exchange pleasantries. Today she wore a starched white lab coat over a crisp suit in light blue. Her blonde hair was pulled back into a low ponytail at the base of her neck and tied with a blue scarf that matched the dress.

"I'm so glad you both could come today. Thank you, Sarah, for letting them in. She'll be accompanying us on our tour today, but first I thought it would be wise to start in here, since you said you had some notes and questions you wanted answered."

"Yes," Ash said, sitting down again on one of the white leather chairs, as Dr. Mallory sat behind the desk. Sarah began writing as soon as she spoke. "Thank you for agreeing to speak with us today. This place is amazing, and your office is beautiful."

Dr. Mallory smiled. "Thank you. I'm not much of a decorator, so I prefer to keep things clean."

"Have you been involved in the arts long?" Ash asked, indicating the certificate.

Her eyes glanced over to the certificate as a broad smile grew over her face. "I enjoyed theatre in high school and undergrad. My favorite role was playing Lady Macbeth, but my graduate studies didn't leave time in the schedule for rehearsal, so I've been an avid supporter ever since I moved here and found the local program struggling." She shrugged. "It brings me joy to see them thrive. So, how can I help you?"

"Can you tell us more about the Borealis Project and what Ted Saunders was hoping to accomplish?"

"I believe I can help a little. Dr. Saunders hasn't worked for Rocky Mountain Labs in about five years. That's around the time the Borealis Project was shut down due to restructuring with the funding."

"Was it just the funding that shut the project down?" Ash said, already eager to know more.

"Yes, we needed to divert resources to other projects. At the time there was a deadly outbreak in Asia that required our immediate focus. That's what we do here. Not only do we store deadly diseases, we study and create vaccines."

"Create or manufacture?" Max asked, his brow narrowed in concentration.

"Create. We are a research laboratory. Once we find a DNA strand and can isolate something to neutralize that virus, we run clinical trials, and if successful, we present our findings to the FDA before sending that work out to other pharmaceutical companies for production."

"Was Ted—Dr. Saunders—working with Borealis initially on vaccines?"

Sarah scribbled away while Dr. Mallory nodded. "That's one modality he had tried. Do you know the origins of his work? His inspiration?"

"We're aware he had a daughter with a physical disability and wanted to focus more research on her condition."

"That's correct. He was looking for new medicine, for a cure."

"Is that ethical?" Max asked.

Dr. Mallory gave a tight smile and looked down at her hands in her lap before answering. "We all have our own reasons for being here. It is better when there is some distance from the work itself. Otherwise researchers tend to want to rush the process and take shortcuts and risks that we have no right to do."

"So he was taking shortcuts?"

"At times yes, and at other times no. The process frustrated him. You can imagine that seeing his daughter in decline worked him into a fervor. Instead of spending much of his time with her and celebrating her life as it was, he was committed to prolonging it, and missed much of it in the process. I'm sorry to say this, because I did enjoy working under him. We made amazing strides because of his work, but he wasn't satisfied. Nothing was enough."

Ash sat up now, interested to know more. "Dr. Mallory, I know you said the project was shut down five years ago, but can you tell me why some people still had blister packs with pills marked Borealis in town in the past six months?"

"I'm sorry I cannot. Were those the attackers? I watched that on the news."

"Yes, we were seeing a pattern connecting people who had worked in security, were single men typically in their twenties to thirties. One of them had that blister pack on them."

"The official Borealis Project was shut down five years ago. As far as what Dr. Saunders was up to since then, I cannot say."

Ash reached into her pocket and put her hand on the book she recovered at Ted's house. He had written all sorts of formulas she had originally planned to show the doctor, but the warning in the cover now stood out to her. Borealis had pushed him out. The lab had forced him to retire and would come for him.

Instead of putting it on the table, Ash asked, "Do you still have any of his research from the original Borealis Project? We were hoping to know more exactly of what it was that he did."

"Of course. That will be in our records department of our library. Sarah, would you get the door and begin pulling those files?"

They walked over to a one-room library that was filled with stacks of medical journals and framed clippings about Rocky Mountain Labs throughout its history. Sarah scurried over to what appeared to be a small circulation desk and brought back a stack of books, files, and bound binders to the table. They all took a seat around it.

Dr. Mallory opened the first one. Her elegant long fingers were free of jewelry and any polish on her nails, most likely because of being in and out of gloves. She flipped open the first file and smiled to herself, as she pulled out a pair of tortoiseshell glasses and put them on to inspect what it was she was reading, before she spun it around to face Ash and Max.

She pointed to one line from across the table like a patient teacher. "Here you can see the beginning of his work. Back then it wasn't called the Borealis Project. He was just out of school and hadn't had his daughter yet."

Ash leaned over and tried to make sense of what it was Dr. Mallory was pointing at. "What was his focus in school?"

"Well, originally he was interested in virology which is the primary mission of this lab. Later, his work shifted to autoimmune diseases and manipulating DNA."

"That's possible?" Max asked, looking up from the file.

"Yes, in gene therapy the cells are taken from a patient, manipulated, and reintroduced."

"How would this happen?" Ash asked.

"Typically through an IV."

"Does it work?"

Dr. Mallory smiled. "Yes, it can. There have been remarkable advances that can lead to a body rejecting HIV, herpes, and other illnesses. The work is slow but progressing."

"Is it possible that gene therapy or something similar could've been in John Burton's IV?" Ash asked, taking notes in a notebook Max had given her to use.

Dr. Mallory leaned back. "If it was an IV, then yes, that would be possible, though that implies Gabriel Silva was able to get access to the research and then knew what to do with it. It's complicated."

"Understandably so," Ash said. "One thing I'm struggling with—if other people are doing this work, why would Ted's and Borealis be so significant?"

Sarah was still scribbling notes of her own and at this point paused to look over at Dr. Mallory, who leaned back with a gentle smile.

"Some people wanted to see if there were opportunities beyond his work."

"How is that different from the others?"

"Good question. As I said, Dr. Saunders was a remarkable man who loved his daughter very much. When he realized how ill she was and how quickly it progressed, he became obsessed with action. That made him reckless. The shortcuts had serious ramifications without people's consent."

"But I thought if people enrolled in clinical trials, they were made aware of the risks and the benefits?"

"That is how it is supposed to work."

"But it didn't in this case," said Max, filling in the gaps. "Did they know at all?"

Dr. Mallory didn't elaborate. "I can only tell you for sure what I personally observed, and take you through the records of what we have here. I was involved later in the process."

"What population did he work with?"

"Children and women who were pregnant, then later the work shifted to include adults. He was following his daughter's age, you see."

Ash felt a hot feeling bloom in her chest, rising to her cheeks. "Did the mothers get IVs or was there another way?"

Dr. Mallory opened the file again and pointed to some

early notes. "Here you can see they were given a new blend of prenatal vitamins, some by injection and some orally."

"These were just here?" asked Max, who had picked up where Ash was going.

She flipped to another page and pointed to a list of doctors. "They were distributed throughout some local clinics before the risks were fully apparent."

"That didn't need approval?" Ash asked.

"The FDA doesn't clear vitamins or supplements, which is why so many exist with questionable results."

"What were the effects?"

"The patients had fast development in certain areas, but it was never predictable or replicable. He kept trying though. Here—see for yourself."

Ash and Max pored over another file, this one handwritten notes on a child who was identified by age and sex only. She hit all her milestones of early childhood development before she showed extreme development in hearing.

The hairs on the back of her neck raised in a rush as she looked at someone who she didn't know, but to whom she felt related. How many more were there?

"Was this reversible?" Max asked.

Dr. Mallory shook her head. "A few patients sought out solutions to the complaints, but they were not able to be resolved."

"But can't you just go back in and redevelop the gene theory to undo what was done?"

Dr. Mallory shook her head. "At this time, viral-based gene therapies cannot be reversed."

Max stood abruptly. "Excuse me, may I use the restroom?"

"Of course," said Sarah, jumping up to walk him out. "Please follow me."

"So, everyone wanted his work because of the potential, but the one thing he wanted…"

"He sadly never achieved anything that could help his daughter's illness, so in his eyes it was all a waste."

CHAPTER 42

Max couldn't wait to get out of the lab. Ash walked out with the doctor, who gave them a smile and handshake before Sarah ushered them out the door.

"I can't believe we had to watch the video, and they wouldn't even let us in the lab. Hey, are you okay?" Ash asked when he didn't answer but just started driving away.

"She said it's irreversible. I wanted to end this project so it could never happen again."

"And we did! It's done. The lab in the mountains is closed. Ted's gone. Gabriel's in custody. It's over. No one else will have to deal with this."

"But I'm fucking stuck like this? You heard her! There's nothing. Not a goddamn thing they can do to help me or anyone else like me."

Ash stayed quiet for a bit, chewing it over. "But remember how you said it's amazing that…"

"Fuck that. This shit is fine when a fucking bear is thinking of attacking me or we're on the run in a blizzard or some psychopath is attacking me in a secret torture lab, but I can't live with it now. How am I supposed to hold a job? I can't even get an apartment."

"It'll take time," Ash said, reaching over, but Max flicked her hand away.

"No, you're not getting it. You can sit over there and think about people, but I'm violent. I hurt people and have no memory of it. No one is going to want to lease an apartment to someone like me. Not like I have any credit or money anyway."

"You can get credit again. I'm sure your records are still there from before. It'll just take one step at a time, and I'll help you."

"Help me? Do you have any idea what this life is going to look like? And for what? So people can be afraid of me or always watching to see where I'll blow next?"

"No one needs to know about your medical history. That's private."

"Oh yeah? Aren't you the one that said the police department would be keeping an eye on anyone involved in the interest of public security and then *encouraged* the public to report anyone involved?"

Ash sat in silence.

"We are not the same. You might think we are, but we're not. You and your friends came out ahead. You have these awesome abilities that help others. You may not be able to control them, but you're not a menace to society. You keep mentioning all of these attacks, the ones like Troy was blamed for. Where are those guys, huh? You mean to tell me they got to go home and live in peace?"

Ash closed her eyes and let her head fall against the seat back. "You're right."

"They're in fucking jail. No one says, 'Oh hey, don't worry about him. He was part of an experiment that fucked up his whole fucking brain chemistry or DNA shit or whatever, and now he'll just fucking go into rages, so just let him be, and give him a blanket when he's done because he'll be cold, tired, and probably naked.'"

"Max—"

"Fuck no. Don't tell me otherwise. You've arrested people. You probably arrested some of them. Did you stop to ask if they had a mental condition or need help or hey, did you get fucked over by some asshole too smart and selfish for his own good? No. I know you didn't because no one does and no one will."

He took a breath, and with it, Ash watched every last bit of hope drain out from his body and face. "A threat is a threat, no matter how it came to be."

"Max," she said, reaching over to take his hand. "We'll keep going and try to figure this out, and if we can't, we'll work on how to manage it. I know you're not a threat to me."

"You can't be with me forever."

"I'd like to be," she said.

"You know what I mean. I don't know how to live a normal life anymore. I know how it works in the mountains, but here everything just feels harder."

"No one said you have to stay here. I like it, but if you need to go back to Pat's place, I'll understand if it's easier for you."

Max nodded. "Yeah, I think that might be better."

She squeezed his hand. "And this time you'll have a library card, and can drive freely. If you want a bank account, great. If not, hey, that's okay. You don't need to do anything you're not comfortable with. One step at a time."

He nodded. "Yeah, you're right."

That night they came home to the dark apartment. Ash lit her candles and made her calming tea with all sorts of vitamins Max had never heard of, before they sat on the couch.

Neither wanted to watch anything, so they ended up watching that same campfire video with some calming jazz playing in the background.

Ash pulled out some of Max's clothing from the laundry basket and laid them on her very white coffee table, before going into her closet. She came back with a padded box covered in sunflowers, and opened it to reveal sewing supplies.

She picked up the sweater Max had borrowed from Troy and found the tears and pulls from the fight in the lab. She turned on the lamp on the softest setting so she had enough light to work without disturbing the chill mood, and began pinning the bits of fabric together.

"You don't have to do that," Max said, looking up from his sketchbook.

"I want to, and besides I haven't done much mending in years."

"I didn't realize you could sew."

Ash nodded while consulting an impressive array of thread colors. She threaded a needle on the first try, before pulling the thread through some wax and stitching the shoulder tear together where the seam had torn. "I have an odd set of skills. Mom insisted upon it."

"You haven't told me much about her or what things were like for you growing up."

Ash shrugged. "I'm the black sheep. It's not the typical story for a cop. They're very crunchy granola types who don't understand my work, and the guys I work with don't understand them, so I'm a bit in between, but hey, at least I can knit you a sweater faster than most."

"That's a hard place to be."

"Yeah, I mean, we still talk, but not that often. Since we're such different people, there isn't that much to talk about. I go and see her at least once a year."

"Where do they live again?"

"California now, on a commune. Years ago, when they first left Montana, they bought hundreds of acres with a lot of their friends and started homesteading. They raise goats and chickens, grow gardens, sell soaps, crystals, candles, salts, fiber arts, baked goods... You know, everything you'd expect."

"That sounds like a wonderful way to grow up."

"It was wonderful, but it wasn't for me as an adult. I had to get out."

Max watched as she finished the stitch, healing the wound so well it was impossible to tell it had ever been there. She snipped off the thread with some small scissors, then pulled out some more tools and a bit of thicker thread.

"I'll have to darn this part. It's something I've only done a handful of times, so no promises, but Troy won't mind."

"Why wasn't it for you?" he asked, transfixed on watching her nimble hands work so fast with the thread.

"It's a long story."

"I'd like to know."

Ash's brow furrowed with a sour memory. "People make bad choices everywhere, including there. One time, the police were called to our house. I was little then—I remember I had this stuffed bunny that I just held the entire time they talked to me, so I was really small. Juniper, my sister, was just a baby, and she was fussing in her high chair when they came to question the spiritual leader on some reports that there were inappropriate actions going on with money and with minors."

Ash got the scissors and snipped the thread with more anger this time.

"Of course, he said nothing of the sort was going on and was shocked anyone would even think that. Blah Blah Blah, the usual crap. Anyway, obviously he was lying, and the smell was so bad, I literally couldn't breathe. It must've triggered some sort of asthma attack or something. So I'm hacking to death with my bunny in the kitchen with Juniper, and mom poked her head in on me and said she'd make me some tea."

"Tea?"

"Yeah, I know. In Mom's defense, she didn't know how bad it was. I was just a kid coughing, but it was scary for me. So, anyway, one of the cops walked right back there and got down on my level. I don't remember his name, but he had the kindest eyes and the shiniest badge. He asked me if I was okay, called 911 even though the spiritual leader said I'd be fine with some raw honey, and sat with me while the paramedics gave me an inhaler. He took the time to ask me my bunny's name and sit with me until it passed."

"Did you have to go to the hospital?"

"Mom wasn't into that."

"That must have made an impression."

Ash let out a laugh. "Yeah, and that was just the first time. The next time there were some gunshots at passing cars and trucks, so they came back and questioned my older brother, Bodhi, and his friend Gus, who claimed he had never even seen a gun. Bodhi told the truth, but Gus was lying so bad I almost passed out, but the cops checked on me then too."

"I'm glad they did."

"Thanks. Me too. It's worked out pretty well. Mom about had a heart attack when I told her I wanted to go into the police academy. We were homeschooled as you can guess, so I needed to get the right math and sciences beyond foraging, and I enrolled in the local high school."

"You enrolled yourself?" Max asked, watching her work on some old BDUs that he could've told her not to worry about, but he loved watching her work and listening to her talk.

Ash laughed again and went to work using a different

stitch, presumably one that was stronger since the thread was thicker and she did a different movement. "Yeah, that counselor's face was priceless. I worked hard, and my family was proud of me at graduation. It was difficult, and actually, that kid Gus was there too. His family had left the commune after a few more incidents. He tried to make a pass at me, and when I brushed him off, he started being a real ass."

Max felt a bit of tension come up on his next question.

"What happened?"

"A few things. Mostly little shit. One time I came out to my car I had just purchased—it wasn't much, but I had bought it myself and I was damn proud of not having to have the bus pick me up at the farm anymore. Anyway, they covered my car in condoms, and he shoved me down when I was walking to the trash can to throw them all out."

Max closed his eyes to try to calm the double vision that had taken over. Shit, he needed to get a grip. It was a story from a long time ago. If he couldn't handle a story, how could he stay here?

"That's really upsetting. I'm so sorry."

"Yeah, I was just a kid, so it scared the shit out of me, but I knew he was full of shit, so I told him flat out I'd go to the cops with every stunt he pulled." Ash smiled over at him. "He tried to act tough in front of his friends to save face, but he never bothered me again after that."

She folded the last of his clothes. "Alright, there you go. All fixed up. I'm a little rusty, but for the most part they came out okay."

Max took the clothes, running his fingers over the small, perfect stitches. "They're perfect. Thank you."

Ash shrugged as if it was no big deal, then took the sunflower box that didn't match the rest of the apartment and tucked it back away out of sight in the closet.

"It's no big deal."

CHAPTER 43

Ash came home from work vibing. For the first time in her life, she truly felt like everything was going well. She'd never been so happy to do paperwork and drink stale coffee from the bullpen in all her life. She felt fresh, light, and happy. She hadn't detected any lies at work. Everyone else was truly happy to see her back.

She parked in a different spot, because hers was obscured by a new snow pile, and grabbed the bakery box with dessert and jogged up the stairs, pulling out her key to let herself inside.

"Hey, Max!"

The apartment was dark. Puzzled, she flicked on a light, and found the space empty except for a drawing of her sewing from last night.

His work was incredible. She had never thought she was a classic beauty, but Max made her look so beautiful with a simple pencil.

She flipped it over to read a note.

Went out to check in with Pat and try to find some work. See you later, Max

She peeled back the window to see the visitor spot still empty with no sign of the truck.

Ash went back to the kitchen and did her normal routine. She stripped out of her work clothes and rinsed off before grabbing a shower, lighting a candle, and doing a little light yoga, but she couldn't fight a nagging feeling that something was wrong.

What if he did have an episode? What would happen?

Ash picked up her phone and checked it. No news alerts which didn't mean much. Work email was empty too. She tried to start a little dinner, but her heart wasn't in it. The usual movements that typically comforted her now were irritating and a hassle.

She took a lap outside, hoping to clear her head, and came back frustrated when it didn't work, then repeated the process. At one point, she picked up the phone to call Marshall and the guys to see if they had heard anything from dispatch that could be Max, but decided against it and washed her face instead, trying to clear her thoughts.

Ash hooked up her phone to a calming lo-fi beat that never failed her after a hard day at work, and it helped, but she was still agitated. At least now she could function.

She put the rice on and let the chicken marinate in an olive oil and lemon mixture, and was just going to check the window again when she heard a key in the door.

A breath of relief rushed out of her when she saw him come through the door. She ran over and hugged him, breathing in the smell and feeling his arms around her.

"Hey, how was your day?" Max asked with a nervous laugh. "Everything okay?"

"Yeah," she said, stepping back and flipping her bangs out of her face. "I just started getting worried about you. How was your day?"

"Sorry I worried you. I drove really slow because of the ice. Day was good. Went to check on Pat."

"How's he?" Ash said, heading back to the chicken and getting her pan ready with a smile.

Max took off his coat, hat, and boots, hanging them next to hers. They looked so natural there, Ash couldn't help but grin.

"He's alright. Same old, same old. Got in a new shipment of reproductions. There was a film crew here about two weeks ago. The costumer ordered all this old west military stuff for the show, but didn't want to take it back with them, so they sold it to Pat at cost. He thought it was neat and he could make a couple of bucks, either in the store or at auction."

"That's cool. Did they say what the show was?"

"No, they didn't mention anything in particular, just that it was set in the 1870s and would be out next year."

"Nice, will you be helping him out again tomorrow?"

Max started setting the table for the two of them just like she had done for other meals. He was a quick study with an eye for detail.

"Yeah, I'll head back, and then Troy and his dad need some help fixing fence and installing a new heater in one of the barns."

"That's nice."

"It's okay."

He wasn't lying, but she could tell how he really felt all over his face. "You don't sound excited."

Max glanced up. "Is it that easy to tell?"

"Yeah. What's wrong?"

"I don't know. It's just a lot to get used to."

"It's very different than spending all of that time in the woods. Makes sense it would take a bit to readjust. You only need to take one step at a time. You've been gone for five years; you don't need to have everything figured out immediately."

"I've thought about maybe going back to my old job," he said when they sat down to eat.

"With Pat or the ones before?"

"Before. I mean, I'm not looking for the marines again, but I did enjoy smoke jumping until the accident."

"I'm sure they'd love to have you. Carter was telling me there were three fires this past summer they were working to contain for weeks. He bought the old bank building in town when Megan moved out. Apparently she was the last tenant, so he bought it and renovated the whole thing. His office is the top floor, so he could see the smoke from his window."

"Yeah, maybe. There's not that many positions open, but I could at least ask around, see if anyone there has known me."

"It sounds like you miss the excitement," Ash said, taking a drink of her green tea.

"I think I do. I feel like I did when I got out of the military. It's like…now what? I mean, I love being here with you, but I just can't shake the feeling that something's not right, like I don't belong here."

"I bet more people feel like you than you realize. It's a big change. I think that's a normal and natural way to feel. Would it make you feel better if we went to Glacier or back to the cabin this weekend?"

Max looked up and smiled. "I'll need to restock the cabin unless you want more MREs."

"You know, I had been missing almost burning my mouth off on some chili."

"Alright, it's settled. The cabin it is."

"Deal. That'll be a nice retreat. Let's just hope nothing crazy happens between now and then."

Later, Ash would regret the moment those words had left her mouth.

CHAPTER 44

The call came early the next day, which was odd. Typically crime liked a later start in the day after being up all night, but then you couldn't argue with crazy, and that was what was in front of Ash the next morning.

"I said freeze. Keep your hands where we can see them."

The man did not freeze. He looked back over to her with a feral look in his eye that was unnatural and unsettling.

They were outside of an old, abandoned school that was now used as a community center. She had been on her way to work and was the first to arrive on scene. Things had already spiraled out of control.

The caller had reported a man screaming obscenities that upset local residents while running around trying to strip his clothes, then rolling around shirtless in the snow.

"Don't fucking come near me! I can hear you all in my head. Why are you all in my fucking head?!"

"This is the Goldvein Police Department. We need you to lie on the ground with your arms outstretched."

Dispatch informed her backup was on the way, thank God. "I will have to use force if you do not comply."

The suspect was unmoved, still twitching and screaming at some unseen force. He looked possessed.

"This is your last warning; stand down or I will have no choice but to use force."

The man was grabbing his skull and clawing at the air around him with a painful scream as if his body was covered in flames they couldn't see.

Ash deployed her taser, which caught the man in the back. He twisted once, twice before bending his body in an unhinged way and pulling the leads off.

His eyes were dilated, green, and completely bloodshot. He let out a primal roar and charged at her, tackling her before she could draw her weapon.

She scrambled to avoid his mouth as he tried to bite her and pin her in the snow. The slick ground was to her advantage. She wriggled out of his hold and kneed him in the groin, before rolling and kicking her way out from under him, but not before his fist landed a clean blow right to her cheek, making her see stars.

Ash's head snapped back and hit the icy snow, before she hauled both her legs up and got vertical as fast as possible. A little unsteady, she tackled him and landed in a good position to pin him until she heard the sirens and the other cops running up behind her to assist.

Between the three of them, they were able to cuff him and sit him upright before reading him his rights. The man was still agitated enough for Ash to call for medical to check him out before they brought him into the small holding cell.

Laura jogged over when the ambulance arrived. "Hey, what's going on?"

"I'm not sure, but he's acting erratic and won't settle down enough for questioning. He's calmed down considerably from where he was before, so he might talk to you. I just want him checked out before we bring him in."

"Sure, let me take a look and see what's going on."

Ash watched as Laura did her standard procedure, checking heart rate, blood pressure, and eyes. She tried to talk to the man, but he kept twitching in odd directions, trying to contort himself against the ambulance door where they had seated him, wrapped in a shock blanket he kept trying to shake off.

Jordan stepped away to answer a call from dispatch, and that's when Ash could again see Laura's healing ability.

Laura took a steadying breath and held her hands over the man's temples. First he tried to shake her off, when a beautiful warm glow bloomed from her hands into his skin. Laura took a few more breaths with her eyes closed, and a thin line formed between her brows as if she was feeling for something and found something else completely.

She took another breath and let go. Some of the golden light stayed on the man's temples before fading like it did from her hands. He relaxed and leaned back against the truck, before his eyes fluttered open and blinked a few times when he tried to make sense of his surroundings.

"Where am I?"

"You don't remember what you were just doing?" Ash asked.

The man looked up at her as if seeing her for the first time. "I'm sorry, Officer, I don't remember what's going on."

Laura glanced at Ash, who nodded. He was telling the stone-cold truth.

"You're being detained for questioning. We got some calls about you running around half naked in the snow, holding your head and screaming obscenities."

He looked down, seemingly amazed to see he didn't have a shirt.

"Heart rate has settled down," Laura said. "It was pretty high when we arrived on scene."

Ash gave the other officers, who were chatting in their cars, trying to stay warm, the thumbs-up, which they returned.

"What's your name?"

"Michael Dwyer. My ID's in my pocket. You can grab it right now."

Ash reached down and pulled out a slim wallet from the pocket he indicated to confirm what he said was true. He was from Idaho, twenty-four, and had two twenties in his wallet, along with an empty blister pack.

"What's this?" Ash held up the small foil with the plastic bit still attached and crumpled.

"It's not drugs, I swear on my life. I didn't drink enough water at the gym, so I had a headache, right?" He was talking faster now, to get out as much of the story before she made a judgment. She wished she could tell him not to worry. "So someone at the bar gave me a pill. They said it was for migraines. I had a long shift, so I took it, and—"

Awareness dawned on him as he started to realize the mistake. The kid's eyes got really big as he shook his head no in disbelief.

"I swear to God I didn't know. I thought it was medicine."

"What did that person look like?" Ash asked, tilting her head to one side.

"I don't know. The next thing I remember was I left work and was walking to my car."

"Where do you work?"

"I bartend a few times a month for a catering company, and work security at night for some extra cash, but I didn't drink or anything. I swear. I don't want to lose my job. I'm new at the gym downtown. I train people. Powerlifting, strength training, and a few group classes. Please don't tell my bosses about this. I don't want to lose my job. They took a chance on me. I just got here. I'm trying to get some more clients and…"

His eyes got real big and panicked as he looked from Ash to Laura and then back again. Ash breathed in through her nose and sensed nothing but the truth.

"We believe you, and since you don't want to lose your job for being charged with assaulting an officer, you need to be available for questioning whenever I call."

"Okay, of course. Thank you, Officer."

"It's Detective. Detective Myers," she said as she took down the address and phone number of the catering company. If she was lucky, she could find out where he had bartended and try to get a guest list. "I'll be calling to check up on you."

"Do you want a ride to the hospital?" Laura asked. "We can check you out."

"Do I have to? I don't have a lot saved up, and I don't want my parents to have to pay a lot. I'm still on their insurance."

Laura shook her head. "No, not at all since Detective Myers is doing you a solid. I'll just make a note that things seem to have settled down and you're refusing care."

"Okay, thanks again. I'm pretty freaked out. I just want to go home and go to bed."

"Can I call your folks?" Ash asked.

"I'll call them later," Michael said, massaging his hands when she took the cuffs off. He looked down, surprised to see the deep red marks on his wrists.

"You were fighting me pretty hard."

Michael scrubbed his face with his hands. "Oh shit, I'm sorry. I had no idea. God, what do you think was in that?"

Ash shook her head and looked down at her plastic-gloved palm. "I don't know, but I'd like to find out."

"You can have it. I never want to see that again."

"Alright, thanks," she said, pulling out a baggie. "Do you need a lift home?"

"No, I'm right over there," he said, pointing to a small two-bedroom house with the front door ajar. "My roommate is coming home from a long weekend with his girlfriend today."

"Alright, I'll swing by to check on you in a few days," Ash said, waving the police cruisers off as they pulled out and drove away.

Laura jogged back to where Ash was after they left. "I let Jordan know I'm riding with you, since my shift just ended. Figured we had a lot of ground to cover, and I never get to see you anymore."

They both waved to Jordan as he turned around and headed back to Station 3. Ash and Laura got in her cruiser, and Laura reached over and touched her hand to Ash's cheek. The warmth was a pleasant heat that felt a little abrasive, like she was lying in the sun on a beach after being in the salt water.

"That's incredible," Ash said, flipping down the mirror to check herself out.

Laura gave her a sheepish smile. "Thanks."

"What did you find out? Can you tell what it was?"

"Not what I was expecting at all. I was looking for addiction—drugs like meth can leave the same sort of imprint on the body—but came up empty. I think I was able to ease whatever's going on. It's not a stroke or epilepsy. If anything it felt like a low grade migraine, like he said, but it wasn't."

"So you've never seen this before?"

"No, I haven't. You think it's from the lab? I thought that was all done like everyone said at the press conference." Laura's hands twisted in her lap.

"Yeah, I hope so. It could be something new on the streets, but I just don't know."

"Sounds like you have a new project, Detective," Laura said, admiring the new cruiser. "I didn't realize your promotion came with an upgrade."

"I know. Figures, the first time I'm driving to work I get a call from dispatch."

"Well, it sounds like it's one you're interested in." They pulled into the spot Ash used to park in at Station 3 next to Laura's car.

"By the way, Carter wants to get everyone together for game night next week. Would you and Max like to come?"

"I'll ask him. I think he'd like that."

"How's he doing? It's a lot of change for him." Typical of Laura to check in on them when she herself had a lot going on at the moment.

"He's okay. How's John?"

Laura blew out a breath. "He's making progress, getting more stable one day but then has a setback the next. It'll be a long road ahead of him, and that's before therapy and getting his life together, but yeah, we're just going one step at a time."

"That's the best way. Let me know what I can do to help. I can swing by and watch Holden if you all need a break. Just let me know."

"Yeah, thanks. I'll keep that in mind. So, Max is good?"

Ash nodded. "He's alright. It'll take time to get used to living in town again, so we might go out of town this weekend just to get some downtime, you know?"

"Sounds lovely," Laura said as she reached over for a hug that felt like it was just as much for her as it was for Ash. "Enjoy it, and don't work too hard, Detective."

CHAPTER 45

Ash took the frozen peas from Max to put on her face when they were sitting on the couch that night. She didn't really need them after Laura's amazing work, but Max wanted to do something and she let him.

"It was insane. One minute he was crazy and the next he was fine."

"Are you going to go and check on him soon?"

"Yeah," she said. "I don't know if I did the right thing or not. Toxicology can't get anything off the little blister pack, and I mean, who even knows if it has to do with that. It could've been something else completely."

"I think you did the right thing. It sounds like he needed help."

"Thanks for saying so. I'm not so sure. I could still go back and charge him with assaulting an officer or lying if something doesn't check out, but"—she shrugged and tapped her nose—"the nose knows."

"It's good there are good cops like you. That's important. Someone else might've handled that very differently."

"Thanks. I'm trying. It's not easy when so much is happening so quickly, and like I said, I could've been wrong." She blew out a breath and let her head fall back against the couch.

Tonight they had a new fireplace video on the screen in front of them, and a brand-new candle lit, this time vanilla. It had become their evening routine. Sitting quietly on the couch, each taking a turn telling the other about their day. Ash had wanted to sew, but it was probably best to rest her eye. Max was sketching again.

"How did your day go?" she asked him while he worked with his pencil.

"The work for Troy and his dad was quick, same with Pat. None of them can hire me on full time or anything like that, so I went asked the librarian, Amanda, to help me search for what's available."

"That's cool. Is that the same person who helped us before and got you your card?"

"Yep, she took the time to help me log back into my email, which was an adventure in junk mail, and then we set up accounts. She said she would also make a few calls and help with my resume."

"What if you come down to the station to help me tomorrow? There are a few open positions, and you'd be a great fit."

"Seriously?"

"Of course, especially with your military service and first responder background. We don't have a police sketch artist on staff. I'm sure they'd love to have you."

"Yeah, if you don't think that'd be weird. I mean you've seen me when I lose control— I'm not sure."

She waved her hand. "If you're the police sketch artist, you wouldn't be in stressful situations. You'd need to go through the academy, but usually the guys who are coming from the military do the best. Want to come tomorrow to check it out?"

"Yeah, it'd be nice to see where you work."

"We have a press conference tomorrow, so how about you stop by after lunch, and I can introduce you again to the people you didn't get to meet at the awards ceremony."

The next day, Max did just that. He made sure to shower, shave, and put on his best shirt that they had recently bought from the store, and he even picked up a couple dozen doughnuts to make a good first impression.

The person at the front desk buzzed her when he arrived.

Ash smiled when she saw how handsome he looked.

"It's weird to hear you called by your official name," he said as they walked through the bullpen back to her office.

Ash smiled and gave him a kiss. "I still pinch myself every time I hear it." She nodded toward the boxes of doughnuts in his hands. "You're going to be popular."

"I didn't know how many to bring."

"Oh, this is perfect. They'll go fast. Here," she said, taking them and setting them down. "Before we go put them by the coffee, I got you something too."

Ash pulled out a small box from a drawer. "I don't know if it's like the one you lost, but I looked it up and this was the most common."

It was the first time she had seen him surprised, when he opened the box and saw the silver St. Michael medal on a matching chain.

He had to swallow a few times before he spoke, and nodded holding back tears before he had to swipe them away. "It's perfect. Thank you."

"Patron saint of smoke jumpers, military, and police, so I figured it's meant to be! I thought it would give you some good luck today, not that you'll need it. They're going to love you," Ash said with a smile when she pulled back from the hug he had wrapped her in.

"Here, I even picked up the application. You can sit here and fill it out and then we'll bring it out with the doughnuts all at once. That'll seal the deal."

Max sniffed again and took a breath. He rubbed his palms on his pants and took her pen.

"Come on, you can fill it out while you sit in the back. It's almost time for the press conference to start."

They went into the conference room, where Max got the last chair before Ash took her place up front.

First the mayor spoke, followed by the chief, and then it was Ash's turn. The reporters had been dying to get statements from her about the whole incident, and the department had stalled as long as they could, but finally the pound of flesh had to be paid.

"John Burton has been missing for over five years, and he was recently recovered by our own Detective Ashleigh Myers. I will now give her the floor."

There were a series of clicks as the cameras all fired off and several reporters started calling for attention.

"Can you tell us if there is any evidence there are more people out there? Anyone Gabriel Silva may have been working with when he attacked John Burton and Dr. Ted Saunders?"

Oof. First reporter went for the throat, but Ash was ready and had been briefed on what to say in what felt like a hundred meetings earlier in the week.

"At this time, there is no evidence to support that Gabriel Silva was working with anyone. Our records show Mr. Silva has a history in government and military service in Brazil where he fled the country after being wanted as a suspect in several murders. Right now, we're in conversations about the trial versus extradition."

A second reporter jumped up. "Has there been any determination of motive for Gabriel Silva?"

"Police believe Mr. Silva was working with Ted Saunders and attacked Mr. Saunders in his own home to take over his research for personal gain. Should any member of the public have any additional information, they can always call our crime stoppers number, but at this time we believe the majority of this situation has been brought to an end."

A tall man in the back stood up and signaled for her attention. "Detective, can you elaborate on a recent attack you yourself sustained by an unknown man who was having an episode in the park? How can the public feel safe when we have people around us who can lash out at any given moment? Are there any commonalities about the people who are lashing out and attacking?"

"All we know is that they are all single men at this time who have a security or military background."

"So men are the only ones who have exhibited these crazed episodes?" he asked.

"Yes, that is accurate."

More camera clicking followed along with a large murmur.

"Do we know why this is happening to these men?"

"We...um, we still do not know, but it may have something to do with their history and the Borealis Project."

"What do you mean the Borealis Project?"

"We believe many years ago, members of the Borealis Project worked with members of the military and prior service to offer solutions to chronic pain, issues, and injuries through gene therapy. It appears now that these men are losing control of their emotions or actions."

The reporters all started talking at once.

A woman in a gray suit raised her phone. "Should people be on guard around men who have military or security backgrounds? Will more of them have these violent outbursts?"

"It is possible, yes, so we encourage the public to be on guard, but we at the GDP are here and prepared to protect you."

Ash glanced over to see the department's head of media walking over and making a chopping motion, before taking the mic from her and saying, "Thank you, everyone. That's all the time we have. No more questions."

Ash rushed to find Max after the media circus had settled down, and found him standing in her office. "Oh my God, that happened so fast. I didn't even get to mention you—"

"Oh, I think you talked enough."

Ash stopped and looked at him. "What do you mean?"

"'These men are losing control of their emotions and actions'? 'We encourage the public to be on guard'?"

"Max, you know that's not what I meant. You're not like them."

"*Them?* What about you? You're okay, but I'm *them?* It's just the people like me? I see what you're trying to do. You never were going to believe or trust me anyway."

"Max, that's not—"

"Are you afraid of me?"

"Max, stop. Don't do this."

"I said,"—Max snapped his head around with an odd look in his eye—"Are you afraid of me?"

"Don't—"

Max started to lunge. Ash jumped back. Her hand went near her taser before she even realized what she was doing.

Max stopped and straightened up with a cool distance in his eyes. "Well, there you go. I should've known you didn't mean everything you said about us being the same."

"Max, please stop. I'm sorry. I didn't mean—"

"Don't. I don't want to hear it."

He spun on his heel and stalked out of the room before she could stop him. Sitting in front of her on the empty chair was the crumpled application.

Ash picked it up and read it, as her heart ripped in two.

He had filled it all out.

CHAPTER 46

Ash went back to her apartment, only to find it a shell of the sanctuary she had come to rely on.

Max's stuff was still there, packed neatly in the corner of the room, a literal baggage to the heaviness in her heart. Knowing Max, he wouldn't be back. He had started over before and could do it again.

Ash ran through her nightly routine. First, she took her shower and slipped into her loose loungewear before settling into some dinner. She had two fillets of salmon in the fridge, but only cooked one. She steamed some broccoli and thought about making a sauce, but then decided it wasn't worth getting the pot dirty. She didn't care enough to wash an extra dish.

The fork clicked against the plate where she ate, alone in silence. Annoyed at the emotion, she turned on the TV to try and find something to fill the void, but every video made her think of him.

The fires, the trees, the snow, the cooking, the rain. Finally, she came to a clip of the ocean. She hadn't been a beach person before, but tonight she was because it had nothing to do with the life she was living.

The mesmerizing pace of the waves grated on her nerves as she ate, until finally she gave in and switched to the fireplace they had been watching last night.

Ash swallowed the last bit of food and cleaned the dishes, trying not to look at the two coffee mugs in the drain board.

Instead, she intentionally dried everything and put it all away so she wouldn't have to look at any of it.

She sprayed down the kitchen counters and table with a lemon-scented cleaner, before digging around in the cabinet for a new candle. She didn't go for the lighter like normal, but instead chose the matches.

The feel of the wooden matchstick in her fingertips rasping against the grit of the sandpaper reminded her of everything Max was.

But the match didn't light. Ash tried again and again, until the stick broke and she had to toss it for another one that did the same thing. Maybe they had gone bad or something. Ash considered the box and put it back in the drawer instead of throwing it away. She reached for the lighter and lit the candle. The flickering glow was a pleasant presence.

She dimmed her lights and pulled out her yoga mat, queuing up her usual string of videos. Each one took place in an ashram in India, which only made her think of Max even more. She couldn't get through the opening centering without his image coming to mind. Ash grabbed the remote and flicked through some other channels, searching for something different and settling for a soft-spoken woman in a room with a dog.

Ash worked through the poses, moving into her usual downward dog, raising each heel to the sky and trying to regulate her breath as she tried to stretch the tension from her body. With each passing vinyasa, her body found the rhythm after weeks without practice. Her calves stretched with her hamstrings, tugging from her back to her heels, as she worked each heel to the ground, which only made her think of running through the blizzard with him protecting her at great personal risk.

Ash shook her head and tried to let the thoughts come and go, noticing them like passing cars or whatever. She lay down for the hip openers, which of course brought back memories from Troy and Megan's cabin where everything had felt perfect. That's where he had told her about his drawings of her.

Ash sat up and looked around, ignoring the soft breathing still coming from the yoga video. She checked on the coffee table before going to the bedroom to find the bedside table empty. With a glance at Max's bag, she saw it.

His sketchbook.

With the final meditation still running in the living room, Ash sunk back down to the floor and opened the small book.

Just like before, the early pages were of a woman far away, looking away, hiding her face. With each page turned, she saw herself bloom into clarity until there she was in the bed, with the sheet around her elbows, leaving her shoulders exposed.

Ash leaned back against the side of the bed, cradling the little book in her hands, staring at the expression on her face. She had never seen herself this way, like he saw her. What Max saw—had seen—was beautiful.

She leaned backed as the tears snuck out from her eyes even though they were squeezed shut. First they fell silently, and she swiped them away quickly, which was useless because more fell in their place. Fast, hot tears came with a choked sob, as she let out the pain of what she'd gained and lost.

Here she was, alone in her apartment like she always had been.

Everything was as it was, but nothing felt the same.

CHAPTER 47

Ash shut the car door after the twelve-hour drive to California. She already had the leave, and needed to go somewhere that didn't make her think of Max, so here she was. Back home.

It was cold. As her shoes crunched over the gravel driveway, the wind rushed over the acres where the lavender was dormant. It sheared into Ash with a damp cold, the kind that stuck to bones and made old injuries ache. The big white house was just as she remembered. It had green shutters, framing windows with golden light behind the handmade curtains. Smoke flowed out from the chimney, filling the air with a rich perfume. There were chickens in the yard, still clucking and scratching the ground around them in the fading light. They'd head in to the red coop as soon as the sun set.

The gardens were mostly done this time of year, hiding under a layer of remaining snow. Behind the side, the goats stood up on a worn down stump to try and reach her over the fencing, mistaking her for the dinner rounds.

The screen door opened with a screech and familiar

thump and rattle as a shorter version of herself stepped out and waved.

"Ashleigh, oh my my my, let me see you," she said with open arms and a warm smile that had more lines around it than Ash remembered.

"Hey Mom," she said, leaning into the hug and the scent of lavender and mint, clinging to the felted wool shawl.

"Come on, let's get you inside. How was your drive?"

Ash stepped in and took her running shoes off and put them next to her mom's pile of clogs and her dad's boots. "It was fine. Long."

"Your dad will be back tomorrow; he had to stay overnight in the park for some night programming."

"That's okay. I'll be glad to see him. I wish I would've been able to go out there, but maybe in the summer when it's warm." Her dad had taken an NPS job a couple of hours north in Oregon at Crater Lake National Park, and sometimes had to stay on the property for programming and maintenance.

"You're always welcome to stay here whenever you want." Her mom just smiled and looked at her. "I'm so glad you made the trip."

"Me too," Ash said, bending down to scratch a tabby cat behind the ears. "It smells good in here."

"I have a nice pot of chili on the stove, and I made some sourdough and there's fresh butter."

"Daisy is still producing?"

"Yeah, she's doing good, but we had to have someone come out and look at her hoof because she had a little spot that got infected. It's healing up nicely."

"I'm surprised you called someone instead of trying to fix it yourself like you used to," Ash said, following her back toward the kitchen and the living area.

It was fairly open concept, with a large eat-in kitchen

facing the living room where an impressive wood stove had a blazing fire going.

The couches were the same comfortable ones that she had grown up with, but they had been recovered several times and now were a cornflower blue in a chenille. Ash ran her fingertip over the piped edge. This was professionally done too.

"I'm not that impossible. I've actually hired a few more people these days," she said, busying herself in the kitchen. "I know you think we're in the stone ages, but your dad and I are progressing."

"That's good. Surprising, but good."

"Well, there's a fine line between being self-sufficient and not supporting your local community."

"Wow," Ash said, taking the plates to help with her eyebrows raised. "That's a very different stance from a few years ago."

"Things are good. People are coming to our shop more and more. We also have a farmers' market here every Saturday, and people pay us to rent their tent space. It's been really lovely and gotten us to meet other people, but enough about all of that. I want to hear everything about you. I was worried when you disappeared and that policeman called us."

"It's been a—" She wanted to say wild ride, but a lump formed in her throat and she couldn't get the words out.

Her mom put the soup down and walked forward, pulling her into a hug. "Oh dear. It's okay. It's alright."

Ash leaned into the hug and then stood up with a sniff and swiped a few tears away from under her eyes before her mom ushered her into her spot at the table, giving her tea Ash couldn't identify in a hand-thrown mug.

"Here, drink up and tell me all about it."

Ash took a sip and found it surprisingly pleasant. It was

her mom's go-to medicine tea, with a few subtle differences. "I'm not sick, Mom."

"Bunny," she said, calling Ash her old pet name. "I haven't seen you cry since you were a teen." Ash cradled the mug in her hands, feeling the warmth in her palms, and filled her mom in on the quick version, going a bit beyond what she had shared in the phone call at Pat's store.

Her mom listened intently, running her hand through the salt-and-pepper hair as she got to the dangerous parts of the story.

"I feel like I was starting to understand everything, and now I'm just left with more questions, and I lost Max in the process," Ash said, holding her head in her hands.

"It's good you came home when you did," her mom said, handing over a lavender-scented handkerchief. "We probably should've talked about this a long time ago."

Ash wiped her nose and looked up. "What do you mean?"

"I've never told this to anyone, but something did happen a long time ago when I was pregnant with you."

"I thought you said on the phone nothing happened with Rocky Mountain Labs?"

Her mom shook her head. "That's right. It was somewhere else. I was pregnant and your father and I were so happy. We both went to every appointment, and read every book we could get our hands on."

Ash smiled but waited for more, feeling herself slip into work mode, as she watched her mom speak and tracked her words.

"We were so excited, and I started having high blood pressure, so I cut out salt. I didn't even have a single chip after she told us that, so you can imagine that when they said there was a new vitamin that could help a baby's brain development, we signed up."

"Wait, when and where was this?"

"At my local clinic. It was very well known because several research doctors frequented it from the Lab and the colleges."

Ash held her breath, waiting for her to reveal more information.

"After that, I gave birth to the most adorable healthy baby with the prettiest eyes since Elizabeth Taylor. Everyone commented. You know, every time I went to the grocery store people commented—"

"Mom."

"Okay, I know, I know. After that, *I* was different."

"What do you mean *you* were different?"

Her mom twisted the wooden bracelet around her wrist, while she looked away and took a breath. "I've never told anyone anything, but I have a heightened sense of smell."

Ash couldn't breathe. *Could it be?* "Tell me more."

"I can tell you what's in something from one sniff."

"You always were a good cook."

Ash's mom looked straight at her with such seriousness, Ash didn't speak again. "I can tell you if they used pesticides on an avocado when they grew it in Mexico."

Ash's mouth dropped open.

"So that's why I had to leave. Your dad didn't understand at first, but he got on board. We sold everything, bought this property, and started from the ground up. Literally. I can't drink city water. It was driving me crazy, and that's before I started researching what it was I was smelling to find out if I was going insane or not."

Ash remained silent, taking it all in.

"You probably think I'm nuts, and half of the time, I'm not even sure I believe it myself, but it's true. I could tell when they added fluoride to the water, or upped the potassium. Bottled water isn't easier. A lot of people think it is, but they haven't looked at how their water gets to them, so we moved out here and dug our own well, started a garden, and tried to keep you and your siblings away from it all."

"I wish I'd known that."

Her mom held up a hand and let it fall with a defeated slap on the table. "The last thing you cared about was chemicals when you were in high school. You wanted to be a cop so bad that I could've told you there was lead in the pipes leading to that old high school's water fountain, but you wouldn't have cared. It almost killed me when you started eating their school lunches over what we had made here at the house."

"I'm sorry, I didn't know," Ash said, seeing her mom with different eyes.

"It's okay; you were just a kid. I got over it, and besides it worked out for the best, didn't it?"

"Yeah, and you know I always feel better when I eat healthier, make my own smoothies, and meditate."

Ash's mom gave her a warm smile that crinkled her face in all of the right places. "Then I did my job and can rest easy tonight."

Her mom laughed, relieved to be free of her burden, but Ash didn't. "Mom, there's something I need to tell you."

A black cloud passed over her mom's face as if a storm had come up on a sunny day, before she pressed her fingers to her lips and closed her eyes.

"I'm so sorry," she said, her voice above a whisper. "I didn't know. I swear to you, I didn't know."

Now it was Ash's turn to stand and come around the table, embracing her around the shoulders and pulling her into a squeeze. They hadn't seen eye to eye since before Ash went to high school. Now, the two of them sat, woman to woman, each with a story, finally back on the same page.

Several questions and answers went by, as they ate the

soup and bread, making up for lost time, finally talking as equals.

"I think it's interesting that it affected us in a very similar way. I can smell people telling lies, and you can—"

"Tell you if food is lying," her mom said with a chuckle, still shaking her head in disbelief.

"What about Bodhi and Juniper?"

"They were born at home under the care of a midwife. I didn't so much as look at anything new when I was pregnant with them, so it's possible, but unlikely."

"Well, that'll be fun to bring up at Christmas," Ash said, cutting herself another slice of the lavender honey cake.

"What are you going to do now?" her mom asked. "This helps you, but it doesn't seem to help your friend."

"As best I can figure, there were almost two projects. One was the study you—we—were involved in. The second was the one that affected Max and these other men, all with security backgrounds."

"It's like some new super soldier."

Ash nodded, churning it over in her mind. "You're right; that must be when it switched and they forced out Ted."

"I wish I could help more."

"If we could get you a sample of what's in that compound, you might be able to tell us what they did and we could work backward."

"But didn't that doctor tell you it was irreversible?"

There was a knock on the door, which made Ash instinctively stand and itch for her gun.

"Oh, stop with that," her mom said, swatting her hand. "I forgot to tell you, Gus had to come by and pick something up tonight. You remember him, right?"

"Gus?"

Before her mom could answer, Gus walked in looking

much taller and leaner than the mean kid he had been in the past.

"Hey Ms. Myers, thanks for making these. Gideon is really sick, and I didn't know what else to do."

"No need to apologize at all. I'm glad to do it. It's lucky you're here because Ashleigh is in town!"

"Hi," he said, looking sheepish.

"Hey," Ash said, not really having any interest in seeing him.

"I'll go run and get those jars. I packed them in a box earlier today."

"I'm surprised to still see you here. I thought you wanted out when you went to high school."

"Yeah, about that," he said, looking down before meeting her square in the eyes. "I really need to apologize to you. I was going through a lot and was really angry back then. What I did to you was wrong, and I'm very sorry."

Ash's eyebrows flew up. "What?"

"You know, I went to school and that was when the counselors helped me, and I got a job working as a truck driver for your parents and their farm. I love it out here and learned to appreciate it more. I know now I was angry and jealous and I shouldn't have taken it out on you."

Ash felt her mouth open and close.

"Wow, um, yeah, thanks for that. It's surprising to hear that from you."

He reached behind his head and scratched in between his shoulder blades. "Well, I'm glad I got to say it. I know you're not here a lot, and I've wanted to apologize for a long time. I have kids now, and I wouldn't want anyone to treat them that way."

"That's good. Sounds like you're a great dad."

"Well, I knew I needed to clean up my own shit so I didn't screw them up, or at least do it less."

Ash let out a laugh with him right as her mom came in with the box of jars. "Alright, here you go. I'll come by to check on him tomorrow after the market if his fever still hasn't gone down."

"Okay, thanks again. See you later, and it was nice to see you again, Ash."

"You too," she said, waving him off.

"Isn't that funny? You two must not have seen each other in years now."

"Yeah, it is. What's all this about you treating fevers?"

Ash followed her mom into the kitchen where she noticed for the first time an even larger amount of note-books, textbooks, and cookbooks.

"Well, since you were born, and I could sense everything in the food, water and medicine, I started learning about the things I was smelling," she said, putting a few books back on a shelf near the coffee pot. "I've taken a few classes, and now I help the people in the market when I can."

"I remember. I barely had any Tylenol or antibiotics," Ash said.

"You did when you needed to," her mom said, giving her the eye.

"But I didn't need them that much."

Her mom shot her a satisfied smile, and did a little head bob before bustling off to carry her canned soup back to her impressive sized pantry.

Ash flipped through some of the notebooks, taking in the meticulous notes. "Hey Mom, did you ever find a treatment for what they did to us?"

Her mom came back over from where she had put more things on the shelf. "Not something that would reverse it, why?"

Ash stopped turning the page. "That makes it sound like you figured out something."

"Well, I have a couple of remedies I put together for myself to lessen the effects," she said, pulling out an old red one-subject notebook. "Because sometimes I don't want to have to deal with it all of the time."

"Because it's like sensory overload," they both said at the same time.

Her mom paused with the book in her hand, and looked at Ash with her head tilted to one side. "You know, I've always wanted to be your closest friend. And tonight, I feel like I'm learning how to do it for the first time."

Ash smiled back. "I'm sorry I didn't make it easy."

Her mom smiled again, her gaze flicking down and up, seemingly taking Ash in for the first time as a woman, an adult, an equal. Her voice cracked as she said with a watery smile, "Daughters never make it easy. But they're worth the wait."

CHAPTER 48

Ash drove the whole way home straight through the next day. In the passenger seat were three notebooks and several loaves of bread for her and her friends, as well as many canned vegetables and dried fruit from her mom's garden.

It had honestly been the best visit she had ever had, and had it not been for what was in her mom's notebook, Ash would've happily stayed a few more nights. The rest of the short visit felt normal. Mom had let her know she never told Dad about her experiences and suspicions, which made it even more impressive that he went along with her plans.

Speaking of Dad, Ash had gotten to hang out with him the following morning. He was doing well and looking forward to retirement, and even ended up doing some family yoga before they all sat around the fire talking and catching up. Ash had promised to come back and help organize their annual yoga retreat for the lavender farm and market, which had become quite a draw for the community.

Her parents had also extended the invitation to her friends, Megan and Laura, who they had met over the years during various visits. Ash couldn't wait to bring them all out here for their first friend vacation. Maybe she could convince Max to come too. It wasn't an ashram in India, but she still thought he would like it.

But all of that had to wait until she got home, apologized to Max, and told Dr. Mallory what her mom had cooked up.

The hours and miles passed without stress as Ash considered everything that she had learned about herself and those around her. She felt lighter now, as if someone had put a missing piece back in her life. Her own self-awareness was the greatest gift she had ever received.

The next morning, she woke up ready to find Max and navigated the Jeep to the cabin, finding it empty before she headed to Pat's store.

"I need to find Max," she said when he answered the door in his usual fashion, with a muzzle near her nose.

Ten minutes later, with Pat's directions, she found Max on a rock outcropping off a hiking trail near where they had first met. He was sitting with his back to the trail, sketching the sunset.

"Max, I'm so glad I found you," she said, running toward him with the red notebook. "You're not going to believe what I found out! I have a way to lessen the effects! This can help you, me, everyone!"

He didn't look at her, but instead stood and started walking the other direction. "That's good. I hope it helps a lot of people." His voice was flat, distant.

"Max, please—" Ash started before she had to take a breath when the tears started to fall. "I know you can't forgive me; I couldn't forgive me either. What I said was hurtful and ignorant, but please, I need your help with this. We can go to Dr. Mallory with this information and come up with a plan. These people shouldn't have to suffer because I was wrong. Once you help me help them, you can be mad at me forever and never speak to me again, because you'll know that I was wrong and you were right all along."

Max turned around slowly. "I don't want to never talk to you again."

Ash sniffed and took a breath, while swiping away her tears.

"Come here."

He pulled her into a warm hug, enveloping her completely as she rested her head against his chest and finished crying.

She felt a hard bump on his chest that hadn't been there before.

Max noticed, and pulled out the St. Michael medal from underneath his shirt. "I haven't taken it off."

Well, didn't that just make her well up again. "I'm so sorry, and I'm glad we're talking."

Max smiled and gave her a squeeze. "I'm glad we're talking again too. Let's go. You can fill me in on what's been happening on the drive."

Ash and Max drove there together and were admitted to see Dr. Mallory that same afternoon.

This time, since more of the snow had melted, more people were in the parking lot, and there was a hum as they entered reception before the admin walked them back, not to the library but to Dr. Mallory's office.

"This a remarkable blend. The properties in some of these herbs are well-documented throughout history," said Dr. Mallory, looking at Ash's mom's red notebook in front of her on her desk.

"Is there a way you can make something like this into a pill or injection to lessen the effects of the changes?" Ash asked.

"That would give people back their lives, allow them to

control the changes when they come and lessen the effects," Max added.

Dr. Mallory stood and walked over to shut the door, her black heels clipping along the floor. Today she wore a black turtleneck tucked into high-waisted wide leg pants with a gold-rimmed belt. Her hair was pulled back into a bun, highlighting gold stud earrings.

"I want to help you, but there are people here who don't want to be involved with Borealis at all."

"But Ted worked here," Ash said. "This gives them the chance to fix what he started. Max is willing to act as a test subject."

Max nodded once in agreement.

"I'm afraid it isn't that simple," she said, sitting back down at her desk which was empty of everything except her computer. "The lab runs on government funding, which is tied to specific projects. At this time, we can't allocate resources to this project without drawing attention, which is something the director doesn't want to do."

"How was Ted able to get resources?" Max asked, his voice low and direct.

"Dr. Saunders had approval for vaccines for childhood diseases like chicken pox. What he did could be looked at as a gross misuse of federal funds."

"Which if that got out..." Ash prompted.

"Would most certainly lead to increased oversight and budget cuts, which is something the director wishes to avoid."

"What if we talked with the director? Could that be helpful?" Max asked.

"We can try. I have a meeting with him later today, and I'll see if I can get you set up with one."

CHAPTER 49

Dr. Saatvik Gupta stood to greet Ash and Max the next morning in his office which was much larger than Dr. Mallory's had been, and much more cluttered with pictures and books. He listened intently to their case, nodding along and pulling out his glasses to read over her mom's red one-subject notebook, giving it his full attention and taking notes with a Mont Blanc pen on a legal pad, which made Ash like him immediately.

"There are some interesting properties that are proposed here that certainly could work to alleviate extreme stress, but the gene therapy that has been done is irreversible. I'm sorry, there is no fix for that procedure at this time," he said, when he passed it back over to her with a smile.

"We understand, Dr. Gupta," Ash began. "We were hoping that you could help point us in the right direction to use this to develop some sort of pill or injection that could make this more potent and accessible."

"Dr. Saunders's research is remarkable and regrettable, but I'm sorry. He hasn't worked here in over five years, before my time even. When he did, the focus of his research was under a different mission statement than the direction we're heading in now."

"Which is?" asked Max.

"Before, we were focused on many vaccines to bring down childhood and other preventable diseases."

"Like chicken pox," Ash said, echoing Dr. Mallory.

"Yes and measles, and now that we have almost eradicated these diseases completely, our mission changed. Now the mission of the NIH is to uncover new knowledge that will lead to better health for everyone. NIH seeks to apply that knowledge to extend the health of human lives and to reduce the burdens resulting from disease and disability."

"But this is a disability," Ash said, glancing at Max and back at Dr. Gupta. "These people can't work and may be targeted by law enforcement when they lash out and have reactions they can't control."

"Yes, I agree with you, but it's the sample size that concerns me. We are expected to keep expanding the knowledge base in biomedical and associated sciences in order to enhance America's economic well-being and ensure a continued high return on the public investment in research. That is one of the latter points of our mission statement."

"Is there a way to figure out how many people Dr. Saunders's work affected?"

"Sadly, no. We do not have records of his independent research. However, even if we did, RML was founded when over half of the adult population in Hamilton, Montana was perishing from what we now know as Rocky Mountain spotted fever. I wish I could offer you help, but the people affected by this gene therapy experimentation do not constitute a large enough percentage of the population to fall under our mission statement."

Max stood up when the doctor did. Ash followed suit.

"Thank you for your time, Dr. Gupta," she said, shaking his hand when he extended it.

"I truly am sorry I cannot help you more. Personally, I'm very interested in Ted's work. I never met him, but I admire what he was trying to do. Please let me know if you find out any more information."

Ash and Max walked down the hall in silence, after the same admin was trapped on the phone and waved them onward alone.

"I'm sorry, Max," Ash said. "We tried."

"Yeah, I can't even be mad at the guy because I liked him so much."

"He was nice to take the time to talk with us."

"He brought up a good point too. We don't even have a list of names to go on, so any work that could happen would have to be reactionary to when they've already been arrested. It's not like we could get ahead of them."

A familiar clip clop of heels walked toward them from down the hall where Dr. Mallory waved them down.

"How did it go?" she asked with a hopeful smile from one to the other.

"Thanks for setting up the meeting, but you were right. It didn't work out," Ash said, watching the woman's shoulders fall in front of her.

"I'm so sorry. I had a feeling he would say that, but I was hoping seeing you both in person might persuade him. Here, let me walk you both out."

They shared with her more of what Dr. Gupta had said until they stepped outside, feeling the rush of icy wind. Max and Ash zipped up their coats, and exchanged a glance when Dr. Mallory followed them out.

"Here's my card," she said, giving it to Ash and looking at her intently. "I've written my personal cell on the back." She lowered her voice so it was barely a whisper and could've gotten lost in the wind. "I wish I could help more, so if anything changes, give me a call."

Before Ash or Max could respond, Dr. Mallory walked back into the lab and was obscured behind the thick glass doors.

Ash and Max ended up going out to dinner at Joe's Diner in town, since he had liked it before and taken to the waitstaff.

They placed their order, tea for both, with a grilled chicken salad for Ash and a cheeseburger for Max.

"Well, was any of that a lie?" Max asked as he dipped a fry in ketchup. "You were pretty quiet on the drive over."

"That's the thing," she said, shaking her head. "None of it was a lie, at least as far as I could tell."

"You've never lost the ability?" Max asked.

Ash shook her head again. "Never."

"Maybe you should test it," he said, flicking his eyes to the approaching waitress.

"How is everything over here?"

"It's good, thanks for asking," said Ash after wiping her mouth. "Hey, quick question, do you guys think you'll ever sell any vegan tofu for your salads?"

The waitress was one of the good ones who had been here forever and seen everything, twice. She blinked. "I'm not sure, but I can ask the owners."

The stench of the lie was overwhelming, making Ash smile like a crazy person. "No, no need. Thank you anyway."

The woman gave her a tight smile and walked away to help another table.

"Massive lie."

"Yeah," Max said, laughing into his cheeseburger. "I could've told you that by the look on her face."

"Well, it's nice to know I can still pick up on it because I was starting to doubt myself."

"You're sounding like me. Is it that hard to believe that everyone at RML was telling us the truth?"

Ash took another bite and shook her head again. "Makes you wonder what it says about us."

"Here's your check; take your time," the waitress said before bustling off.

Ash went to reach for it, but Max picked it up.

"Max, you don't need to—"

He held up his hand, stopping her. "Listen, I've been wanting to tell you. I know I was upset, but I did some thinking and I went to the station and dropped off my application. I have an interview next week."

"Oh my God! That's wonderful!" Ash said, jumping up to give him a hug.

"Hey, at least it's something. Not sure if it will work out, of course, but this way we can say we didn't just get bad news today."

CHAPTER 50

Ash and Max walked hand in hand to the Jeep after leaving the restaurant. The snow was starting to fall, and the downtown Goldvein area felt magical. Even though they hadn't gotten the answers they wanted, Ash felt happier than she had in a long time.

Max smiled as he told her a story about how he had managed to tinker with some farm equipment enough to impress Troy's dad, Hank, who called him mechanically inclined and made him feel good. It was good to see him spend a lot of time with them, becoming friends in his own right. Turns out, Max and Hank liked the same magazines, *Guns and Ammo* and *Backwoods*, which got him extra points in Hank's book.

The snow and the streetlights from above made his blond hair sparkle so he looked more like an avenging angel than a big-ass Viking, especially when he smiled and his dimples came out.

A trash can lid fell in an alley next to them, before a skinny man in a military jacket walked out. It was the same man she had pursued after the drug deal what seemed like forever ago now. In his hands, Ash could see the glint of a silver blister pack with white circles still inside.

Ash took off after him. When he started pulling ahead, she yelled, "Police, stop!"

She was much closer than she had been before. He was about five eleven, maybe six feet. Around one eighty. Muscled guy, little on the wiry side, but not as thin as before.

There was a patch on the sleeve of his jacket, which Ash couldn't make out before a Honda pulled up and someone threw open the door.

The skinny guy practically dove right in while the car took off, burning rubber into the night.

"Goddammit!" Ash said. "I didn't even get a good look at the fucking plates, and did you see? Did you see? He had the blister pack on him! That's the guy! The same friggin' one!"

"What do you mean the same guy?"

"I saw him before I went to Ted's house. He was trying to hustle someone, but I couldn't see what. Tonight, I saw it. He's the one! He's selling these blister packs that are making men turn violent."

Ash wanted to punch through a brick wall. "He was right there, and I couldn't even grab him or enough detail to track him down."

"Ash?"

Ash rounded on Max, ready to unleash all of her frustration. "What?"

"I think I can work up a sketch which might be enough for you to go on."

"Oh. My. God." Ash reached up and kissed him. "Yes, perfect, and we can tell everyone to be on the lookout for him and a white Honda."

"I also think we need to talk to Pat. He might know him."

Ash rounded on Max, making him take a step back. "What do you mean?"

"That's a 2nd Armored Division patch on the jacket, which caught my eye because it's Patton's."

"Think he was military?"

Max shook his head. "That division was closed in the nineties. It's probably from a surplus store, and Pat's is the only one for miles."

"Let's go."

When they got to Pat's store, he had already pulled the remaining jackets with 2nd Division patches, since they had called ahead.

"Alright, well, we don't get a lot of these, since we have mostly navy vets around here in this part of Montana, but the first thing you got to understand is you can buy these patches anywhere. I got a ton off some guy in Virginia whose wife was on his ass to clean house. So, he could've picked one up anywhere and stitched it on."

"Does this picture ring a bell?" Ash asked, as Max showed Pat the sketch he had drawn up in the car on the way over.

"Oh yeah, that's Speedy. His real name's Brian. Weird kid, kinda twitchy. Was shy before and super into Vietnam stuff, so I was surprised when he went for more of a WWII vibe. He said he needed them and a bunch of other stuff for a play down in Hamilton; said he's working at a playhouse in an old schoolhouse building."

Max's face broke into a wide grin, and even Ash couldn't help but smile. "That's a huge help. What else did he buy, by the way?"

"Oh, let's see." Pat pulled out an old box of notebooks that had seen better days and started flipping through. "Couple of boxes of ammo, back before I sold out."

"You mean your gun isn't loaded?" Ash couldn't help herself from asking.

"That's from my personal stash. The store has been sold out for months, but"—he patted a locked ammo box behind him and smiled—"you don't need to worry about me. Anyway, he also wanted a lot of medical stuff, said he was doing some stuff on a MASH unit."

"That's been a huge help. Thanks for everything."

"You're welcome. Glad I could be of help. I haven't had this much excitement around here in a long time. In fact, here, take some ammo from my stash. You kids looked white as a ghost when you came in, so you might need it."

CHAPTER 51

Ash and Max pulled up at the Hamilton Playhouse using the address Pat gave them. They had followed a little two-lane road at the foot of the Bitterroot Mountains, crossed over a small creek, and had gone about a half mile outside of town, past a field that looked overgrown and underfunded before they arrived at an old, renovated schoolhouse. Another snow was starting to fall, making the whole scene reminiscent of a winter wonderland.

In the middle of the night, the building was more of a dark spot that obscured the stars than a presence on its own. When they walked closer, they could make out more detail. It was two story, brick with several windows on both floors and a bell tower up top.

They pulled up and parked before each grabbing their preferred guns from underneath the usual hiding spots. Max forewent his long rifle and pulled out two nine millimeter pistols. Ash went for the one Pat had lent her and her police issue.

They caught each other's eye when they were ready.

Both of them armed. Both of them standing in the snow.

Both of them about to walk through an unknown door together.

Max pulled her in for a quick, fierce kiss before they gave each other a squeeze.

"I'll try not to freak out unless I need to."

"You know I love it when you do, though," Ash said with a smile. "He's like my other friend."

"Don't even say that, or he'll come out just to say hi."

"Well, keep him handy. I have no idea what we're going to find."

They crept forward and made a circle around the perimeter, checking for any cars. Seeing none, they peeked in the windows and shined a light inside.

It was a wide open space with a wooden plank floor, before a wall of doors leading to what would be the stage area. There were stairs in the back corner that led up to what presumably would be the offices for the playhouse.

Max waved her around past a propane tank to the front entrance, which had an old brass lock and no deadbolt. With a flick of her credit card, they were in.

He went high, she went low. The only thing they heard was the floorboards creaking underneath them.

They both stepped into the empty but heated space, seeing nothing out of the ordinary. They made their way through a long, open foyer, which was easy to clear since it had what appeared to be a small reception and waiting area, before a brief check upstairs revealed a few offices that were fairly empty, along with a costume shop with several tables of covered sewing machines and racks with hanging costumes in garment bags.

After clearing upstairs, they came back to the entryway to the theatre with a small counter acting as concessions, now shuttered for the off season. There were a few framed posters on the wall, showcasing old programs, including *Les Misérables*, *Miss Saigon*, and *South Pacific*.

"I can see why Pat's a fan," Max whispered.

"He's not the only one," Ash said, flashing her light over a bronze plaque.

Ash stepped forward with her light and read the bronze in front of her. "Hamilton Players thanks Rocky Mountain Labs and Dr. Ted Saunders for their generous donation and support of the arts."

"Ted wouldn't use the same trick twice, would he?" Max asked before he gave the plate a good couple of tugs. "I guess not."

They checked it over for anything that could twist, pull, or lift and came up empty.

Ash squinted and checked the plaque again looking for a word puzzle, and grabbed Max's arm.

She pointed to where he looked. There in bronze, under "Special Thanks," Dr. Rose Mallory's name was listed.

"Why would she get a plaque here?" Max asked.

"She did say she interned for Ted. It looks like this old schoolhouse was one of the original labs for RML before they sold the property," she summarized from reading the text. "Maybe she was around when the sale took place. She also said she was an avid supporter, but didn't mention how. Maybe she bought it or renovated it for them to use."

"Come on, let's clear the stage," he said, his voice hushed.

Just like before, Ash took a breath and went low, while Max went high. There was nothing to see inside the small theatre that she wouldn't already expect.

"Theatres creep me out," she said, whispering to him as they checked each dark row.

"How come?"

"It's all a lie, isn't it? Nothing on that stage is real."

"I guess I never thought about it that—"

Ash heard it too. Both of them froze in the dark and pressed the flashlight against their legs, plunging them into a thick, dusty darkness.

There was a faint song, coming from a radio somewhere, deep in the recesses of the building. Ash crept forward down the padded aisle, listening.

John Denver kept singing from somewhere, but it could be anywhere with the echo. Ash kept going, following the sound until she reached what would have been the orchestra pit if there was one at the foot of the stage. It was very faint, but she could make out the glimpse of a red light coming from underneath the stage.

Max gave her two nudges, which she took as a nod, and looked for a door, but found none.

They walked on the stairs, painstakingly slow so as not to make any sound, brushing past the thick velvet curtain into the wings of the stage, which were empty.

The song was muted now, but coming from beneath them.

They followed the wings to the back where they found a few dressing rooms, and stairs down to a door beneath the stage with a red light coming out from under it.

Ash walked forward with Max, who stepped in front of her. She started to protest, but he held up one hand and that was the end of it.

The small brass knob to the door looked pitiful in his hand as he twisted it to reveal exactly what Ash had been looking for.

Where there should've been music equipment or props, there were tables lined with large bottles of pills, vials of clear liquid, and under a red light in a clear box reminiscent of a fume hood, blister packs with white pills.

"We need to grab those pills!" Ash said, popping the door open and rushing inside. She grabbed a few vials and had just thrown open the hood to grab the blister packs when a weight crashed into her from the side and threw her onto the floor. Her gun went into a distant, dark corner. The glass vials scattered across the floor, some breaking, some not. Speedy, the skinny kid she had seen, was on top of her, trying to pin her arm.

Ash thrashed around, yelling and wriggling out of his grip before giving him a knee to the chin and a foot to the jaw, which stunned him, letting her get away. She heard Max swear, and saw he was being pinned by Michael, the kid from the park she had let go. He was jacked now, muscles and veins bulging out from his arms like thick ropes on his neck.

"Michael! Stop!"

His head swirled around like an owl, and his eyes didn't even look human or seem to register her existence. He also maintained his hold without even a change in facial expression. He had gone into his own rage now.

Max let out a roar and went into a rage, flinging Michael off like he was nothing, throwing him into a metal set of shelves. Michael didn't even flinch when his back bent the steel behind him and instead picked himself up and charged back at Max, crashing into him and flipping a table, sending vials everywhere. It was like watching two bears fight each other, neither willing to back down.

Ash wanted to help, but she wasn't going to match that. She grabbed as many vials and pills as she could and ran outside, right as Speedy had recovered and came out, running at her like a ram. She made it out the door and shut it behind her, just as he barreled into it before ripping it open to give chase.

She was a good runner, but she knew there was no chance against the rages. The cold stung her lungs as she ran as hard as she could toward the Jeep across the field. Footsteps pounded behind her, crunching fast over the ice and snow. She clutched the vials and pills to her chest but knew she was losing ground. If she could get to the car, then she could call for help, but there was no way to reach her phone now.

She was thirty feet, then twenty, then ten, when someone grabbed her coat from behind, and she slipped and fell, sending the pills and vials everywhere into the field. Speedy didn't even hesitate and was on her in an instant, trying to stab her with a syringe, when a roar ripped through the night.

Backlit with the glow of the red behind him like an avenging angel from the depths of hell, Max ran toward her.

Speedy took his eyes off her and snarled, abandoning her to square off with Max, punching him straight in the jaw, snapping Max's head back like a toy. Max used that momentum to bring up his leg and kick back, straight to the gut.

Ash wasted no time and pulled out her cell. "Dr. Mallory, we found the lab and I have the evidence. I'm bringing it into the station now." She didn't wait for a reply, but hung up when Michael emerged from the playhouse, heading for Max.

Ash dropped to her knees in the dark and scrambled around, hoping for at least one pack of pills and vials before sprinting to the car. That's when she glanced behind her and saw Max.

He was being strangled from behind, and his face was twisted in horrible pain as they overpowered him. Michael had a syringe in his hand and was aiming for Max's neck.

From somewhere in her gut came a scream that could only be counted as primal. She ripped open the car door and pulled out Max's ancient long rifle, taking aim and not finding a clear shot, with them all over him. She pulled the bolt and tried to breathe, when she saw the propane tank to the side of the building.

She pivoted, and with two clean shots turned night into day.

The blast from the fireball came from the second round, pushing all three men into the ground. Ash ran forward toward Max, with the gun now ready to use as a bat, if needed. She grabbed him and ran.

He focused on her face, but it wasn't Max. It was the rage. He nodded once, acknowledging her, reaching out.

"No, don't lift me. Let's go to the car."

Message received. Max beat her there, but was behind the wheel and cranking the engine as she hopped in the seat. He sped off once she was inside, leaving physics to close the door. Michael and Speedy tried to catch up but were no match for the car.

"Oh my God," she said, finally taking her first good breath since entering the lab, then seeing it go up in flames behind her. "I can't believe it. There won't be any evidence now."

Max grunted while driving remarkably well, if not a little jerky on the country road. He reached in his pocket and handed her a pack and vial.

"That's what I'm fucking talking about! I knew I loved you too, you Big-Ass Viking!" she said, wrapping her arms around him and planting a kiss on his cheek.

"Let's go to town and show everyone what we have. Turn up here; it will be a shortcut to get us to the GPD faster."

CHAPTER 53

They pulled into the Goldvein Police Department and ran inside. It was empty, which wasn't unusual in a small town in the middle of the night, so just Dr. Rose Mallory and Chief Smith met them inside the bullpen. The chief was looking rumpled like he had been called out of bed for this, whereas Dr. Mallory looked elegant even in the middle of the night in black boots and a long, fur-trimmed puffer coat, with her hair pulled to one side.

"Detective Myers, I'm so glad you called me," she said when they ran inside. "You have done a wonderful job of finding this all, Detective. I can't imagine anyone else handling this better."

"Thank you. Most of the evidence was destroyed, but we managed to get this, so now we'll be able to get a sense of what they're doing to people, how many might have been affected, and how to treat it."

"Good work, Detective, Max," the chief said, giving a nod to them both.

"I'm so glad you found that evidence," Dr. Mallory said. "May I see it?"

Ash started to pass it over but hesitated, sensing something other than the truth for the first time.

"Please, Detective. I admired Ted very much when I was younger, and I know how much this project meant to him. I want to do more. Please let me help."

"I think I'll keep it with me now, until I log it," Ash said, backing away.

The chief frowned, looking more stern than usual. "Dr. Mallory, I know it's highly volatile, but per our policies, Detective Myers must—"

Ash tossed the vials and blister packs to the chief who caught them and looked at them in his hands.

"These are the pills and vials that are making people go insane in town. These are the ones that have been used to experiment on people. This is what Ted was talking about in his writings when he said his work was being used to create more harm than good."

"Ted didn't appreciate what he had built and couldn't see the power of it for himself," Dr. Mallory said, holding out a black gloved hand to the chief, her voice taking on a new depth and clarity.

The chief's face changed. He hesitated and looked uneasy as he passed them over to Dr. Mallory without even a glance at Ash. Her mouth fell open and she took a step back toward Max, who stepped forward in front of Ash, making the doctor laugh.

"See? He listens to me. Honestly, as if you could be any match for me, when I made you what you are," she said, pointing to Max. "And got you," she said, pointing at Ash, "in with GPD. Both of you are here right now because of me."

"Chief?" she said, flicking her gaze over to him in one last attempt for hope.

He opened his mouth to speak, but Dr. Mallory spoke first. "Don't you think it's a good idea for the police to have access to people with extraordinary abilities? Wouldn't they want officers with extreme strength, speed, and stamina? Or perhaps," she said with a smile, "the ability to detect the truth?"

Ash looked from her to the chief and back. "That's right. He benefits from my work, and has agreed to receive my help, and he's not the only one. We are making better humans. This country is filled with people wasting potential. You think you can stop me, but you are less than a tooth on a cog of a wheel of the machine I've built, and it goes right to the top."

"That's insane."

"That's efficient. Humans are resources and we need to capitalize."

"Now, you," she said, looking at Max. "You were fascinating from the beginning. Everything about you matched my target audience. Broken home with no surviving family, military background, and you were all busted up, needing someone to put you back together again."

Her perfect red lips formed an ice-cold smile that chilled Ash's body down to the bones.

"You're welcome," Dr. Mallory said.

Max didn't flinch, but instead glared at the doctor. "I'm not like them."

"Yes, you are," she said, rolling her eyes, seemingly bored with him. "But instead of a thank you, what was the thanks I got? You blew up one of my labs, killed my staff, a few other test subjects, and then vanished." She made a tsk-ing noise with her tongue. "So rude to keep such power all to yourself when there are people and countries around this world who are willing to pay top dollar to have a Berserker like you. You were the strongest one we've seen yet."

"What's a Berserker?" he asked.

"Do you like the new name? I've taken it from the Vikings

and their berserker rages in battle, which rendered them seemingly above human, enabling them to fight in a trance-like state. Borealis was too hopeful, no offense, dear," she said, looking at Ash. "Ted Saunders devoted his life's research to coming up with prenatal medicine delivered through vaccinations that would prevent the conditions that affected his daughter. He then went on to take data on these babies as part of studying the long-term effects. The project was named Borealis, because they would go look at the stars and he liked Galileo. Honestly, ridiculous," she said, with a flick of her gloved hand.

"So, when I took over, we named Max and the other men Berserkers. Instead of focusing on children, we sought out strong men, who were then given the gene therapy after a tragic accident to help them repair and regrow as soldiers and men with high intensity jobs. It took a while to perfect because some can't handle it. They just have a heart attack and die, while others attack people around them and have no memory of the event. This leads to distress and suicide."

Ash listened in disgust as the doctor rattled on about this just like a medical ad on TV as if it was no big deal, since they had troubled backgrounds or a lifetime filled with trauma.

"That's why they were out on the street."

She shrugged. "Larger pool. The target audience is more comfortable getting hope in a quick hit in an alley than in a research study."

"You were working with Silva all along to keep John," Max said, with a menacing glare.

The doctor laughed a high-pitched, shrill, menacing laugh and grinned. "No one appreciates my work. Once he realized what was happening, he became difficult, and encrypted our master list of subjects from both Borealis and Berserkers, so he needed a timeout. Once I crack the code, he'll be of no use. Silva was an excellent assassin who hunted people who got out of line, however it just goes to show you can't have good help these days. You have to make it yourself."

Ash glanced back at the chief who at least had the decency to look increasingly uncomfortable with what was happening.

"I'm never going to stop trying to end all of this, not until I'm dead," Ash said.

"Which is such a waste of your talent, but at least we agree on something."

"What are you going to do? Kill me right in the police department?"

"No," she said, popping a vial in a tranquilizer gun and shooting Max right in the chest. "He is."

Max screamed and fell to the ground right as the door behind them opened, and Michael and Speedy walked inside, standing on either side of the door.

"Run!" Max yelled, a deep guttural tone she recognized as him turning into a Berserker. Ash didn't need to be told twice.

"Detective!" yelled the chief, but he was outmanned, outgunned, and took shelter under a desk the second the bullets started flying.

"Don't let her get out of here!" Dr. Mallory screeched behind them. "I'll call the others."

From her long black coat, she pulled out her phone and slid a red button across the screen. Ash ran through the offices, heading for the emergency exit.

Michael jumped out at her first, his eyes more crazed and bloodshot than before, the veins in his neck straining like cords.

He launched himself at her, trying to swing for her face and neck, but she ducked down to avoid him at the last minute, taking a filing cabinet to the leg. She swore and reached down to grab her leg before limping down the hall to where she saw Max fighting off the skinny kid, Speedy.

A printer bit the dust as Max flung it at Speedy, who dodged in time for the thing to shatter to pieces against the wall.

Ash hid in a supply closet and grabbed a broom as a weapon. Through a window, Ash could see Mallory run to a blacked-out Tahoe with the engine running in the parking lot.

A dozen more men with the same stare came running toward the police department. Could she summon them all at will?

Ash opened the door and saw Max.

Max tossed Speedy into a stack of boxed paper and spun around, following after her, his eyes wide and bloodshot as he snarled and shook his head like he was trying to clear water in his ear.

Ash stepped out into the hall where he could see her and called out to him.

"I don't know what this will do to you, but you didn't hurt me before, and I don't think you'll hurt me now. We have to leave; more are coming."

Max looked at her and his nostrils flared. He stood up slowly and twitched his head before he started walking toward her with a menacing look on his face that looked nothing like the Max she knew.

Ash ran toward the emergency exit, right as the door opened and two more Berserkers came through. She was trapped as they walked toward her and Max, and Michael and Speedy came up from behind.

She would not go down without a fight. Ash grabbed her broom and got into a brace position, ready to fight until they ripped her apart.

Max was the first to reach her, and he pressed his face

right up against hers, breathing hard and ragged, looking at her like he wanted to break her in half. Ash couldn't bring herself to hit him, and closed her eyes as she braced herself against the wall behind her.

She could feel his hot breath on her cheek, and wanted to cry for what it reminded her of. All of the time they spent together. His tenderness that was lost. His delicate art. His love. Their love.

There was a mighty roar that deafened her right ear, and then the most violent sounds she had heard yet from Max, but no pain came as he took on the others one at a time.

Ash could've wept. "Max..."

A squeal of tires from outside was the only warning before a loud crash, as a series of large glass vials broke through the windows and spontaneously combusted as they hit the floor, sending a blast of heat and fire down the hall.

"Detective! She's going to kill us all!" yelled the chief.

"We've got to get out of here! There are more coming!"

"Let's head to the roof! Come on!"

Ash wasn't sure if it was a trap, but Max couldn't take on any more people who had already breached the main entrance. She followed the chief leading the charge to a supply closet, barricading the door behind her with the copier before climbing up the access ladder to the roof.

She ripped away the drop ceiling tiles and kept going with Max behind her. They could hear the beating of the door behind them right before it cracked open as the copier nudged away, and then opened farther, sending in thick dark smoke which cloyed at her lungs.

"The panel is stuck! I can't get it!" Ash yelled while coughing, right as the door failed below them.

Max swung around her and braced his legs on the top rung before shoving it open with a yell. They all clambered out, just as the Berserkers below grabbed ahold of the ladder.

Ash climbed out right as Max slammed the panel shut, grabbed the broom handle, and jammed it in the seam so it couldn't be opened. He looked up at her then almost attacked the chief.

"No, stop!" he pleaded. "I'm sorry! I knew about your ability and that she was testing on people who might be more focused in the police department. That's all I knew, I swear! I had no idea she was some crazy arms dealer out making super soldiers and explosives!" He held up both hands.

Max swung his head over to Ash, like a guard dog looking for confirmation before she gave the final word. Ash took a deep breath to clear the smoke out of her nose, and stepped forward, smelling again.

"At least you're telling the truth now."

The panel next to them hopped up with a loud metal thud, as the other side got punched and rammed repeatedly from the other side.

"Why are we on the roof again?" she asked, taking a step back on instinct, seeing the smoke billow out from below them.

"When the chief of police calls for backup, we get back-up," he said as the sound of sirens pierced the night. That wasn't the only sound though.

A familiar beat of helicopter blades came from above and to the west, as a chopper approached.

"It's a lot less terrifying when I know they're on our side," Ash said.

Just then, Max let out a shudder, as he collapsed back into himself, weak and drenched in sweat. "Hey, it's okay. We're getting out of here," Ash said as the chopper landed behind her. She and the chief got him inside where the police pilots were ready to accept them.

"Get us out of here and somewhere safe," he said to the pilots, who began to lift off.

The beat of the helicopter blades pounded over the roar of the flames below them, sending the smoke away from them as they ascended into the black clouds.

"Wait!" Max yelled to the pilots. "She was right. I'm no different than them. I'm going back."

He slid open the door with a loud clang. The clouds of smoke behind him glowed with the orange light from the fire below. Sparks flew upward from the hellish nightmare. The wind swept through his loose hair and long beard, making him look like a god of war.

"Max, don't! You don't need to do this!"

He was already leaning out. "I love you!"

"No! Stay with me!" Ash screamed.

"I'll be fine!"

Ash reached for him the same moment he let go.

Max fell into the smoke below. All Ash could hear was her own screaming. All Ash could sense was the most powerful lie she had ever felt, and the only one Max had ever told her.

CHAPTER 54

Max hit the roof with a bone-shattering thud that stunned him into stars. He recovered quickly when he heard the screams beneath the trap door.

He limped forward and ripped the mop handle away.

The metal was bent. He grabbed the handle, which felt warm to the touch, and pulled. He tried to will the Berserker into him just as he had tried to will it to not harm Ash, as he strained against the bent steel.

"Come on… one… more… time…" he said, before he felt his vision get blurry.

The effect was like swimming under water. He could smell more, hear more, and he felt like he was walking through sand, while his mind tried to process everything that happened so fast around him as his body went into autopilot.

First the panel was wrenched up and free, releasing a plume of black smoke and several men, who all tumbled out, crawling toward fresh air. More and more came, until it felt like there were dozens.

He wanted to go in himself and see if anyone else was there.

No one should have to die for something they didn't choose. They didn't have a choice in the matter of what that bitch had done to them. It wasn't their fault. It wasn't his fault. It wasn't…

The squeal of the tires pulled him back to conscious thought. He crawled over to see the Tahoe peel around the back, and Dr. Mallory got out and tossed another glass into the window where it exploded on impact.

For the first time, Max let the reins loose on the rage he had fought so hard to keep at bay, and willingly succumbed as his vision blurred on command.

He laughed as he leaned back and felt himself let out a mighty roar, this time keeping some of his awareness. It was like looking through watery goggles, where everything was blurry and moved too fast. He thought of something, and his body took over in survival mode, leaving his brain scrambling to pick up the pieces.

He could see the others around him, and with something that sounded like a snarl to his own ears, he called to them. Recognizing him as one of their own, they followed now, until they all stood at the edge of the roof watching Dr. Rose Mallory torch the police department, records, and all evidence within, including trying to kill them all, her own *test subjects.*

Max felt the anger rise up in his throat where he let out a scream that snapped every other head in his direction. He sensed he was speaking, but couldn't make sense of what he said. At the end, he let out something that sounded like a roar, and he and the others synced in a sort of hive mind and started scaling down the building, using each other for support, working together as a team. All of them with the same goal.

Revenge.

Once on the ground, they began sprinting toward the Tahoe and the doctor, who had her back turned and didn't see them coming.

Not that taking her by surprise bothered Max, since she was about to get what she deserved. He relinquished control and watched as his body acted on its own accord, chasing her down with the others.

Dr. Mallory heard them now, her shrill scream piercing the air, as the whites of her eyes showed wide and round with terror. She scrambled for her phone and tried to hit buttons, but it was too late. The fire and nature's survival sense had overridden whatever godforsaken control she had implanted in them all. Nature, in all of its forms, wanted to live no matter what. That was always the primary objective.

The Tahoe was the first casualty. The swarm ran forward and covered it, smashing the windows, ripping the doors open and finding the vials, which were set off in one spectacular fireball after another. With that done, they all turned toward her and pounded in a feeding frenzy, every man wanting his pound of flesh to get what he was owed, to even the scales for what she had taken from them all one at a time.

The screams were terrifying, as the angry mob of her own creations, her own Berserkers, descended on her and justice was served.

Each man tried to climb on the others' backs as at least two dozen piled on, seeking the same confirmation—that she was dead and this hellish nightmare was over. The remains of the body were thrown in the Tahoe, feeding the angry, spiteful fire.

There were sirens approaching quickly now. Max felt the energy subside as a soft goodbye, like a large bear who was retreating back to its cave, tired and satisfied, leaving him in control again.

Max collapsed onto the ground, surrounded by a literal hell. The fire from the police station and the Tahoe lit up the night sky so it looked orange like a beautiful new dawn, with black clouds billowing to the heavens, purging everything bad and evil from down below. Could it be possible that he could still make it to heaven like this? It had never occurred to him before.

Max reached up and held on to his St. Michael medal and prayed for forgiveness for what he had become and everything he had done. Tears streamed down his face as he watched the men like him, the test subjects, all collectively lie down and take a deep breath of the smoky, night air, before shuddering back into their conscious selves.

Knowing the real danger was gone, Ash was safe, and his fellow Berserkers were okay, Max blacked out and succumbed to complete exhaustion.

CHAPTER 55

Ash sprinted out of the helicopter the moment it touched down in the parking lot of the supermarket about a half mile away from GPD and sprinted faster than she had ever run. All of the training in the world was no match to the adrenaline that was coursing through her veins the moment Max threw himself out of the helicopter. Every cell in her body was screaming for her to get to Max as fast as possible, and no matter how fast she ran, it wasn't fast enough.

The sight of the GPD all lit up like a fiery sun in the dead of night brought out a choked sob, as she started yelling for Max through the thick, black smoke, cloying through the air. She searched the roofline, spotting only billowing black smoke and angry orange flames licking up from inside windows.

Another blast came from the back, where she heard glass shattering and many men screaming, interspersed with the sound of the fire engine and ambulance echoing through downtown Goldvein. She ran through the parking lot right as she saw Buzz driving the fire truck straight toward the scene.

Buzz and Megan hopped out. He set up the hoses. Megan suited up.

"Check for people inside!" Ash yelled out to her as she ran by.

Megan didn't hesitate; she threw on her helmet over her flaming red curls and dashed in the front entrance which looked like the doors to hell itself.

The ambulance was next. Laura hopped out before it even came to a complete stop, and ran behind Ash toward the back. Ash heard Laura scream, "Holy shit," when the bodies came into view.

There were dozens. All of them men, between the ages of twenty and forty. All of them strong. All of them lying motionless or moaning softly while trying to crawl away from the blistering heat.

The building was on fire, but so were the remnants of the blacked-out Tahoe, its windows shattered all over the ground, glistening like diamonds from the flames. Dr. Mallory was nowhere to be seen.

Laura checked for major wounds and injuries, then took one at a time, going from person to person, touching her hand to them and giving them light. More paramedics from station three came forward, treating the various lacerations, breaks, and head wounds. Laura didn't even bother to hide her hands as she worked, pouring her life-giving energy into each one.

The back doors flew open, as Megan walked forward with one more on her shoulders, calling out to Laura, who came right away to attend to the burns.

Megan headed for the burning Tahoe and pulled out the remains of what once had been a person. There was a gold belt, still intact, on the torso.

Ash scanned, looking through the crowd for a mess of auburn hair, starting to panic when she didn't see one immediately, but there he was, at the back, closest to the fire, his face turned away. Max lay unconscious, his face turned away from the flames as if he wanted to run, but his body had failed him.

Ash ran forward, the tears streaming down her face. As she got closer, she could see his skin was pink and damp with sweat. His hands were red and blistered. One leg was lying at an odd angle, and he looked completely ashen.

"Max!" she screamed, when she ran and slid on her knees to his side. Ash collapsed on his chest, trying to swipe the hair away from his face to get a better look at him, talking the whole time, hoping he would wake up and snap out of it.

"Ash! We need to get him away from the fire, but don't touch him," Laura said. "We need a backboard over here!" she called out on the radio.

Laura rubbed her hands together, took a breath, and pressed her palms to Max's head. Ash watched, still as Laura furrowed her brow and breathed out slowly through her parted lips.

Megan ran up behind and crouched down on the other side, giving Ash the thumbs-up, before she saw who they were crouching over.

Ash and Megan watched as, surrounded by what looked like the depths of hell, Laura's hands emitted a pure golden glow that was absorbed into Max's temple, leaving a slight glow on his skin, as she moved her hands down to his palms and then to his leg.

Ash and Megan caught Laura as she fell back, then she took a breath and sat back up, looking exhausted and tapped out from this much healing. "His leg is broken, but it's clean and can be set easily. He won't need surgery."

Ash let out a choked sob and thanked her before Megan

and Laura wrapped her in a hug, as Jordan and the other paramedics ran over with a backboard and started stabilizing Max.

"Stay with him," Laura said, reaching out to Ash. "We've got this."

"Don't worry about us," Megan said, giving Ash a squeeze before running back to help the others put out the fires on GPD.

Ash nodded and wiped the tears as she stood and helped carry Max back to the waiting ambulance, passing all of the men he had saved.

CHAPTER 56

Ash was there when Max opened his eyes. There in the upper floors of the hospital, Ash held one of his bandaged hands and spoke softly as he woke up to find himself admitted to the hospital with his leg in a cast. She hadn't needed to brace herself because instead of panicking like before, he blinked a few times and tried to sit up.

"Where are they all?"

"Easy," she said, pressing her hand to his chest. "Some are here; some were sent home. They're okay, thanks to you."

"And the doctor?"

Ash's lips formed a thin line. "Gone."

Max nodded once. "So it's over?"

"Yes."

He let his head fall back and threw an arm over his eyes to cover his tears. They sat in silence for a few minutes.

There was a knock on the door. The chief poked his head around and asked if it was a good time. Ash looked to Max for confirmation. Max wiped his face with a tissue she handed him and sat up. Once he gave her the signal, Ash waved the chief in and stood, ready to salute, but he held up his hand.

"No need for that, Detective. How is our patient?"

Max smiled. "Doing as well as I can, considering."

"That's pretty damn good for falling out of a helicopter without a chute."

"I'll take what I can get," Max said.

"May I sit?"

"Please," Ash said, having a seat herself.

"I want to apologize for what ultimately destroyed GPD. I was made aware by some higher-ups in the government that Dr. Mallory would be seeking out individuals who were gifted and 'recommending' them to the force. I was highly encouraged to cooperate, and I had no idea what was really going on. We see now that she was using this to ultimately try and take over the GPD with people she could control and manipulate. Ignorance is not an excuse. I should've known, and I didn't. That's on me. I'm going to resign next week."

"Was there anyone else like me?"

"Not that I know of, but that was her plan."

"Chief, I don't think it's your fault."

He held up his hand again. "The buck stops with me. It's my responsibility. That being said, you never should've been a person of interest, and I want to apologize again, formally."

"Thank you."

"You're welcome. Your promotion was overdue. You're a good cop, and it's been a failing of the department, and of mine, not to recognize that sooner."

Ash had the decency to look down. Why was it so hard to hear praise? The worst part about it was it all was the truth. There wasn't a hint of a lie anywhere.

"She is," said Max. "We were out in the woods, and she still wanted to help others."

"I'm glad you brought that up, because I have something to say to you as well."

Max's eyebrows went up.

"I've been a cop a long time, and I've seen a lot of good cops sacrifice themselves for another person, whether they deserve it or not, whether they know them or not."

He looked at the floor for a second, then leaned forward with his elbows propped up on his knees, his hands clasped loosely in front of him, before he looked up at Max.

"I understand you want to apply for a job as a sketch artist."

"Yes, sir."

"Considered yourself hired. Once you heal up, you will need to call this number, and they'll schedule your onboarding."

Max accepted the card and held it in his hands. "Sir, I think you should know, I'm one of those men. I'm—"

"Gifted?" he said with a smile.

Max opened his mouth to protest, then stopped.

"I saw extraordinary bravery and courage to protect others. Look, if you have a little something extra that helps you do that, I consider that one hell of an advantage."

"I don't know what to say."

Chief Smith smiled. "Think it over, and give me a call. I'll still the chief for another week. Rest up. You too, Detective. Take a few days off."

They both thanked him as the chief left. The nurses came in to check vitals and to change the bandages on Max's hands, right before lunch was delivered. After that, Max started to doze, and Ash stepped out into the hall once she was sure he was asleep and comfortable.

She walked down the long hallway of Goldvein's hospital. It should've creeped her out after what she had been through, but even though the hallway and the equipment were the same, the people inside gave it an energy. There were nurses working, talking on the phone, laughing with coworkers, and families talking with loved ones.

Ash walked down the corridor, seeing some of the same men she had seen last night. A few of them caught her eye and stood up to shake her hand or nod in her direction. Ash returned the favor before stopping at the nurses' station to inquire about another patient. The nurse wrote down the number on a slip of paper and passed it over with a kind smile. Ash thanked her and took the elevator, riding up to a quieter floor and finding the door ajar with soft voices floating out into the hall.

"Okay, now, make sure you color this yellow," said Holden. "No, that's gold. We need yellow for this."

Ash peeked around the corner to see Holden sitting on the edge of the hospital bed with a coloring book, pointing to where John Burton should be coloring.

Laura spotted her and waved her in from where she was sitting in a chair in the corner.

"Sorry, I didn't mean to… I can come back later."

"No, you're good. Holden will be excited to see you!"

Holden had ears like a champ. "Who's there?" he asked, running over to investigate for himself.

"Guess who!" Ash said, backing around the corner to pull a peek-a-boo at the last minute.

"Ash!" He gave her a classic tackle hug, which she caught and returned with a squeeze.

"Come in and meet my dad."

"That was quick," she said, looking at Laura who nodded.

"I asked a child psychologist the pediatrician recommended, and we're just keeping it simple and taking it one step at a time."

"Hi, John," Ash said, a little unsure about what to say or

expect. "We never met, but I'm one of Laura's best friends. We met when she started running calls."

"It's nice to meet you," he said with a shy nod.

His speech was slow and a little slurred, which was to be expected given everything he had gone through. He looked better than when she had found him. For starters, he was conscious, upright, and able to hold a chunky crayon, and was slowly making small marks on the page. It probably was excellent therapy after the coma.

"He's a good colorer and his favorite color is blue," Holden said, smoothing over any awkwardness between the adults. "He can't color really good right now, since he was sick, but he'll get better like I did. See how good I'm doing at staying in the lines?" Holden held up a Mickey coloring sheet for approval.

"That's wonderful, bud."

"Yep, I'm getting pretty good, so I can help. It's a good thing I'm here."

"Yeah, it sure is, buddy," John said slowly, with a smile as he looked at his son in awe.

"We've been coming for a few days now. Mama said he has to stay in the hospital for a while until he gets better. Once he gets a house and stuff, I might be able to go play over there."

"That will be a while, but I'd like that," John said.

"Yeah, me too. Do you think you can be by the park or the playground? I think that would be the best place."

"That's a great idea."

Ash looked from where John was patting Holden on the back as he colored to Laura, who sat in the chair opposite. Her elbows were propped on her legs as she watched with her chin resting in her palm and a soft smile. Ash walked over and leaned up against the wall, so they could watch the gentle scene in front of them.

"Everything good with you?" Ash asked.

Laura nodded. "Yeah, I'm good."

"Holden seems to be handling it well, and you're doing remarkably well."

Laura looked up at her and let out a laugh. "Funny enough, I forgot some things I liked about John. I was angry and stressed for so long, I forgot the good parts."

Ash raised her eyebrows, but Laura shook her head.

"Don't worry, I'm not getting rid of Carter. John was a friend first before we grew up and apart. It's nice to see him as a friend and a co-parent."

Ash smelled only pure truth and peace.

"I'm really happy for you."

"Thanks. Things are going to work out for John too. Some doctor from Rocky Mountain Labs stopped by."

Ash was stunned.

"The director, Dr. Saatvik Gupta."

"Oh yeah?"

"He offered John his old job back. That's where he was the analysis and computer science guy when we were together."

"What did John say?" Ash asked.

"He said he'd be excited to take it and put his life back together."

"That's wonderful."

Laura looked over at John and Holden again. "There's more."

"What?"

"Dr. Gupta found Ted's old laptop in Dr. Mallory's office. John is the one who encrypted it. On it is the list of names of everyone ever affected by Borealis."

Ash's mouth dropped open.

"Yeah, I know. We'll have a master list, and Dr. Gupta said once he has that, he'll go to the board about next steps for community outreach, research, and therapies to help manage the consequences and study the long-term developments."

"Holy shit."

"I know, I'm still in shock. Speaking of shock, how's Max?"

"Well, he'll be glad to hear what you just told me, and he just got a job as the GPD sketch artist once his leg and hands heal up."

"Hey," Laura said, "that's awesome! Tell him I said congratulations!"

"Thanks, I will. He's resting now, but we might be able to go home in a few days."

"Good. Let me know if you guys need anything. Carter and I can run by."

"You have enough on your plate."

"That's what we do for family, and you're in mine." Laura reached out and held Ash's hand.

"Have you heard from Megan and Troy?"

"Oh yeah, they've been incredible. She's been dropping off so much food and even calling Mom to check in, and they've started taking Holden on little day trips out to the ranch for some fresh air. Hank got him one of those tractors you can ride in and started letting him ride horses, so the next birthday is a cowboy party at the ranch."

"Now we're talking. Classic. Sign me up."

"If you need anything, Megan's making the loop since her semester at school ended early with the snow."

"I can't wait to see everyone together."

"Yeah," said Laura with a smile. "I think we've earned a few girls' nights."

Ash laughed.

CHAPTER 57

T*hree months later*

———

ASH AND MAX left work together at the new Goldvein Police Department. Only one floor was finished so far, housing detectives and support staff. Traffic and the other departments were in the next town over until the brand-new, state-of-the-art building was complete.

The days had finally gotten longer, and the snow had melted into luscious green grass as Montana came into bloom. The rivers were high with all of the snowmelt, and full of tourists ready to ride the rapids in rafts that could be seen from every highway bridge.

They held hands as Max drove the old blue truck he had bought off Pat with his first check. He wanted to pay more for the years of interest and rent Pat was owed, but Pat wouldn't take it so long as Max continued to help out when he could at the store. It had been incredibly busy, since he had personally helped outfit the entire GPD when everything inside had been ruined during the fire. As a thank you, Pat let Max keep his access to the old cabin, where Ash and Max went to decompress when they both had time off work.

Carter had run a donation campaign which fixed the building and then some, but when the GPD needed body armor and ammo the next day, Pat had been the number one supplier. Business had been booming ever since.

"Alright, here we go," Ash said, as Max turned into the long gravel driveway up to Mountain View Ranch. The ranch sat at the base of the Sapphire Mountains, which were a pleasant feature on the landscape with a now ever-present memory of how Max and Ash had run through them during a blizzard. The fields were green and lush, filled with a few crops for the horses. At Hank's insistence and with Troy's management, they had gotten back into growing alfalfa and timothy for the horses and to sell the extra. This, plus the booming bed and breakfast, was bringing in enough revenue to supply Troy's passion project.

From where they crested the hill, they could see the beautiful, renovated farmhouse that acted as the bed and breakfast, next to the much-improved barn. That barn housed several truckloads of horses retired from army service. The first few had almost died in a barn fire last year, until Megan had run in and saved them.

Troy had since gotten more, and with the help from his dad, welcomed all sorts of people onto the property for therapy a few times a week. Veterans and people with trauma would come and work with the horses. As he had told them at a dinner party last month, sometimes people would come to ride or learn how to ride, and sometimes people would come to work with the horses because of their calming presence. The main clients had all been a part of Borealis and the Berserkers.

All of the men who had been test subjects for Dr. Rose

Mallory had an open invitation to come and work with the horses while talking with others like them who had the same shared experiences. Several had also started working on the ranch full and part time, under the careful supervision of Hank, who enjoyed getting to know all of the young men who reminded him of both Troy and his late son, Adam. According to Megan, Hank was almost always riding around in the truck to check on something, or talking on the phone checking in on someone. Most of the time he was so exhausted, he fell asleep in his chair before *Wheel of Fortune* even came on, but he was active and happy.

"Looks like Mom is already here," Ash said when she saw the parking lot.

Max parked the truck in the spot next to the old van with the California plates. Ash could see Carter's new van too. He had bought it to help move Holden and John around more comfortably. Laura had told her that if Holden sat in the very back, they could fit her mom in there as well for visits outside of the assisted care facility where she was still recovering from a debilitating stroke.

Megan bounced out through the door in a light-green dress and down the front porch steps, her red curls shining in the evening sun. "Great! You're finally here!" She wrapped both of them in a hug and accepted the Crock Pot of chili from Max. "Thanks for bringing this. How did you get this hot? I thought you both had to work today."

"I cooked it in my office, so everyone in the bullpen was jealous all day," Max said with a smile.

"I can smell why," Megan said, leading them inside. "I'll put it in the kitchen with the other food. You guys go ahead; everyone is out back already."

Max grabbed his drink from the truck and took a sip. The herbal remedy her mom had put together had helped him and others maintain a better sense of control over the rages.

It was even being studied at RML as part of the ongoing research. Ash led Max through the house, holding his free hand, until they stepped out onto the back porch. When everyone saw them they cheered, as Ash and Max gave a wave.

Ash stood and looked at the scene before her.

It was beautiful.

The backyard of the bed and breakfast was complete with a new slate patio surrounded by a garden in full bloom. Back when they had gone on a girls' trip out to California, Ash's mom had talked Megan into planting everything, and the two had struck up a regular friendship over plants and baking. Ash's mom sat on Megan's new patio furniture, draped in a silk scarf that looked like it was painted with watercolors, her salt-and-pepper hair flowing away from her clip. She was chatting with Laura's mom, who was in her wheelchair, sitting in the speckled sun under a tree. Even though she was in the shade, Laura's mom had on a smart summer hat with a button-down white shirt, slacks, and some of the biggest pearl earrings Ash had ever seen. Complete opposites, the moms laughed together and waved when they saw them. Ash and Max waved back.

On the other side of the new patio, Hank and Pat sat, both wearing blue jeans. Hank had on a blue button-down shirt and a cowboy hat. Pat had on a plaid shirt open to a Creedence Clearwater T-shirt. The two men both sat wearing boots, knives on their belts, and with Levi at their feet, while they talked about the price of things.

Holden was running around on the grass with a bubble wand around where John sat, giving him a turn to blow the bubbles. John reached out and was able to hold the wand, creating an impressive amount while Holden danced around and tried to catch as many as he could.

He gave an enthusiastic wave, but kept playing with the bubbles.

Laura and Carter, who had been watching, walked over just as Megan and Troy came out from the house. The girls all gave hugs, while the men shook hands and clapped each other on the backs.

"Looks like a great turnout," Ash said, nodding over to where picnic tables had been set up near a smoking grill where most of the men who came to therapy were milling about with Jordan and Buzz, who was in the middle of acting out one hell of a story.

"Yeah, everyone came," Megan said. "Troy's been grilling for hours."

Troy gave a quiet smile. "It's my mom's old recipe for chicken BBQ and a couple of new ones I've been working on."

"I can't wait," said Carter, with his megawatt smile. "I'm going to bring out the football here in a second and see what happens. Gotta test out the old arm," he said, warming up the shoulder.

"Don't get hurt again," Laura said with a laugh.

"You'll be the first one to know!" he said, laughing and giving her a kiss.

"I was worried Troy was going to get burned when he fired up the charcoal," Megan said, wrapping her arm around him.

"Not as worried as I was watching you stick your hand right in the flames to fix it," Troy replied, shaking his head. "I don't think I'll ever get used to it."

"Well, I feel completely useless," Ash said, smiling.

"Unless someone says the food is crap," Megan pointed out.

"I'm sure they won't, but I think we'll all be able to tell that's not true."

"Alright, you three," said Buzz, coming forward. "I want a picture of my girls with their guys." He hiked up his good jeans and squatted a little to get a good shot. "Say cheese!"

"Cheese!" everyone said.

"Alright now, with a kiss!"

"Seriously?" Ash said.

"Come on!" Pat called out from where he was sitting.

"Live while you're young!" Hank said.

"Fine," she groaned as she turned to face Max, whose blue eyes were twinkling.

"I love you," she said.

"I love you too," he said.

Ash heard the others say the same, and as they kissed, she knew that everyone was telling the truth.

ACKNOWLEDGMENTS

There are so many people to thank, but I must first start with a heartfelt thank you to my family and friends for their endless belief and encouragement in my writing. I cannot thank my husband, Kevin, enough for believing in me and encouraging me. I'm also profoundly grateful to my dear friend and writing buddy, Jenn Gosselin, who has been with me throughout this series. Her invaluable feedback and calming presence helped me navigate this story's twists and turns.

I always owe many thanks to Ann Suhz and Ann Riza for their insightful comments and suggestions that helped shape the story and series. I learn so much from their invaluable feedback and constructive criticism.

A huge thanks to Lynn Andreozzi for her dedication and creativity in bringing this cover to life. Her work has not only matched the story but also brought a new energy to it. I am so grateful to have her as a partner to bring my vision to life.

Finally to my readers, I am continually humbled and grateful for your unwavering support. Your love for my characters and stories is a constant source of inspiration for me.

ABOUT THE AUTHOR

Kathryn K. Murphy writes action-packed, small-town romance novels bursting with emotion.

If you want to know when Kathryn's next book will come out, please visit her website at www.kathrynkmurphy.com, where you can sign up to receive email updates.

www.ingramcontent.com/pod-product-compliance
Lightning Source LLC
Chambersburg PA
CBHW061636190726
48289CB00006B/1621